The Eye Unseen

By
Cynthia Tottleben

JournalStone
San Francisco

JOURNALSTONE
YOUR LINK TO ARTISTIC TALENT

JournalStone books may be ordered through booksellers or by contacting:

JournalStone
www.journalstone.com

www.journal-store.com

The views expressed in this work are solely those of the authors and do not necessarily reflect the views of the publisher, and the publisher hereby disclaims any responsibility for them.

ISBN: 978-1-940161-10-5   (sc)
ISBN: 978-1-940161-11-2   (ebook)

Library of Congress Control Number: 2013950838

Printed in the United States of America
JournalStone rev. date: January 17, 2014

Cover Design: Denise Daniel
Cover Art: M. Wayne Miller
Edited by: Dr. Michael R. Collings

For my mother, Carolyn Houck, who would want the world to know she is not the model for the character in this book. You have blessed me with many wonderful days, not to exclude the incident with the ghetto blaster or your warped gingerbread houses. Thanks for being my greatest supporter.

The Eye Unseen is creepy, unsettling, moving, surprising, and utterly impossible to put down. This book started out strange, and then becomes totally insane, in all the best ways, and from the first few pages I was completely hooked. Cynthia Tottleben has created an absolutely beautiful novel about a twisted relationship and even more twisted circumstances. Don't miss this one. – **David Liss** – New York Times-bestselling author of *The Twelfth Enchantment* and *The Whiskey Rebels*

Acknowledgements

I cannot thank my writing group enough. The members of the Quad Cities RWA who have tolerated my high drama and bloodbaths despite their gentle natures: Theresa Davis, Jan LaRoche, Jan Steffens, Crystal Donahue, Ellen Tsagaris, you are a fantastic group and have taught me a tremendous amount about the craft.

My beta readers, Maria Del Mar Carrasquillo, Judy Brosche, Kerri Miller Ebright, your help and input have been invaluable. Thank you for taking the time to read and let me bounce ideas off you! Howard Olson, the quiet keeper of Rancid, has tried to lead me in the right direction though I often refuse to follow. I appreciate all of your support. You are an excellent friend.

Ann Pierson D'Angelo, who has endured the bone-chilling neediness of my offbeat creative talents since she performed my piano composition in high school. Thank you for listening, reading, giving feedback, and inspiring me with your artistic talents.

Simon Wood and CJ West, my Bouchercon buddies, who never hesitate to answer my questions or dole out advice and encouragement, you guys are the best!

I am forever indebted to the crew at JournalStone Publishing for their patience while I've learned the ropes: Patrick Freivald, fellow author, kind enough to take me under his wings, my editor Dr. Michael Collings, for not only his hard work on my project, but the headache of breaking in a newbie. And, finally, to Christopher Payne for giving me this opportunity.

Chapter 1

Lucy

The prelude was subtle, as insidious as a gradual infection. For the past several months Mom had done a slow waltz around the sanity drain, the mutations in her behavior spreading like tumors through all of our lives.

But the snap was instantaneous. The flick of a match. A camera capturing an image.

Nuclear detonation.

I could see it in her eyes. Like someone had finally turned on the garbage disposal and cleared out the bits and pieces of her that still existed. A flip of the switch, and Mom was all but gone, mush corroding somewhere at the bottom of a pipe, barely a remnant of the woman I remembered.

She came at me fast, pinned me against the wall. I dared not fight, for I knew the repercussions. I had experienced them once months ago and still trembled each time I approached the shed in the back yard. Looking out the sliding glass doors I could see the building cast shadows across the grass, inviting me back in.

Tippy ran up beside us, her nails clattering on the linoleum as she hurried to my rescue. I mentally scolded her as she began barking, but Mom was on her in a flash. I watched as she kicked my miniature dachshund and sent her flying next to the kitchen table, Tippy whining and then running off in a panic. She couldn't protect me from my mother and both of us knew it.

Tippy was much better off in the other room. While I appreciated her efforts, I was also so embarrassed by my predicament that I didn't want her to witness it.

The left side of Mom's mouth curled up in a sardonic grin. My flesh shivered as her expression broadened into a twisted sort of joy. I half expected her tongue to flick in and out of her mouth like a snake's.

The first slap stung as Mom's hand found my face. I had anticipated it the moment Mom walked in the door and challenged me with her stare, the second I felt the air shift in the kitchen with her approach. My toes ached from walking on constant egg shells, and for a second I was relieved that the violence had finally begun.

"Your coach called me at work," Mom announced, her words coated in bile.

I could taste the rotten stench as it crept out of her mouth, a blend of soured milk and eggs left in the heat for three days. With anyone else I would have politely walked away and wrapped my long hair under my nose to filter out the nastiness. But with her I lacked such freedom.

I stood chest to chest with her. A voice punctuated my panic, screamed up my spine that I could poke my fingers in her eyes, kick her in the jaw as she flailed around blindly. But that thought caused my legs to jerk and I almost fell in place, Mom pulling me back up by my hair. She pressed her palms flat against the wallpaper, directly over my shoulders. I was wary that both hands might jump out at me as our interrogation proceeded, for they often worked as if they had a life of their own.

"I'm sorry, Mom." I tried not to move. I struggled not to vomit from the odor that oozed out of her pores, came at me on her dragon's breath.

"Do you know how embarrassing that was?" Mom's body scooted a quarter of an inch closer to mine. "Not knowing that your daughter had quit the team?"

My instinct was to run. Open the sliding door, escape the treachery of the outbuildings, flee like the deer into the rows of corn that bordered our side yard.

But I knew better. Mom no longer had boundaries. Even if she couldn't catch me on foot, I didn't doubt she'd come after me with her car or even the shotgun. Although our land in rural Iowa had plenty of hiding spots, I didn't want to live like the animals in the woods that adjoined our property, hiding in the trees, always on high alert.

Constantly waiting for someone to kill me.

"I didn't know what else to do. I'm sorry."

I gripped the kitchen chair, waited for the pain to come. Again.

"I'm ashamed of you, Lucy. School hasn't even started yet and already you're in trouble?"

The worst part of her psychosis was trying to squeeze the truth in between the walls of Mom's irrationality.

"I'm sorry. The other kids, they were talking about me…."

Her hand switched to my neck. I flinched when I thought she would slap me, but instead she traced the edge of my mouth with her index finger and then spidered her whole hand across my jaw until it settled with her thumb stroking my jugular.

"Yes?" Mom directed me to finish.

I didn't want to answer. I contemplated lying but knew that Mom would see straight through that. Making up even half-truths had never been a skill of mine.

"They were looking at…and the coach…."

"Lucinda Shay Tew, you have about ten seconds to spit it out before I get really mad."

Fingernails bit into my skin. Mom's face was no longer just florid with anger, but I could tell she had started to enjoy this. My suffering. Tippy, whimpering in the background. All three of us knowing that soon that would be me as well.

Brandy has always told me not to talk about it. To tell no one but her what really went on in our house. Not to even acknowledge the abuse to Mom.

Of course, my sister was immune to the cruelty. Her worst offenses were my bruises. Even when she'd snuck out one hot August night, taken Mom's car and driven to the quarry to hang with her friends, she was sent to her room while I endured the punishment. Mom could never believe Brandy had flaws. Brandy preferred not to rock the boat.

Then again, she had never joined the swim team and couldn't be blamed for my current condition.

I couldn't pad the truth. The situation with Mom was lose-lose.

"I could hear them talking about my bruises," I began.

This time my head bounced off the wall.

Mom moved back a step, uncurled her fist, and rubbed her knuckles. All expression exited her face.

"What bruises, Lucy?"

"Mom, please. You know." Shame catapulted through my entire system. I couldn't believe we were having this conversation.

"No, Lucy, I don't."

At school the girls talked about everyone, even their own best friends. In the locker room I had listened to many of these conversations, virtually unseen as I showered and changed after practice. But lately when I entered the pool area or hit the showers, all chatting stopped. Even among the boys. On the day I quit, I had dared to glance at my own skin. All I could see was the imprint of Mom's fingers colored onto my thigh.

"Please, Mom. People notice, on the swim team. It's not like I can wear a full body suit in the pool. I had to quit. What if the coach called someone?"

I closed my eyes for a second and waited for the blow that did not come. Instead Mom moved her hand under my chin, pulled my face up so that I had to look directly into her mad eyes.

"Say it, Lucy." The words slithered out and curled alongside my face. My belly lurched from the odor. "What do people notice?"

Brandy had warned me never to talk about it.

"The bruises you gave me."

Brandy was right.

This time when my head hit the wall it left an indentation.

* * *

Brandy snuck into my room after Mom left for work. We both listened for the crunch of tires on gravel before so much as breathing.

"Hey. You okay?" My older sister asked.

"I can barely open my eyes." I held out my hand and Brandy grasped it.

After Mom had finally gone to bed, Brandy had been the one to take care of me. We both imagined that our parent instinctively knew this would happen and let nature play its course, for she never chastised my sister. But then again, Brandy rarely got in trouble for anything.

"You really took a whuppin' this time. I'm sorry, sweetie."

Brandy crawled into my bed, pushed my hair up and over the pillow. I felt a rush of relief as she spooned around me, pressed her face into the back of my neck. It amazed me how she always made me feel protected, loved.

"I think she's getting worse," I told my sister. "You should've seen the look on her face. It's like she's an entirely different person."

"I know. I could hear her muttering all night. I swear it sounded like she was fighting with Dad. She said his name enough times."

Chills raced up my back.

"What are we going to do?" I relied on Brandy to make the big decisions. She was smarter than me, had experienced a lot more. "What if she goes completely crazy?"

"You mean she's not already?" Brandy giggled and tried to lighten the mood.

"I'm serious."

"So am I, Luce. So am I."

* * *

"I don't want you to go to school," Mom said flatly, sipping her coffee while I finished my oatmeal.

"But Mom, it's the first day. I can't miss that." I knew my bruises would set off a few alarms with my teachers, but I had prepared a story about having a bike accident and running into a tree. With my face.

"No, you're right. If you miss the first day you might as well skip out on the whole year." Her lips left the mug, and I could see Brandy relax a bit when Mom chuckled. "I'll tell them you moved in with your dad."

"What?" Brandy and I asked as one. We looked at each other, then back to Mom.

"But don't think for a minute that I'm going to let you off that easy. While I'm working I expect you to clean the kitchen, top to bottom. The oven, the cabinets. Even the walls. You know how to use the oil soap." Mom set her coffee back on the table.

"Are you serious?" Brandy spat with disrespect and then physically retreated. I took note of how she moved back in her chair as fragile as a secret, as if she immediately regretted her bold question.

"Lucy is perfectly capable of washing the walls. Do you think I'd just let her stay home from school all day and read?"

"No, Ma'am." Brandy stepped back into formalities. "What would you like me to tell people at school?"

"I've already called them. Say just what I did. Lucy has officially moved in with her father. That's why she quit the swim team. Because she no longer lives with us." Mom flexed the morning paper, folded it open to the business section.

I sat still as a bird. Transfixed. Transparent.

Silently I glanced at Brandy, pleaded with my eyes. Neither of us had anticipated this.

"But, Mom?" Brandy dared ask. "Everyone knows Dad is dead."

Mom continued reading for a moment, unbothered.

"Whoever said the two of you have the same father?"

The second the car scooted down the drive, I grabbed the sponge and started cleaning. I knew Mom's expectations.

I also knew I could never meet them.

* * *

"Keep away from the windows. You know Mom'll freak if people see you!" Brandy warned.

I had served my first week under house arrest and was aching for fresh air. In my new regime I was only allowed to open the door in the blackest of night, and in no other situation, not even an emergency like a house fire or gas leak, but with all the inside lights off and nothing to help me see outside. Mom let me walk Tippy around our five acres in the pitch dark and only on the backside of the house, away from the road. Once I moved from under the cover of our magnolia, I was in forbidden territory.

She never had to spell out the consequences if I did not follow her directions. Misbehavior was not an option.

"Brandy, when you look outside what do you see?"

"Corn."

"Row after row of it. No roads, no other houses. Just corn. No one will see me, not even the Hanleys," I reminded her as I stepped forward and cracked the window. "Besides, the air in here is stagnant, don't you think?"

Brandy had spread out her homework, ready to give me a lesson in College Algebra.

"Why do they call it College Algebra if you take it in high school?" I quizzed.

"Because it's college level. But it's really not that hard."

Jealousy gripped me as I looked at my sister. She was one of the prettiest girls in her class, with long, glossy dark hair, and freckles that accentuated her hazel eyes. In the past year Brandy had developed a much more mature frame and looked at least twenty, not the eighteen she was soon to become.

"I've always liked math, but this isn't so bad. Plus my teacher is really cool. You'd like him. He's new this year."

"Really? What's his name?" I sat next to the open window, let the breeze coat me with its warmth.

If I closed my eyes I could see the yard I already missed worse than any of my classmates. Behind the house, our picnic table sat empty, staring at the pine trees that guarded our land. Was it covered in bird poop? Had anyone washed it? Were the frogs that lined our creek wondering what happened to me?

"Mr. Meller. Now, look at this equation. It seems really complicated with these other problems set in parentheses, but they're all the same...."

I couldn't concentrate on my sister's lesson. A thousand questions filled my head as she rambled on about her classes. Had the principal cared that Mom removed me from school? Did anyone in town find it strange? Was I still considered part of the Class of 2003, or would I not graduate with the others, even if Mom allowed me back on school grounds?

"What do they say about me? In school?"

Brandy's lip dropped open like she was going to say something and then thought better of it.

"The girls in choir were concerned about you, but after I told them about your fantastic new living arrangements, they were insanely jealous!" Brandy sparked back up.

Her energy egged me on. "Really? Who?"

"Oh, that loud girl with the freaky glasses. And her funny friend who belches all of the time. I can't remember their names. Freshmen...who cares who they are?" My sister tried to act cool, but then stopped.

We both realized that if I weren't confined to the house I'd be a freshman, too.

"Becky? Becky asked about me?" I screeched with excitement. "What'd you say?"

"I told them you've gone to France to stay with your father for a while...."

"France?" I was surprised.

"Tours, more directly. He works for the University there, you know."

"Of course. And what exactly does he look like?" I played her game.

"Tall. Extremely tall, for a Frenchman. He has reddish hair and a little moustache that he combs and curls up at the side."

We started laughing at the image of my mystery parent and couldn't stop. When the tears came I crawled into my sister's lap and shared with her the terror that gripped me constantly. Her hug lent me camaraderie, but even the slight touch made me yelp in pain.

"Maybe he's my father, too. You never know. Just because I don't have red hair doesn't mean a thing."

Four minutes before Mom came home, the table was set and dinner ready to come out of the oven. Brandy and I decided that we would never give her another opportunity to lash out at me again.

* * *

Sundays were the worst for me. I had always loved church. Well, maybe not so much the sermons, but the music and the picnics and the activities of our youth group. Mom didn't allow Brandy and me to go out with friends very often, but she never challenged the leaders of the First Methodist and gave us free rein to attend almost every get-together they had.

Now, instead of Sunday afternoon skate parties or our Thursday trips to the nursing home, I was in charge of preparing a family meal and having it on the table by the time Mom and Brandy arrived home.

I loved setting a formal dinner table. In the past Brandy had done most of the cooking. We always relied on Mom for clean-up duty, as each of us took our turn with one segment of the chores, and quite frankly she was much better at scrubbing the pans than getting them dirty in the first place.

But since I had moved in with Dad, I had taken over all of these responsibilities.

I still enjoyed table setting. Last Christmas Mom gave me several books on napkin folding and building center pieces that she found at a yard sale. Every Sunday since I have used one book or another to create my very own masterpieces.

Looking at my presentation, I was pleased with the autumn assortment I had picked out of the linen closet. Pumpkin was my theme color and also the flavor of our meal. Brandy and I had baked pumpkin bread on Saturday afternoon. Now Mom's favorite pie sat cooling on the kitchen counter, the crust delicate yet as picture-worthy as the one on the cookbook cover.

Even so I couldn't help but be nervous. Mom and I hadn't had an episode since the one over the swim team, and I could feel it brewing in the air. As I glanced at the mashed potatoes growing cold on the stove and again at the clock, I worried about the condition of our main course. Mom liked to amble in the back door, put down her purse and jacket, and then take a three-minute break in the restroom before sitting down to eat. She performed like clockwork. She expected everyone else around her to do the same.

Which translated into having a hot meal ready to be moved to the dining room table the moment she entered the house. Usually I poured the side dishes into serving bowls as soon as I heard the car approach. Brandy would follow Mom into the house but immediately start carrying food so there was no delay.

But not today. I wondered if the congregation was sharing lunch or if Mom and Brandy had had some tragedy coming home. Since we no longer used a house phone, I couldn't call. Plus I would never be able to explain why I was calling Mom from France to see why she wasn't home for dinner.

I stood vigil by the stove and waited. While the buns warmed with the ham in the oven, I contemplated rolling the potatoes into balls and blasting Brandy with them when they finally came home. Tippy and I had a good laugh over this, but we both knew it would never happen.

Instead I refolded the napkins, did cleanup work, wrapped saran around the pie after it had cooled. When my family was two hours late, I cut a bit of meat for myself and gave Tippy a couple of scraps. She was overjoyed at the treat, and I had grown incredibly hungry while waiting.

At 4:30 the car sounded warning, crunching up the gravel drive.

Tired and not knowing which way to jump, I kept my post by the oven. The meal was ruined, although the meat and rolls were still salvageable. Mom would be furious, either that I had wasted food or that I had eaten part of the ham without permission.

I had no idea how to proceed.

Brandy's voice drifted into the kitchen as they hurried from the car. Mom was even laughing! I desperately wanted to run open the door or pull aside the curtains and wave at my family.

But this was forbidden.

"Hey, Luce." Brandy smiled at me as she hurried through the kitchen and then caught sight of the table. "Oh, wow. That looks fantastic!"

For an instant I was offended by Brandy's happiness. The fact that she hadn't wasted hours, emotionally spent, waiting for the disaster that lurked behind the kitchen door. My sister could have hurled one of the potato balls at Mother and fallen over in hysterics as the food fell out of her hair while Mom chased me for the outrage it caused.

Life was not fair. It was not a circus, either.

Mom entered the house and glared at the inedible food. I could feel goose bumps marching up my arms in double time.

"What is this all about?" She waved her hand at the stove.

"I kept trying to keep it hot for you, but I think I've cooked it too long. I'm sorry."

I watched Mom's hand hover in the air. But instead of hitting me, she put it to her side.

"Well, I'm not surprised. You certainly can't cook like your sister."

"No, Ma'am, I can't." I lowered my eyes.

"Clean it up. We've already eaten."

Brandy reappeared and rolled up her sleeves. She started to draw dish water and made herself immediately comfortable working around Mom and me.

The woman continued to glare. My skin grew hot with tension.

"Here you go, Luce. Let's scrape these for the compost bin and I'll run that out in a second...." Brandy stepped in front of Mom and gave me a chore list.

I hopped to it.

Later, after the threat of violence had dissipated, I asked Brandy where they had been.

"Don't you remember? The second Sunday of September is always the autumn banquet. God, I wish you could have gone. It's so boring without you, and Mrs. Bradford made that Jell-O salad you love so much...."

"Thanks."

"Lucy, I can't do anything about her. You know that."

"No, I wasn't being sarcastic. Thanks. For what you did, getting her out of the kitchen." I had no trouble holding eye contact with my sister.

"Listen, kid. It's getting better, can't you tell?"

My nod brought tears. Brandy took her dish towel and wiped them away.

"Are you hungry? I bet you haven't eaten a thing, have you?"

Brandy made me a ham sandwich and stood guard while I wolfed it down.

* * *

"I wish she would let us listen to the radio again," Brandy said as she dipped a canning jar into soapy water.

"Yeah. I get so lonely during the day that I could go just as crazy as...." I didn't need to finish my sentence.

We were doing Saturday chores, an often random list that Mom developed to keep Brandy and me busy. Last weekend we had recaulked the bathtub and cleaned the floor vents. This time we were assigned the dusty job of cleaning the often bug-infested canning room.

"I listen to the music the kids play at lunch. I get so jealous sometimes! I wish I could sit in my room and chill out and put on some country tunes...well, you know what I mean. I suppose it's just as bad for me to want it as it is to listen to it."

"I sing all day," I announced, sharing my secret with Brandy. "Tippy and I make up songs or try to remember the good church hymns and sing those."

"Remember the music Mom used to buy? Faith Hill? She was the best."

Unfortunately Brandy had lost music for us entirely. Even after Mom had disposed of the television she used to let us listen to the radio. We each had one in our rooms, and one in the kitchen for family time. Many evenings when we were playing board games at the kitchen table, a song would come on that we loved, and all three of us would jump up and put on a stage show while the dog howled along.

Until Brandy discovered rap. Why she would ever listen to such nastiness, I can't figure. But the night Mom caught her reciting gangster lyrics was the night Brandy couldn't stand up from her bedroom floor and actually peed herself while Mom punished her.

After that, no radio. No music. Very little singing.

* * *

My nightmare startled me awake. I lay on the bed, panting, my dark thoughts still clinging to my hair and jabbing at my face. My heart ran in a flat out panic.

When I sat up in my bed I could barely breathe.

I concentrated on bringing reality back, coaxed myself to be calm, and drew a few deep breaths until my lungs stopped burning.

It took only a few seconds to get my surroundings, but when I did I thought my heart would explode this time.

Standing in the corner of my room was Mother.

She said nothing as she pulled herself from the shadows. I took my cue from Brandy and made myself smaller, wilted back onto my sheets, felt the heat from my body dissipate instantly.

Mother waited. I closed my eyes but could feel her holding court near my dresser, hovering and casting judgment upon me.

I wished her away.

Silently prayed and wished her away.

* * *

After Brandy and I cleaned up from dinner, we were usually allowed to entertain ourselves. Brandy completed homework and gave me quiet lessons in some of her subjects. I read her textbooks, practiced math techniques, and voraciously inhaled the books she checked out from the school library.

Together we started a yoga routine and stretched on her bedroom floor. Since Brandy's room was twice the size of mine, we could both spread out and not bump into each other while we exercised. Plus, her room had so many more amenities: a scrap of blue carpet that was thick and much more comfortable than the rag rug decorating my floor, a mirror attached to her dresser, which allowed us to watch ourselves and improve our form, and two windows.

From one, I could witness the solitude of our neighbor, Mr. Wyckoli. Even though I couldn't open the curtains and look directly out, I hid against the wall and spied from the side of the window, ensuring he was sitting in his kitchen and still alive. The tiny TV he kept cast enough light that I knew he was home, enjoying his game shows.

Television had been banned from our house for so long I could barely recall the names of the programs we once watched. We spent our entertainment time playing cards, Scrabble, the board games barely contained in old boxes bound with rubber bands. Usually on Saturday afternoons—when all chores were completed—Brandy would pull out the Monopoly board and we'd set up a game.

Before Mom became mentally challenged, more often than not she'd join in. The three of us had a great time, teasing each other and relishing the cinnamon toast Mom prepared as a treat.

Now Brandy and I continued our traditions but did so under great duress. We had no idea what Mom did with her time after dinner; she would retreat to her bedroom, lock the door, and stay there for hours. Not that we complained.

Brandy, the risky one, would sometimes tiptoe to Mom's door and listen to the chanting that drifted into the hallway.

"I don't know. It sounds like she's talking to some guy named Jerry about delivering groceries in the springtime."

"What?"

"Oh, come on, Lucy. Have a sense of humor. I can't understand any of it," Brandy said. "Do you ever go in her room while she's at work?"

We switched to silent mode. In the past month we had both become incredibly adept at reading lips.

Once. I mouthed.

What does she have in there?

I didn't touch anything. All I saw was a Bible and her tea mug. A photo on her nightstand of some old woman that kind of looks like Grandma, if she had worn her hair in a braid. I hadn't dared to snoop through Mom's things. One look at my face and she'd know I was guilty of something.

Brandy sat thinking for a moment and then dropped the subject completely. She started talking about school, giving me the gossip about couples and friends who were fighting, kids who had gotten arrested for vandalizing the gymnasium. She was my only outlet to the real world and took her role seriously.

* * *

"When do you think this will end?" I asked Brandy as she brushed my hair.

"I don't know. Sometimes when I talk to Mom, I think she'll start yelling 'April Fools!' and the whole town'll be in on the joke. She'll let you out of the house, people will clap and joke about how easy it was to fool us, and everything will go back to normal."

"Yeah, I get that same feeling. But then it goes just as fast as it came." I couldn't help but gasp when she hit a big snarl and my head hit the back of the chair.

"Exactly. I look in her eyes and wonder if there's anything left inside her."

"So what do we do?"

"Nothing yet." Brandy sighed.

"When is it too much? When do I get worried?"

"Oh, sweetie, this is a cake walk. What would someone say about your situation? Everyone here spanks their kids, so getting slapped a few times is nothing. You aren't in classes, but Mom could just say she's homeschooling you. So you do some extra chores. We don't have TV. Is it really that horrible?"

I turned in the chair and faced my sister. One look at my anger and she started laughing, letting out a hideous cackle that made my freshly straightened hair start to curl again.

"Luce, honey. You don't have to glare at me like that. I'm not the one responsible for your problems."

Brandy put the brush on the top of her dresser, wrapping her arms around my shoulders in a giant bear hug. I felt her lips kiss the side of my head and watched our reflection in the mirror. My sister stared straight back at me, her embrace growing tighter.

"Or am I?" she whispered.

I pushed her off me, knocking the chair backward as I jumped up.

"Jeez, Luce, I was only kidding. Lighten up! I know she's got you stressed out, but I'm on your side, remember?"

Chapter 2

Joan

No one in my family had crimson hair.

You fought me for twenty-one hours, and when you finally arrived I saw nothing but your red hair coated in all that muck. Never have I felt such horror.

When you started crying, I did the same. The nurses thought I was just exhausted, and maybe that was part of it. Looking at you I couldn't help but shriek. I begged them to take you away, and they did, for a few hours. What I had really wanted was for them to make you disappear.

But Brandy fell in love with you.

"Mommy, she looks like Christmas," Brandy told me when the staff let her visit.

She had been excited to be an older sister. For my entire pregnancy I had gorged on fear and could barely get out of bed, I missed poor Alex so much. But Brandy had planned for everything. She drew a hundred pictures of what the new baby might look like, made up names, and told everyone in town that you were on the way. When we went shopping for baby things, I told her what I needed and she ran around, filling the cart while I stood behind it, not even double checking what she picked out.

I couldn't nurse you, didn't really want you near me at all. The staff brought you to my room, but it was Brandy who fed you. I just lay on the bed, staring at Alex's daughter, then following her eyes down to you.

No one in our family had red hair. I knew this wasn't a coincidence. You were everything I'd been raised to fear. Cunning, even at birth, like Satan himself, your tiny dimples a constant reminder of the fiend I was born to bear.

Where were the women in my family when I needed them the most? They had been quick to condemn me as a child, blame me for what was yet to come. But now that you had arrived, set their ancient fears in motion, none of them were left to help me.

Not even Mother.

I would have left you in the hospital if Brandy hadn't taken to you so fast. She and I were a team, and I hated to let her down. If you hadn't come out covered in all that hair I might have shared her delight, but instead I fought through my revulsion just to hold you and faked enjoyment at birthing a second daughter.

The nurses called it postpartum depression. I called it postpartum terror.

Brandy mothered you while I prayed for my own mother, dead since the moment of your conception, to help me. She would have known what to do. My mother would have taken care of everything for me, just let me lay back and close my eyes while she dusted it all under the rug.

How I missed her. Missed all of them.

Alex most of all.

In the end I brought you back to our apartment. Dutifully I smiled while the neighbors kissed the top of your head and told me what a beautiful child you were. I nodded, I laughed, I did everything a mother is supposed to do.

"What's her name?" people asked.

"Lucy!" Brandy said proudly.

She hadn't been there when the nurses named you. Brandy had still been safe with Mrs. Belast, the secretary of our church, when the doctor raised you as they cut that damned cord that bound us together.

"Lucifer!" I had shouted, my voice muffled under your first cries for air.

The nurses had started calling you Lucy right away. Although Dr. Smythe had certainly understood my cry, his helpers had only heard the first half of your name.

"Lucinda," the blonde nurse had said. "What a pretty name."

And so you became mine.

Chapter 3

Lucy

My instructions became much more specific. Brandy called Mom's notes an exercise in micromanagement, but I didn't mind. The more direct her orders, the less doubt I had about my performance.

I was handed a timeline. Mom also gave me a very detailed verbal explanation of her plans. From across the room, I could see Brandy mouth the word *Cinderella.*

Mom must have seen a flicker of light cross my face as I tried not to laugh.

"Pay attention!" She backhanded me.

"Yes, Ma'am. I'm sorry."

"When you get task #5, you will find all of the materials you need in the pantry cabinet."

I scanned the list and discovered that Mom wanted me to bake and decorate Brandy's birthday cake.

Wow! I couldn't believe she was turning eighteen. How had I forgotten?

"No problem. Thank you." I wanted Mom to know that I had this one covered. For a nanosecond I even felt a sense of camaraderie with her, but that passed the instant I looked at her face and saw the same rigid features that greeted me every day.

"We'll be home at the usual time."

With the addition of my exciting mission, time flew. The materials Mom purchased were fabulous: a pan shaped like a butterfly—Brandy's favorite—and a cake-decorating kit to match.

I got to work early on it. The cake hit the oven at nine o'clock sharp, allowing it ample time to cool and be ready to ice in the early afternoon.

I had just started cleaning the black specks from the refrigerator seals when Mom came home for lunch.

The second I heard the tires crunching gravel, my heart jumped. The car sounded just like Mom's, but what if someone else came by? What if one of the church ladies was bringing a gift for Brandy? I couldn't answer the door.

I couldn't even be seen. Everyone knew I had moved to France.

I put my cleanser in the sink and scurried to the hall closet. Claustrophobia entered alongside me, clutching my legs like a small child wanting to play. I batted the fear away, but it bit in deeper. Shutting the closet door opened up too many memories of my time in the shed. I almost started screaming. When a coat sleeve touched my arm, I jumped, certain the devil himself had shown up, ready to ram his horns into my side.

"What are you doing in here?" Mom yelled when she found me.

"Hiding." Relief flooded my body as I stepped out. "I didn't know who was here. I didn't...."

She placed her high heel on the top of my foot and pressed down.

"You didn't what, Lucy? You didn't want to get caught slacking?"

"No, no, no...I didn't know it was you. It could have been anyone...."

Mom grasped my hair and pulled my head to the side, marching me into the kitchen.

"I gave you a very specific list this morning, didn't I?"

Spittle hit my face as Mom dragged me toward the list sitting innocently on the counter.

"Yes."

"Why didn't you follow it?"

She shoved me backward, into the table. My rear end hit the edge and almost toppled the heavy oak.

"I did. I am. Right now I'm on the seals...."

"I don't care what you're doing *right now*. *Right now* all you're doing is sniveling. *Right now* you're trying to figure out how you can get out of trouble. *Right now* you're annoying the crap out of me. But *right now* you're not doing what I told you to do."

I stared at her, blankly. What rationality she had drained from her face with every word. I couldn't fathom what she wanted from me.

"You weren't supposed to bake that cake until this afternoon, were you?"

When the pounding began I lost sense of time. She hit my ear viciously, and the explosion that followed muddled my vision. Constant action flipped into slow-mo for me, the battering a clumsy waltz in which Mom spun me to and fro and I kept tripping over my own feet. The second time I bounced against the table, it spun and landed on top of me, protecting my torso from Mom's shoes.

"When I give you direction, Lucy, I expect you to follow it. Look at how much time you've wasted. You can count this as your lunch break."

In my daze I could barely comprehend her words. They sounded as far off as the chanting Brandy and I heard coming from her bedroom at night.

"I expect a great party for your sister tonight. You had better not ruin it."

She left as quickly as she came.

My senses were all askew, but I did not breathe until I heard the tires crushing the gravel on their way back to the main road.

I eased a Kleenex into my ear while I cleaned the refrigerator coils, hoping that by the time I decorated the cake it would stop bleeding.

* * *

Brandy burst into the room and halted the moment she saw my face.

"Oh, no. Lucy…."

She was cut short as Mom entered behind her, carrying several big bags.

I had hidden the new scuff marks on the table with the pink plastic cloth Mom had purchased for our party. Streamers and balloons decorated the kitchen, the railing on the stairs, even the toilet handle. Since it was way too early for dinner I had put together a fruit and cheese tray for our appetizer.

"Well, ladies, shall we get this party going?" Mom asked.

Brandy and I exchanged glances. Sometimes we referred to the Mom of the last few months as New Mom, the woman we loved and cherished as Old Mom. The woman in the kitchen was definitely Old Mom, come for a visit.

"Honey, did you put any ice on that bruise?" She asked, touching the side of my face in an amazingly gentle fashion. "I swear, you need to be more careful or one of these days you'll do permanent damage to yourself."

I didn't know whether she was slipping me a secret threat or if Old Mom really had no idea what had transpired between us today.

Part of me didn't want to find out. I stayed silent until she finally walked away.

"I can't believe you're turning eighteen!" I congratulated my sister. "Wow. You're so old!"

"Now I can vote! Well, tomorrow I can...why are we having this party today?" Brandy turned and asked our mother.

"Because tomorrow I have to work late and we have a meeting at the bank that will run forever. I didn't want to ruin the festivities!" Mom answered.

She opened the junk drawer in the kitchen—now fastidiously organized, thanks to my cleaning—and pulled out the deck of cards.

"Gin?" Mom handed the cards to Brandy and went to fetch a pad of paper.

"Lucy, I love the cheese, but let's break out the cake!" Mom had candles in her hand and slid them into mine.

I pulled my masterpiece from the oven so she could admire it. Mom kissed the top of my head and whispered that it was beautiful. My fingers shook while I lit the match, I was so excited by the sudden change in Mom's demeanor.

We sang while Tippy danced around us and barked. Brandy was quick with the candles, blew out the flames with her eyes closed and a formidable wish left hanging in the air.

If she hadn't asked for Mom to be like this all of the time again, Brandy would have made a dire mistake.

Mom kicked our butts at Gin and then gave us some pointers at poker while dinner sizzled in the oven. I was thrilled not to be cooking, but also excited about the menu Brandy had chosen for her special night; frozen pizza and Doritos, a rarity in our home.

We gorged off pink paper plates and at one point remembered to get the Birthday Princess tiara out of the closet for Brandy, a tradition we had carried on since she was seven and Mom found it at Kmart.

Another round of cake brought us misery in the form of stomach aches, but Mom egged us on to continue with the party. At eight o'clock she presented Brandy with her gifts and together we sang again.

"This has been the best night, Mom. Thanks for the party. And the cake—wow, Luce, you could go pro with that!" Brandy said as she sat in front of her unopened presents.

Jealousy struck as my sister opened her largest gift first. She gasped, "Mom!" as she pulled back the tissue paper, beaming. Brandy held up the new winter coat, and it hit me hard that in it she would be leaving the house, going out with the kids from church, attending school, and running errands with Mom. In that coat, Brandy would have a life.

Here, in this house, I would inherit her old clothes and shoes, study the homework some faceless teacher had already graded. Brandy could go sledding down the hill in our front yard, attend bonfires and hayrides, bike to school if she missed the bus. And I would remain in the kitchen, waiting for her to return home, hiding when someone else came to the door.

I had always heard that life in France was much more fascinating than this.

"It's beautiful, Brandy." I complimented her. I did not want to let my sister feel the envy that vined through my heart.

"Oh, my goodness! I just love it!"

Mom made us all hot chocolate while Brandy continued to open gifts. She picked up a small box from Tippy and unwrapped it to find matching accessories for her coat: a faux fur hat-and-glove set.

"These are going to be great when it gets colder! Can you imagine how warm these are?"

I held a glove to my face and cherished the softness on my cheek.

"Lucy? You got me something, too?" Brandy winked, grabbing the last package.

"Of course. I'm an excellent shopper." I would have winked back but for my swollen eye.

The gift was rather hefty, fatter than the coat box, but a bit narrower. I raised my eyebrows in anticipation and was excited to see that I had given my sister a new backpack. Bulkier than the one she used for school, this pack looked ready for a camping trip or a hike across Europe. France, even.

"This is excellent, Luce. Thanks." Brandy said and then turned her attention to Old Mom. "It's all fantastic."

"Well, don't bother putting it away. We've only got three and a half more hours until you're emancipated. You'll probably want to start packing."

She pulled the mug of cocoa to her lips, but I could have sworn I saw Mom smiling.

New Mom. Back again. Or had she ever left?

"I'm sorry, what did you say?" Brandy asked. I had never heard such panic in her voice.

Even Tippy let out an exhausted groan.

"You have three and a half hours until you're eighteen. My contract is up the second that clock hits midnight. I suggest you start packing."

The air in the room shifted as Mom's demeanor changed. Brandy looked to me, back to Mom, at the clock. Mom never even blinked.

The hair on the back of my neck slowly crept up, as if the house teemed with ghosts and they had all just joined us at the table.

"I don't get it." Brandy shook her head. "Is this a joke?"

"No, Brandy, it is not. We've had our giggles here tonight and that's your grand farewell. But this is the deal: at midnight I am done with you. You are no longer my child, you are no longer welcome in this house, you are no more burden of mine." Mom sat her mug down hard. "This is what is NOT going to happen: as of midnight I am changing the locks on the doors and you will not be inside this house. Nor will you ever be again. If you don't leave willingly, I will take you out by any means necessary."

Mom had just threatened her life. Brandy might not have understood New Mom, for she had had so few dealings with her. But I did. Her threats were not to be taken lightly.

"This is what WILL happen: you and your sister are going to pack your new bag. I would suggest taking some extra tennis shoes, because you'll probably be walking quite a bit. If you are done by eleven I will personally drive you to the Amtrack station and buy you a ticket anywhere you want to go, as long as you end up at least one thousand miles from here. I will give you three hundred dollars. And then we will be done with each other."

Neither of us had seen this coming. Brandy sat like a popsicle, stick-straight and frozen solid. The three of us sat in silence while Mom nursed her cocoa.

"Hey, Brand, let's get moving. We don't have long to get you ready." I pulled her arm, took the backpack out of her hands, and dragged her from her chair.

"I don't get it."

I led my sister to her room, watched her fold up on her bed.

"Brandy, this isn't a game. You've got to snap out of it. Please."

I opened her dresser and started picking through her underwear. Brandy was always cold, so I grabbed her thermals and thickest socks first.

"But, Luce, she likes me. Why would she get rid of *me*?" Brandy broached one of our unmentionable subjects. We rarely discussed Mom's favoritism.

"Who knows? She's not right anymore. Just get up and get moving. Don't upset her. She seemed pretty serious, and after my problems with her this afternoon I don't think you want to push her buttons."

"Where will I go?" My sister clutched her pillow to her chest and let the tears flow. "I don't know anybody. I've never had a job. I haven't even finished high school!"

"Winter's coming. Go someplace warm, like Arizona or California. Mom gave you the winter gear for a reason, but you need to make an excellent decision right now about where you're going to live." I hated taking the role of the responsible sibling. All of my internal alarms were screaming, and I kept promising them I would attend to their concerns once my sister was taken care of and on the road.

Neither of us even suggested bringing in the authorities. We had spent so long following Mom's rules and reacting to her fire drills that Brandy and I didn't consider contacting outsiders.

"Lucy, I can't do this."

"Yes, you can. Now tell me which jeans are the most comfortable. Ones you can get long johns under and still fasten." I held open her pants drawer and yanked out some denims.

She finally came over and helped. We shoved as many clothes as possible into the bag, found a flashlight in my room, and rolled up a blanket that we tied under the pack. While Mom sat in her room casting spells, or whatever her constant muttering produced, I snuck into the kitchen and loaded Brandy up with some food.

"I'm sorry, Luce." Brandy wrapped her arms around me.

"No, Brandy, don't apologize. You didn't do anything."

"I'm sorry you'll be here alone with her."

I stared at my sister. I had been in such a race to get her going that I hadn't even considered this consequence.

"When she came home tonight I really thought that she had changed again. How stupid am I?" Brandy said.

"We haven't done anything wrong," I reminded her.

"Yeah we have. We were born!"

"What else can we do?" I asked, still looking to Brandy for advice.

"Kill her?" My sister suggested, crying.

Despite the gravity of our situation, Brandy's idea made me chuckle. Which in turn made me start bawling.

"Or is it too soon for that?" Brandy muttered, glancing at her watch.

I could barely hear her over our sniffling, Brandy's words so inexplicable I knew I must have misinterpreted them. But Tippy jumped on the bed, joined us in a group hug until Mom yelled for us to come downstairs.

They left the house a bit past ten, Brandy bundled for a Canadian winter, Mom humming a hymn as she opened the back door.

When she spoke to me her black eyes forced me to look away. "You can sit outside with the dog."

I held my hand out to Brandy, a last wave, a goodbye, a desperate attempt to drag her back inside with me.

"But don't get used to it," Mom snapped as she slammed the door.

My insides dropped as I bid my sister farewell.

* * *

Mom returned within the hour. I met her at the back door, helped usher in the bags from Menards, and set them on the kitchen table.

We didn't mention Brandy.

Just like that, my sister was gone. Erased. Eradicated.

Escaped.

Mom lilted about the house, singing to herself, petting Tippy, occasionally letting out a muffled chuckle. Once when she laughed I caught sight of her eyes and instantly felt her claws reaching through my back to rip out my spine.

I wondered if Brandy had actually left the area. What if Mom had hurt her? Could she be in the cornfields somewhere between here and town? Would she run immediately to some authority figure and let them know I was left behind? That France was simply the confines of these walls and Mom's dwindling grasp on reality?

My heart deflated. Brandy was proud and kept our family secrets to herself. She had too much loyalty to Mom. She would never turn her in.

When Mom ventured back outside I put Tippy in my lap and prayed. For some reason I felt dirty inside, whispering to God. Talking behind Mother's back, the fear crawling along my skin as though I was covered in thousands of scorpions. But Brandy needed help, and I fretted that she didn't have the strength to ask for herself, let alone me.

While I loved my sister, she had never understood the gravity of my situation. Because she had survived a few whippings and knew that eventually the bruises healed over, Brandy ignored a lot of the badness in our house. She went to school but never revealed our dirty secrets. Even at church, when she left for Sunday school or youth group, she could have suggested that someone look into my unexpected trip to Dad's.

My sudden visit with a father who didn't exist.

Brandy was hot headed. She would be freaked out and fuming, concentrating only on herself and the dilemma her birthday had created for her.

For us.

I listened while Mom installed the locks. Stood ramrod straight, staring out the open kitchen door, Tippy at my feet. My fists flexed open, closed. Mom crouched outside, hanging onto the brass knob, the door a giant eye exposing the moon-drenched yard.

I stretched my fingers. Held my breath as the wind strode in to caress my hair, the fragrance of autumn filling the kitchen. Looked at the cornfield. Dared not look at my mother.

My legs twitched, and I could feel myself making a run for it. Grabbing Tippy by her collar and yanking her into the curve of my arm. Slamming the door with my right hand as I leapt over the threshold, knocking Mom backward and onto the concrete. My head start would be small, but my agility and speed would nurture it.

Over the sidewalk, into the backyard. Past the shed and old swing set. Into the corn. Into the darkness.

"Done!" She said, curbing my getaway before I ever took a step. Mom checked her handiwork, then walked around me without a word to fix the front door.

I didn't move. The slight hope that I could always run while she was at work shattered as Mom pounded her way around the downstairs, nailing the windows shut, changing all of the locks. Installing new ones on the outside.

Thwarting any escape.

My stillness became stiffness and even Tippy begged me to move, jumping against my legs before attacking her water dish.

"It was a great party," Mom said after completing her chores. She gripped the hammer tightly, the look on her face daring me to give her an opportunity to use it.

"Yes, it was lovely. I think we all had a good time."

* * *

I jumped from bed, terror taunting me from sleep. I flipped over and encountered Mother, sitting by the edge of my bed, her eyes red and alive with an energy that made me want to scream.

Her fingers stroked the wooden hammer handle, her knuckles pale as the moonlight that seeped under my curtains. Tippy laid beside her, cuddled against her thigh. Still trusting the woman who had fed her for the past six years.

My eyes moved from dog to woman and I held my mother's glare.

"God loves you," she said, standing. "Try not to forget that."

She left my room but not my head. Her face decorated my dreams. Each time I awoke it was all I could do not to roar and break the windows so I could flee the dreadful house.

God might love me, but someone else loved Mom for sure. Someone whose name was so horrid that I dared not even think it.

Chapter 4

Joan

You were supposed to be my miracle baby.

Alex and I had planned to have another child. In fact, we had been trying for months. *Ovulation* became the code word for wanton sex, the lust we had for one another quelled only by our love for Brandy. If she was awake we would entertain her with a video tape and run off to the laundry room for six minutes of intense stain removal or, if we could hold off until nap time, twenty minutes of insanely quiet love making in our own bed.

His parents had passed away when Alex was only eight. He had bounced through the foster system until the state emancipated him at seventeen.

My husband valued family, wanted one of his own to cherish. I simply wanted to be surrounded by Alex. If that meant having more children who looked and laughed and told horrible knock-knock jokes like he did, then I was all for an enormous clan. Four kids with his chocolate curls? Glorious. A dozen, their hazel eyes shifting from brown to green, just like their dad's? Nothing would have made me happier.

"I drove by the cutest place today. Three blocks from a park, nice sized back yard, two car garage." Alex told me one afternoon when he returned home from work.

"Yeah? How much?"

"Don't know. I wanted to make sure you liked it, too. How 'bout I take you and the kid to dinner and we can check out the neighborhood on our way home?"

He wanted my opinion, but I could tell by the flicker in his eye that his mind was made up. Alex had great instincts and often made life-altering decisions on his gut feeling alone. I could tell that this was one of those occasions.

"Which school district?"

"Hammond. Which, I don't have to remind you, is the best!" He dipped me so that I was facing Brandy and left me hanging backward while our daughter smeared peanut butter on my mouth with her kiss.

When Alex lifted me back up he licked my lips. "No jelly, Brandy?"

"Dad!" She ran over and clung to his legs.

"Good to see you, too, Pumpkin!" Alex let go of my arms and reached down to pick up his little girl. "I think you got prettier while I was at work today."

"Of course I did," Brandy announced, and we all laughed.

My heart melted, watching the two of them together. Brandy resembled her father so much that I often wondered if I had anything to do with her creation at all. Watching my daughter's eyes, I knew that she idolized this man almost as much as I did.

Almost.

We were a family full of promise back then, our house alive with the anticipation of growth and the strength of togetherness.

At that moment you might have been a shimmer in my eye. Just being in a room with Alex made me all fluttery, my belly doing flops when he held me, my breasts so tender from his touch that I constantly felt pregnant. My husband used to tease me that we should buy stock in EPT, I purchased so many of the pregnancy tests.

I waited for you. When the world crowded around me, when all was black and I could barely rise from bed, I longed to join you in your watery tomb and watch you develop into another little Alex. You could have been my miracle. You could have saved me from the sorrow, as it pressed in.

Instead you were a leech on my life. Cumbersome and relentless. An incessant reminder of all that should have been, but never became. Sucking the life from my every bone as you grew and thrived.

Chapter 5

Lucy

Silence startled me, at first. I whistled a lot and talked to Tippy while I worked, but once my mother came home and retreated to her room even the dog refused to make noise. The house was chilling. A tomb. I jumped each time a fly passed.

During dinner Mom often discussed her work at the bank or the issues in town, how the flooding in Iowa would have ripple effects on the local economy.

She spoke as though I were one of her colleagues, issued her daily robotic recitation of polite conversation.

"So how does that affect the price of gas?" My questions were scholarly, impersonal, a vehicle to carry her conversation forward. Although I didn't understand her motives, I cherished any time we had together that resembled normalcy.

"It really shouldn't. But in today's market…." I listened intently, eager for words to fill the void that surrounded me.

In Brandy's absence, Mom and I had become civil. We did not joke, hug, or express much concern for one another, but the beatings stopped, and each night we ate at the kitchen table like two strangers paired up in a cafeteria.

My sister became one of the topics we never discussed. One Sunday afternoon Mother slid all of our family photos off the walls, the dust outlines ghosts of the antique frames that once decorated the living room and stairway. The naked markers orphaned me. I sat on the landing, Tippy curled in my lap, my stomach churning as Mom carelessly dropped our pictures into the garbage can.

Brandy and me with the Easter Bunny when I was three. Our hair long and perfectly combed, the dresses Mom made identical except for size. My sister had her arm wrapped around me, protectively. I remembered being terrified of the giant rabbit. In the picture you could tell I was trying hard not to cry, not to disappoint Brandy with my fear.

Mom and Brandy when Brandy was a baby. Mom's face beamed. I couldn't remember ever seeing her so ecstatic.

Dad at his high school graduation. I had spent hours studying his shaggy haircut and toothy grin, trying to find myself in him. To see if, just maybe, some bit of Dad swam in my cerulean eyes, or if he was the model for my rather pointed chin.

My sister had the faintest memories of riding Dad's shoulders at a summer parade, streaking through the yard while he sprayed her with the garden hose, his soothing voice reading to her as she fell asleep. How many times had I imagined myself in her place, feeling the warmth of this man I had never met but through her fragile thoughts?

The three of them. Before Dad died, before I joined the ranks. Everyone smiling, Brandy forever caught with her mouth open during a fit of giggles. Mom pressed under Dad's chin, her head balanced against his neck, Brandy held tightly on her lap. Although it was a lovely picture, it had always made me feel misplaced. I was forever on the outside, looking in at this happy family. I could put my finger on the dusty glass and touch them. But I could never be them.

Glass crashed as the frames stacked up. Mom didn't even hesitate as she pulled down the black and white photos of her parents, the grandparents I never knew, her own baby pictures.

Why was she giving all her memories away?

Mom suddenly looked at me as if she had had no idea I was there.

"Go somewhere else. Go to your room. Go to the basement, I don't care. Just stay away from me," she growled.

My movements were swift and silent. I had learned stealth from my sister and practiced it at all times now.

Sitting in Brandy's room, I tried to smell her. Her pillow contained a smidgeon of her scent, and I sucked it in, trying to imagine her life without me. I wondered where she was, if she had found a place to stay, a job, a new family. I couldn't imagine her fear. The bravery it took to survive on her own.

As I listened to Mom's frustration grow, I quietly crept back into my room. Mom didn't need the aggravation of finding me on Brandy's bed.

While I waited for her anger to settle, I realized that no one had ever come to ask about me—not the police, not the school, not even Reverend Baxter from church. Brandy had been gone long enough now that someone should have come after me.

I swallowed my heartache and tried not to give way to tears. My sister was dead, smashed like the photos in the trash bin. She had to be. Brandy would have told. She never would have left me alone like this.

With Mother.

* * *

I pilfered. I knew it was wrong, taking things from the house and hiding them in my closet.

The adventure began with my sister's tablets from school. I stole two from her bedroom and added them to my bookshelf. Then, when Mom didn't notice, soon more of Brandy's possessions became my own.

Her knitting needles and the pile of half-started projects she had in an old box under her bed slid easily under my box springs. An old pair of jeans I was certain my sister couldn't even wear became mine. Her orange-and-white nail buffer. A ceramic kitten that I strategically placed on the window sill, in the corner behind my curtains.

From the bathroom I took a few aspirin, some cough drops, band aids and added them to the pockets of my dressier clothes that hung unused. Then boldness settled in and I started to lift things throughout the house.

Small things, at first. Food. Kleenex. The Lois Lowry books Brandy had left behind.

Then my priorities changed. I cut through the thin sheath covering my box springs and started a collection of goods that I tucked up under my bed. Water bottles, snack foods, a flashlight that I found under the bathroom sink. Brandy's barrettes and the stuffed rabbit, Bernie, from her bed. Pencils. Lots of colored pencils.

Sometimes I felt like a feral cat, chasing after anything whimsical while also keeping my eyes peeled for fresh food.

Old Mom never returned. I liked to imagine that Brandy had stolen her away, could picture the two of them strolling down city streets in Phoenix, talking about the harvest weather back home and how they never missed it.

Or me.

My sister hadn't been gone three weeks when everything changed again.

I had become complacent. Not content, not slacking in my chores, still tiptoeing around Mother. But as each day passed without a steady threat of violence, I eased out of the fortress I had built around myself. Let the walls down. Found pleasure in life's small moments.

Tippy and I took to singing loudly while I pressed Mom's work clothes or prepared dinner. We boogied about the kitchen, sometimes even daring to flash through the living room in a bold ritual dance of our own creation, striking bizarre poses and chanting while we dusted or ran the vacuum.

Sometimes we just needed to burn off a bit of pent up energy and smooth out our edges. Tippy never argued with my decisions to run amok while Mom was at work.

Perhaps she should have.

I had the dog in my arms, waltzing by the head of the dining room table, when Mom came home sick from work. She didn't drive all the way to the back of the house as was her habit. Instead she parked near the front and collected the mail. Mom startled me when she stepped into the living room; I was so wrapped up in my mid-morning talent show that I hadn't even heard her key in the lock.

For an instant I was relieved that the person entering our house was Mother.

Until I saw the look on her face.

She swung the door shut with such force I thought for certain the windows would crack.

"How dare you!" Mother screamed. Red streaks shot up her neck, settled in her cheeks.

"We were just dancing." My defense was lame.

"Dancing? So close to the windows that I could see you from the road?"

I noticed the part in the curtains, the sunlight that stopped right by my feet. Mom's brow creased and turned such a dark shade of red that I thought she might have a heart attack before she ever took off her coat.

"I didn't realize...I'm sorry, Mom." I knew the apology would do no good.

"You didn't know? How could you NOT know?"

The coat came off. Mother dropped it into the recliner and came at me so fast I almost fell over. Tippy jumped out of my arms and fled the room without so much as a goodbye.

"Don't you get it, Lucy? Don't you understand that I don't want people to know you still live here?"

I had understood that for quite some time now, though I was loathe to admit it.

"Yes."

"Have you ever thought how much happier I'd be if you were really gone?"

Mom backed me into the corner. When the wall stopped me, my heart fell. After the shed incident I no longer tried to run from my punishments. But I still wanted to have that option. This time I knew I was trapped.

I tried to maintain eye contact but instead found myself cowering. Her words pained me almost as much as her fists.

"Go to your room. Don't come out until I say you can."

I rocketed away, Tippy quick to follow. We bolted into my room and shut the door.

* * *

That evening Mom allowed me downstairs for dinner. After running to the bathroom, I fed Tippy and then joined Mom at the table for a somber meal.

She had calmed down but her unpleasant mood lingered.

"I'm sorry you don't feel well," I said, trying to start a conversation.

"If I wanted to speak to you, I would. You're lucky I let you out to eat."

For an instant I stared at the steak knife in her hand, the glint it made under the lights attracting my eye. I wanted it. My heart jumped a beat as I realized that I had been assembling the wrong types of things in my box springs.

I shook that thought out of my head. Mom might be crazy, but my idea was even worse, lusting after that blade like I might have to use it against her.

My cheeks colored with shame.

I finished my meal and sat politely, waiting in the quiet for her to do the same.

* * *

My eyes flicked open when Mom started working on my door. I had been sleeping for hours and thought her rage had finally dissipated.

I was wrong.

Tippy jumped off the bed but ran back up with me when she felt the waves of anger radiating off Mom.

"I wouldn't get upset if I were you. You made your own choices. I trusted you, and you shit on that trust."

In my sleepiness, I hadn't even really pieced it together. I watched Mom with the hook and eye lock and realized that she intended to trap me in my bedroom.

"Mom, I'm sorry! It was a mistake! I didn't know anyone could see me!" I sat up but had to put my hand over my mouth to keep from screaming.

"You knew exactly what you were doing. You were flaunting it. Why didn't you just stand right in front of the windows and let the world know you're still here?"

"I was just playing with Tippy. I wasn't paying attention to the windows like I should have."

"And it has cost you. Big time."

The tears came and amplified my shame. I hated breaking down in front of her.

"Please, Mom. Please don't do this to me. I'll be good, I promise. I won't leave the back of the house." I gave my best effort, but it only angered her more.

"You and I both know that this would have happened sooner or later. I'll get a dead bolt tomorrow."

With a quick slam of the door, Mom sealed me in. I heard her click the temporary lock into place and clung to Tippy while fear roiled inside me.

Panic made the room spin. I found it difficult to breathe, to even open my eyes and acknowledge my surroundings, the four walls that barred my exit. The flowered wallpaper that seemed to smile and ridicule me, its captive.

I put my hand on my battered white nightstand and tried to regain my balance. Looked across the room at its older sister, the matching dresser, furniture I'd had as long as I could remember. Besides Tippy, these were the only things to keep me company now that I was locked inside. I didn't even have so much as a picture of Brandy to lend me comfort as Mom's steps creaked down the hallway toward the stairs.

But at least this time it wasn't the shed.

* * *

Mom was thoughtful enough to come home for lunch every day after that.

While she let Tippy out for a run across the yard, I was allowed bathroom time. By then my bladder was so close to exploding that I almost had to crawl to the toilet for fear of peeing myself in front of Mother.

While she was busy with the dog, I refilled my cache of water bottles and snuck them back into my bedroom.

We ate sandwiches or sometimes soup, had iced tea and fruit. Once Mom developed a routine it rarely changed, so day after day we consumed the same meals. I wished I hadn't lost my privileges and could still be the one in charge of cooking.

"You have fifteen minutes," Mom would say each day.

I ate standing up, leaning against the sink. She could not have cared less; she was absorbed in her newspaper, ignoring me as usual. But from my vantage point I could see the world outside our windows. The road. The wall of corn, frail and yellowed from the weather, ready for harvest.

I could spot the three trees in our front yard. Every year Brandy, Mom and I had had an autumn contest to see who could decorate their tree the best. Our family competition had gathered quite the following in town. Friends from church would cruise past our old white two-story on their Sunday afternoon drives to see what we had accomplished. Some of our teachers and those of Brandy's friends who had cars and could navigate the country roads would pause and wave as their tires kicked up the gravel dust that coated all the vegetation girding our lawn.

They were never allowed to stop and join us, even if we promised not to venture off the front porch or take our conversation across the road where the Hanleys kept their cows. Mother wouldn't allow it. Instead, Brandy and I stood right at the edge of the terrace, giddy with all the attention, gesturing as the cars passed and worked their way back to the paved road, the four miles back to town.

Mom usually lost the contest; she liked corn stalks and pumpkins, which we girls thought pretty boring. My decorations usually centered more around Halloween, with ghosts and bats hanging from the branches.

But Brandy always put us to shame.

She worked on her tree plans for months. Sometimes she would ask me for my input, but often Brandy didn't involve me until she needed someone nimble to climb the tree and help her drape or dangle things. Mom gave her free rein with her creativity and even footed the bill for supplies without question.

Last year—when I was still alive to the outside world—my oak had held fifteen cardboard bats and two dozen fabric ghosts. I had had a fantastic time pulling myself as high as I could, balancing against the sturdy trunk as I tied my creations to branches and watched as they instantly spooked about in the breeze.

I loved being so high up I could spy on all our neighbors, even the Millers, who were never home. From my vantage point I could see they had added an old bath tub to the collection of trash strewn between their outbuildings. If I looked the other direction, and really strained my eyes, I could see the blacktop and the occasional car that cruised along it like a tiny ant. This high up, I felt close to God.

As Halloween neared, I carved three pumpkins (one for each of us!) and lit them every evening around my tree. At night the bats could barely be seen. But I knew they were there, floating about like the faintest of whispers.

Brandy's tree usually attracted the most attention. Last year her theme had been a bonfire. She managed to get the Thompsons, who went to our church and owned the feed store close to town, to donate a dozen huge pumpkins for her display and spent two months' allowance on orange and yellow fabric at Joanne's in town.

We had fun that day. Buying her cloth. Mom tucking the cash in Brandy's hand. The two of us getting on our bikes and pedaling the four miles to town.

Closing my eyes in the kitchen, I could jump into that earlier me. I could feel the sting of the wind as it hit my face and caused tears to cloud my eyes, the absolute freedom of my hair flying behind my head as I raced down the road. Brandy was always ahead of me, turning back to check and make sure no one had clobbered me with their John Deere, smiling in anticipation of her great plan.

We were not only sisters then, but co-conspirators. Brandy's look of unfettered joy, the devotion with which I shared her secret, made us members of a special club that no one else was allowed to join.

When we arrived we were breathless. I propped my bike next to the Hallmark store and had to lean over for a second to catch my breath.

"That was a great ride!" Brandy, as always, hadn't even seemed to break a sweat.

We left with two big bags of cloth, then rode straight to the hardware store to pick up nails and a little rope.

"You'll have to drive by. If it goes as planned, I'm going to call the paper to have them come take pictures." Brandy bragged to the clerk, her confidence amazing. Her project was still only in the planning stage, but already she considered herself successful.

"I shore will, honey. I shore will." Mrs. Leighton told my sister as she bagged our goods.

The woman never even glanced my way. But I was the quiet one and used to being ignored. Brandy, on the other hand, was the center of attention everywhere we went. Not one person we passed didn't know her name. I felt like a wilted flower beside her.

The ride home was never as long or as exciting as the trip to town. Our dreaded return to Mother dampened even the best excursions. Now the road seemed bumpier, the weather colder, my nose running as well as my eyes. Yet I could barely contain my excitement. I couldn't wait to help my sister assemble her masterpiece.

We carved pumpkins for two days. Even Mom entertained us by adding some flames to the front of a gourd, then taking all of our seeds and cleaning them for later. She encouraged our artwork, brought us cider and leftover cornbread for a snack.

"This has been a great weekend," I told Brandy as we dragged hay bales to her oak tree, which towered over the others in the yard. The leaves were a brilliant red, in stark contrast to the yellow of the hickories by the creek. Brandy was lucky hers still retained most of its leaves. Mine was nearly bald.

"Yeah. Who needs to hang out at the movies when we get to be so...organic?" Brandy winked and started aligning her pumpkins around the edge of our hay circle.

We didn't finish until Sunday evening. Brandy assigned me the task of attaching the fabric to the uppermost part of the tree. I didn't really want to nail it in and had to apologize to the tree for hurting her. Brandy crossed the road and yelled directions to me.

"Move the part by your knee to the left about six inches," she bellowed.

Mom heard us and came outside to join the fun.

The finished piece created the illusion of a giant bonfire. Each pumpkin had flames carved into its face, and they were stacked three levels high. The top pumpkins almost met the fabric, giving the illusion that the fire practically touched the sky, the wind moving the cotton like unencumbered flames.

We watched from the porch after we had lit all of the pumpkins. My tree looked pathetic next to my sister's, but I was fine with that. I just enjoyed having fun with my family, carrying out our traditions, knowing that Brandy's tree would cause townspeople to drive past our house and see how creative we were.

Pretty soon one car paused as it sped past, then another. The third stopped, driver and passengers staring with delight, and by nightfall we had a steady stream of visitors past our house. Brandy loved the attention.

But this year Mom had decorated all three trees. I ached for my sister. For her goofy smile, the hee-haw of her laughter, the warmth of working together in the kitchen.

"When did you do the trees?" I asked, forgetting that she didn't want me to speak.

"Last week. It's never autumn unless we decorate the yard," Mom said, agreeing with me. For once.

Three trees. Three sets of cornstalks tied around the trunk, with pumpkins stacked at the bottom. Boring. How I lusted after the fun I could have had outside, playing in the leaves with Tippy, laughing with my sister as we took in the comforting scent of fall decay.

"Your time is up. Go back upstairs," Mom said as she put her dishes in the sink.

Tippy and I ran up. Mom followed, shutting the door, turning the deadbolt wordlessly.

I missed my sister. Finding her stuffed bunny, I curled up with him on my bed and hugged him close to my chest.

* * *

On day twelve of my bedroom confinement, I started counting corn.

Row after row. Over two miles worth, thirty thousand seeds an acre. Three hundred fifty acres between my room and the Hanley's house. Despite the wicked storm that had rolled in, I could still see each row, nearly ready for harvest.

Mr. Hanley had told me years before that this crop was feed corn. Next year he would raise soybeans on this same field, planting them in the opposite direction to ensure that the earth maintained her integrity.

I waited until late in the afternoon, when the sun stopped blocking my view. By that hour I was usually consumed with boredom, having read in the morning and done a limited exercise routine after lunch. I perched on the floor with my eyes just over the sill and gazed out at the fields that surrounded our house. Even my bedroom detention could not diminish the beauty of an Iowa autumn.

The squall kept my window at a constant staccato, rain pat-pat-patting against the wooden frame. The corn danced to this same rhythm, the stalks waving and rippling like water, almost flattening in spots. I could hear the branches from the magnolia tree bang against the side of the house like they were knocking for me to let them inside. The sky started its night ritual of casually darkening, with chasers of flamingo shooting across the horizon.

My spirit needed this. To crack the window and let the outside trickle in, absorb the snappy scent of the crisp air, imagine myself buried in the leaves Mom still hadn't raked. I could close my eyes and see my sister traipsing around the back line of our property, picking up pine cones to decorate for Christmas, singing to herself as she twirled and danced through the fields. She always made me carry the bucket, but I didn't mind.

This afternoon brought magic. I had occupied myself with the corn again, starting on the west side of Mr. Hanley's crop, working my way toward the edge of the house.

Row 2254. I counted in patterns, imagining a giant grid and multiplying the vertical rows that I could see by the horizontal ones that I could only imagine.

The deer shot out of the field and seemed surprised to find themselves in an open garden, our back yard. Nine of them stood, looked about, mellowed. I was fascinated by the silent signals they gave each other, one keeping guard while the others looked for food. Eyes catching bits of sunlight glowed back at me. I tapped my window, hoping they would hear and look my way, but the creatures simply helped themselves to my mother's mums and then ambled out of view.

I strained to see them. If Mother weren't due home at any moment, I was tempted to fling the window open and stick my head out, but I stopped myself.

"Look, Tippy. Aren't they beautiful?" We both felt an instant kinship to the animals. In my heart I even hoped that they would somehow rescue me.

Chapter 6

Joan

Your infancy dragged on forever.

Some days I could barely haul myself from bed, and there you were, screaming for food, a diaper change, and someone to hold you. You demanded attention. You demanded clean clothes. The neighbors could hear you wailing. But I didn't care.

Instead, I cradled the paring knife I'd received years earlier as a wedding gift. Made it my constant companion. While your eyes begged me to release you from your crib, I just stared back. Literally clawed my own skin to keep myself from smothering you, the lines from the blade almost as thick as the scars the devil had left to haunt my skin, the night he had created you. But what does a mother do if she doesn't want to touch her own child? I would gawp at you for hours, and all I could think was red hair, red hair, red hair and how to eradicate it.

I had even attempted it, once. My ultimate fantasy. I grabbed your stupid, kicking feet, my blood as hostile as your hair, and fancied myself a Nazi soldier. Walked you toward the wall, where I planned to swing your legs and beat your head repeatedly until the blessed moment when I could hear your skull crack and feel the warmth of your blood spray my face. I could see myself, licking the

~ 47 ~

fluid that had splashed against my lips, wiping the gray matter off my shoes once your body had been discarded.

But someone else could see me, too.

When I noticed Brandy in the doorway I pretended to be playing, gently swaying you back and forth, even though you were upside down and no mother would hold her daughter in such a way.

I would take deep breaths and run movie images in my mind of eight hundred ways to kill you and eventually I would calm down. You would stop with the freight-train racket, your wails giving way to gaspy sobs, until you gave up and realized that I wasn't going to come for you. Disappointing, wasn't it? You should have been in my shoes. I had nowhere to push my rage but into tiny boxes I stacked deep in the closet. You, on the other hand, could cry all you wanted and no one batted an eye. Except, of course, for Brandy.

When I looked at you, at the blood dotting the floor around your prison and the fresh wounds overwhelming my arms, I knew that I had to do something to control myself. Or else you would die. And while that concept really didn't faze me, I certainly didn't want to go to prison. What would happen to Brandy? She would become a foster kid and wind up being adopted by some ratty rednecks who kept sixteen other kids in their trailer and only ate meat when someone ran over a possum on the way home from the bar at night. I couldn't paint that picture.

Church really helped me. While I couldn't reconcile the thought that you were my child, I was able to see you as a kid that needed altruism. My daughter? No. Brandy's young friend who had a bad home life and needed to crash here 99.99% of the time? Yes. I could envision that.

Even before you could walk I had two dozen stories for your birth family. These untruths comforted me, put a healthy distance between us. You became the discarded child of my meth addicted neighbor, a girl from Brandy's daycare who was starving and needed a good home, an infant I picked up at the local shelter like some forlorn, forgotten dog and brought home to be a playmate for my real daughter.

Of course I never shared these stories with Brandy or anyone else. But they soothed me. One time you were sick and screaming in a fevered rage. I had gotten dressed and put on my face, ready for work. The look of you made my stomach churn. You had vomit streaked all over your cheeks and in your hair. The stench of shit surrounded you. Worst of all, I knew that the sitter wouldn't come if you couldn't hold down food.

I didn't want to miss a day's pay wiping away your filth. To be honest, I didn't want to miss a day's pay doing anything with you. And your constant bawling drove me over the edge. What, exactly, did you want from me? What did you think I could possibly give you? Why had I ever brought you home in the first place?

I was six seconds from leaving you alone in the crib while I went to work.

But then I looked again, and you were Patty, the neglected child my pastor had asked me to watch while her parents were in rehab. It tore me apart to see you so ill with no one to pick you up. No one to hold you or love away your discomfort. God, my heart ached for you and your vomit-encrusted soul. I couldn't begin to fathom your loneliness, how desperately you needed a good mother.

I dropped my shoulder bag and grabbed a dishtowel. Except for a few minutes to call my boss and let her know of your sickness, I spent the entire day rocking you and singing soft songs that had always helped Brandy fall asleep. You perked up after your bath, and it thrilled me when your little head nuzzled against my chest, your tiny fingers wrapped around my own.

I cursed your immature, irresponsible mother and truly bonded with you that day. How easily I allowed concern to consume me, as long as you were *her* child and not my own. Without that permanent tie I could walk away from you at whim, I didn't have to vow my life to protect you, I could care about you without being forced by societal rules to love you. Your red hair wasn't a barrier between us. Some other mother would carry that burden.

But once I set the vehicle in motion I also had to deal when it backfired.

The looks at the park when I accidentally called you "Brandy's little friend." The night when, after working a twelve-hour waitressing shift and my muscles were as flexible as a brick wall, Brandy referred to "her sister," and I argued with her for five minutes. The times I wished you away and literally waited for your negligent crack head mother to come back and fetch you. Stood by the door, even. Put out because that horrible woman had abandoned you with me. Again.

We had to move after the day-care incident.

I was proud of Brandy on her first day of school. She wore her hair braided and carried a small backpack full of crayons and craft-making materials. We took pictures, had a special chocolate chip pancake breakfast, and I bawled in my car after dropping her off.

Afterward I picked her up for a mother/daughter excursion. I had the entire day off work and planned a glorious afternoon, just the two of us. We went to a local pizza place for lunch, complete with six rounds of PacMan and enough breadsticks to feed her entire class. I could barely contain my joy.

We went shopping for more school clothes and then hit a three o'clock matinee. We chowed down on popcorn and soda, held hands while the animated movie played and all other children fidgeted and talked and constantly left the theater to go pee. But Brandy was transfixed. I loved her silence, the stoic way she sat upright and ate her snack one kernel at a time, eyes glued to the Disney characters she loved so much.

We ran a couple of errands for me, grabbed a burger about five thirty, and headed home.

Of course this was before everyone had a cell phone or pager.

The day care had left three messages on my answering machine. The first one asked if I was running late; my daughter was hungry and needed picked up. While I listened I stared at Brandy, wondering what the idiot woman was talking about. The second one said that they were closing in fifteen minutes and that I really needed to contact them. The third expressed great concern for my safety, since I had never been less than diligent with picking up my child on time. The owner also informed me that she had called the police to come get my daughter.

If she hadn't said my name I would have assumed she had dialed a wrong number. Brandy had her toys out and was playing with them when she looked up at me and asked, "Where's Lucy?"

My pleasant day soured instantly: It hit me that I had forgotten you at daycare. I cursed the stupid teenager from the clinic where I volunteered, since if she hadn't abandoned you with me, I wouldn't be embarrassed by this mistake.

I didn't know where to begin. I honestly thought about just getting in the car and slinking away, leaving you behind so your birth mother could parent you. But Brandy wouldn't let it drop.

"Mommy! Mommy! Where's my little sister? I want Lucy!"

A couple of minutes later, the police were at the door, accompanied by a woman from the state. How desperately I wanted her to take you away. Silently I begged her to just get it over with and make me a whole person again. To tour the apartment and see the evidence of my hatred, polka-dotting your floor. To lift my sleeves and know how keeping you around was killing me.

Instead I lied.

"Oh my goodness, I am so sorry. Brandy and I were celebrating her first day of school and I think we overdid it. Between the pizza and big bowl of popcorn at the movies, she got incredibly ill. During all the turmoil that caused, I lost track of time. I was just about to call the department to see how I could find Lucy. Poor thing! She must be terribly afraid! I know we've been worked up since I realized my mistake." The smile I plastered on my face must have worked. The policeman expressed concern, and I told him how embarrassed I was at not getting home on time.

"Being a single mother is really rough sometimes." I told him about Alex, that the father of my girls was no longer in the picture.

After we moved, I tried to change my ways and look at you like a mother should. But it made me feel so vile inside that I couldn't tolerate it for long.

I could spend all of my time praying to God, but in the end I was still saddled with you, Lucyfer. Even God wouldn't take you away.

Chapter 7

Lucy

The Hanleys didn't harvest until mid-October. I was insane with loneliness and boredom by the time the combines arrived, lumbering like drunken beetles up the field from the farmer's house. I couldn't help but adore their enterprise, the welcome respite their machinery and team work brought to my silent existence. But I hated them just the same. Despised the way they invaded my field, the hostility of annihilating the corn just a kernel when compared to the destruction dealt the wildlife.

The sheer number of animals sheltered by the plants amazed me. Early on I could barely make out the forms running from the comfort of their seasonal home but assumed they were coyotes. As the Hanley's continued working I saw pheasants, foxes, raccoons, and, of course, my deer, barrel in terror from the brigade. The farmers stopped for nothing. The animals meant diddly-squat to them. Once, I swear Mr. Hanley swerved just to run one over, a dog that had been raiding garbage cans since his owners had dumped him on our road early in the summer.

"Oh my God! Stop!" I hollered against the window pane when I saw the golden retriever get wedged into the corn head.

The poor dog was a stranger to the countryside and didn't understand farm equipment. The machine swallowed him whole. Within seconds, a flurry of blood misted the field.

"Don't look, Tip. Get away from the window!" I didn't want my dog to have a breakdown, watching the tragedy as it played out in the corn.

As Mr. Hanley moved forward, bits of something blonde spewed from his combine, but he was too far away to tell if he was harvesting corn or the remnants of a broken-hearted creature long rejected by his family.

My heart wrenched in fear and agony. The dog had done nothing to deserve such a wretched death, to be threshed alive. And who but me was left to stand up for him and deliver a eulogy?

And how many mice had died? Rabbits? Feral cats that roamed the stalks and kept the rodents from overrunning our house? A hundred obituaries, unwritten.

Of course I cried. I had watched the animals night after night as they snuck around our property, grazing on whatever greenery they could find. I did not want a single one of them to die or become so terrified of the field that they wouldn't return.

I cheered the beasts on. Celebrated each life as it escaped the clutches of the machines. Then realized, in a sudden and profound moment of truth, that these animals were blessed with the ability to flee.

Unlike me.

I fell to the floor. Covered my eyes with the edge of my curtain and bawled into it, drenching the material while I let my emotions rip through the room completely unfettered.

I had needed a good cry for a while. Tippy bounced around my legs, nipping at my skin, and battled me for control of my tears. Her tongue sought out the moisture before it had time to drip from my cheeks, her little face wedging between me and the curtain.

When I pushed my dog away, she growled and feasted on me with her one eye, her look a warning that I was losing precious water and shouldn't be so liberal with my tears. Which made me wail even harder at the thought of catching my own fluids in a water bottle just in case Mom never returned.

By the time the combines were at the edge of our yard, I was standing in front of my bed, screaming in an uncontrolled rage. I took my pillows and flung them around the room, then picked them back up and pounded them repeatedly against my mattress.

Tippy retreated under the bed.

After my tantrum, I returned to my window. I could almost see eye to eye with Mr. Hanley's son, but he didn't pay any attention to me.

"She hasn't let me out for two days!" I shouted. But of course, with the window closed and his combine fast at work, he couldn't hear me.

Every cell pushed me to flee. Every voice trapped in my head hollered with such force I thought my skull might explode. I looked at the Hanley boy, drinking a big plastic bottle of pop, wanting desperately to gulp it down myself. I knew I could break the window. Then crawl out onto the roof, wave my arms at him until he realized my distress.

But I restrained myself. What would Mom do to me if I acted so bold? Would she put me in the shed again? Even in the cold? How many times could she pound my face against the wall before it became Swiss cheese?

When Mom didn't show at lunchtime on Thursday, I at first worried about her safety and then as the hours passed began to panic about my bladder.

Tippy just said 'fuck it' and peed right on the floor.

"If she doesn't care, why should I?" my dog asked.

"Because I don't want to stay in a room that reeks, it's bad enough as it is," I explained.

"Then open the window and climb out to safety," Tippy told me, her snout in the air. At least she had had the decency to go in the corner and hadn't made a puddle by the bed.

I had the luxury of using my waste basket. Drip-drying was controversial, but after the third trip to my closet, I gave up trying to find old tissues and decided to go with nature. The stench overwhelmed the room. Even Tippy acted repulsed when she jumped on the bed to cuddle.

We shared my stash of water, a couple pieces of beef jerky, and played thirteen games of Monopoly. Tippy liked to be the banker, and because she usually won, I understood her to be a quick cheat.

"This time I get to hand out the money," I ordered as we cleared the board for the next game.

"Then good luck finding someone else to play," Tippy barked. She jumped onto the game board and pieces went flying all over the room.

By ten p.m., each time the house creaked I jumped off the bed and hovered by the door. Mom had stripped the room of light bulbs so the Hanley's wouldn't see that my room was occupied, leaving me without so much as the promise of hope.

I had never been left alone overnight. Brandy and I hadn't even had a baby sitter since we were in school. Mom was always there. Even since I had been locked away, I still took comfort in her footsteps, her routines, the sound of her bedroom door opening at three in the morning when she took a trip to the bathroom. In my room I listened to her every movement, every sound of her socks on the carpet, water running, the vacuum as she performed Saturday cleaning chores. Her motions became my own as I closed my eyes and imagined the thrill of doing dishes again or the luxury of a scalding hot bath with lavender scented bubbles.

But without Mom I had less than nothing. I had stuffy air that I could only relieve at night when no one noticed a cracked bedroom window. I had Tippy, who blamed me for our situation and would occasionally crawl under the bed and go mute with rage. Mom controlled my everything.

The darkness clawed at my every thought. I could feel someone standing behind me, breathing on my neck, making me jumpier than my lack of sleep had.

Then I realized that not much could be worse than my current situation. Burglars? Ha! Maybe they'd set me free. Steal me and take me home with them. I'd probably be much safer. And well fed.

I thought of them, these masked men, invading our house, tip-toeing in the darkness, looking for the electronic loot that other families would cherish. A television. Nintendo. A fancy fitness machine.

Instead, they'd stumble upon my locked room, thinking it must contain the household's treasure. Break down the door. Find me sitting, Tippy glued to my side, ask me why I was kept by myself in the pitch black.

When they opened their cloth bags, they'd be full of food. Hot soup. Macaroni and cheese. Pork chops, fresh from the frying pan, covered in apple slices.

The smells of their delicious spoils filled my room. Made me open my eyes. Brought me back to my current situation.

My stomach had a growling match with Tippy. We had such a limited food supply under the bed that I began to panic. What if Mom never came home? Could I eat the wallpaper? The sheets? And how long would Tippy and I make it without water?

When we heard the car drive under the bedroom windows, Tippy ran to the door and cried softly. I warned her not to get too excited, but her hopes were soaring and she was practically screaming by the time Mom finally made it upstairs to let us out.

"Dear God, you reek. Get in the shower. I want to go to bed soon, so make it snappy."

She carried a small suitcase into her room, and I ducked into the bathroom for a much-needed break. As I warmed the shower, I returned to my room and fetched our water bottles, the wastebasket, Tippy's piles. The toilet filled fast with our waste, the stench sickening.

Showering had never felt so sweet. And even though Mom interrupted my time, I cherished the fresh squeak to my hair and the droplets of water that clung to my skin. Tippy appreciated them, too. While I hurried about the room in my towel, she chased behind me, licking the moisture before I could dry it off.

"Are we that desperate?" The look in Tippy's eye told me everything. "At least she came home. We didn't have to eat any books!"

Chapter 8

Joan

You have always been part of my family.

Not because you shot screaming from between my legs or even because you inherited my mother's beak nose. It's not so simple.

You are as ancient as the wind, a disease that has rippled untamed through generations of my blood line. Every century at least one like you has emerged. A devil of sorts. Waiting patiently until the time to strike has come, then causing untold damage to kindred and community.

Alex always laughed at the family legend. My mother, though she rarely discussed the issue, quietly believed. She would whisper about it on occasion. Only in extremely private moments. Never at the dinner table, or a neighborhood barbeque, or even with God. Just with me, alone, her hand in mine.

She knew you would come. I'm certain of it. Mom always carried that wariness about her, almost a resignation that horror might emerge at any moment. A passive understanding that this was her fate, her turn to deliver the beast upon the world. Through me.

How could I have missed it? Was the depression after everyone was gone so all-encompassing that I somehow went blind? And stupid? And forgot everything? When all was upon me, did the terror close my mind to the truth?

My great-aunt Evelyn had spent years researching our heritage, following the stories from Mongolia to Alaska and all through Europe. When I was younger I found her eccentric, an old woman on a first name basis with Earth, who would pull my chin up and bore through me with her eyes. Her bangles skittered back to her elbow as she held my face under the hard light, the slight jingle of the silver bands offering comfort as I stood noiselessly, afraid she would yank out my eyes and gorge on them while my mother stood by and watched.

I listened to their conversations. She had maps and charts and old journals passed down from so many generations that I could barely see the script still on the page. Yet Aunt Evelyn could not only see the ink but translate each from the original language. Her intelligence amazed me. Her words terrified me.

The last time we visited she had spelled it out quite clearly, but none of us heeded her warning. Even after they carried her lifeless body from the room.

"Sixty years have passed since the last sighting," she reminded my mother as she wrapped her boney hands around a mug of hot tea.

"That's good, then. The longer the better." Mom hated these conversations with Evelyn.

"No, it's not good!" My great-aunt pounded her fist on the table, the silverware jumping upon impact. "One is upon us! I can feel her! I can feel her in this room, clawing to be free!"

Grandma silenced her sister. With one firm hand upon her shoulder, she politely told Evelyn to calm down.

Aunt Evelyn moved her gaze toward me. I clung to my mother. Wrapped my arms around her stomach and held on as tightly as I could.

"She's in you, child." Her pointed finger forced me to burrow my face into mother's side. "She taunts me. I have followed her through time. The wench knows who I am! I can smell her even when she's not of this earth. I saw her once, in Spain, and who won that time?" Evelyn raised her eyes heavenward, pointing at God. "Who was left standing?"

"That's enough, Evelyn. Quiet down." Grandma hovered by her sister's chair.

When Evelyn shot out of her seat the room took a collective gasp. I felt Mom's hands wrap around me protectively.

"I wear her blood on my hands! I was the victor! I took the eye and pulverized it, let the flames take the damned thing back to Hell where it belonged!" Evelyn lifted her fists in the air, as though she were scorning God Himself.

"We know, honey. You have fought this thing for decades." Grandma patted Evelyn's shoulder, her tone condescending. Behind her sister's back, Grandma rolled her eyes and shook her head.

"You know nothing. Don't even pretend to understand. The year is coming. Does no one care anymore? The year is coming!"

Grandma eased Aunt Evelyn's hands down. Both women looked drained.

"Evie, we all care. But sometimes when you work so hard on a project you get blinded by it."

"Mom, what's she talking about? What year?"

My great-aunt reared her head again, her torment twisting her features until she resembled a vicious dog on the brink of attack.

"Have you not told her? How could you be so insane!" The fist landed on a plate this time, shattering it. "The year 2000, prophesied as the Year of the Woman. The millennial change in seats above and below. When She assumes the role for which She was destined."

I had no idea what Evelyn meant, but dread settled in my stomach. A deep and somber ache with tendrils reaching into my adulthood.

"The bitch has been chasing her dream for centuries. I've seen what She's done! I've stood on the same ground where She let loose her horror and could smell the blood, fresh as the day She unleashed it upon the soil. I've watched it drip from her teeth while She gave me her maddening grin. Babies, dead at her feet. The world behind her, burning. Satan is nothing compared to her. If we don't stop her, She'll destroy humanity!"

"Mom, I'm scared," I whispered, practically crawling into my mother's lap.

"As you should be," Evelyn screamed. "She will rise from you. From your womb the witch will come!"

"Stop this!" Mother stood. "Mom, can't you shut her up?"

"We have to stop her! We have to end this now!"

I moved behind Mom as Evelyn grabbed her arm.

"I have no idea what you're saying and I'm just going to pretend that you're talking about our conversation. Which is one we will never have again." Mom used her firmest voice, spoken through tightly clenched teeth.

"The bitch is laughing at us. Can't you hear her? How many times has She crawled from our bellies? Every one of us carries the guilt. Not only did we birth her, but we fed the devil and taught her how to walk! All of us!" Aunt Evelyn beat her fist against her heart, the color draining from her face.

"Calm down, sister. You're reading too much into this."

"No. Joan's mother knows. Don't you, Gladys? I can see it in your eyes. You believe."

"I..." Mom started.

"She lives in our every cell. Trust me, she's just waiting for the right time and vehicle to emerge. Joan will bear her. But who will destroy her? Do you have the strength?"

I cowered, afraid of her questions.

"Of course you don't. My grandmother's cousin, Ruby, left her flopping in the yard like a chicken after she cut her head off. The beast was only four at the time. That morning, she had set fire to her brother in the kitchen. As the flames rolled off him, Ruby saw the color rise in her daughter's eye and knew then what she had borne. Ruby marched the spawn to the yard and took the ax to the child's neck. Of course her husband shot her straight through the heart before she ever laid the weapon down." Aunt Evelyn slowed her words a bit. "The men in our family have never understood."

"I have the strength." My mother's voice shocked me. She did believe.

"I know you do, Gladys. But your courage isn't enough for this one. She'll obliterate you before you ever lay eyes on her." A coughing fit racked Evelyn's chest.

"You need to deal with the child you have now. It is the only way. She is destined." She nodded my direction.

"No. If the child is hers I will take care of it. I will not harm Joan because you have bad feelings about her."

"Yes! You will! You must!" My great-aunt screamed as her hands flew to her chest, clutching her breast.

For a split second Evelyn held my gaze, surprise touching her face. Her upper lip curled as though it had a faint wisp of laughter stuck underneath it. Even as her eyes rolled back in her head, my great-aunt nodded at me in acknowledgement. Pinning the future to my collar with her words. Understanding that no matter what, you would come.

Her chin slammed against the table as she collapsed. I heard her jaws snap at the collision, the spray of blood bursting from her nose, decorating us all as her body plummeted to the floor.

As Evelyn drew her last breath, broken teeth fell from her mouth and skittered across the linoleum, collecting under the kitchen table. I could hear laughter that I first thought was a man's until I felt it pass through my lips and pool around my great-aunt while she convulsed on the floor.

Her fall was like an enormous tower crumbling to the ground during an earthquake. In my child's eye, she was the dragon slain by someone small.

Like a little girl. That I had yet to know. One that could kill someone as powerful as Evelyn with just the promise of her birth.

Not to mention all the other people I'd loved along the way.

After my mother died I could barely function. But you know that. You were with me then, clinging to life by devouring every drop of hope I had left. In my madness I forgot my legacy, the shadow that had always lurked on the edges of my existence.

But I couldn't hide from it forever.

You were six when I first remembered. The heat clung to us like Saran Wrap that miserable summer's day. We were at the park. I kept the bottles of water on the bench, and you came to me, sheltering your eyes from the glaring sun. Casting a shadow over your face. Letting your secret slip for a split second.

"Mom, I'm thirsty," you said, holding your hands out for some water.

I opened the spout on your plastic bottle and let you gulp down the cold sweetness, mesmerized by what I had never noticed. Your left eye, an iris within an iris. The birthmark of the girl yet to come.

The light hit it exactly, lit it up like the beginning of a solar eclipse, the second iris the moon just edging across the sun. My body trembled, paralyzed with fear. And you just tilted your head. Smiled. Handed me back your water.

"Thank you," you'd said, pretending your veins didn't hold all the horror of the world to come. "I love you, Mom."

Aunt Evelyn was right. I did not have the courage.

That night I sat in your room, my pillow in my hands. I wanted to smother you. Visions of my mother entered my head. She would never have hesitated. Her stride would have been swift, her actions to the point, her decision made twenty years before in that kitchen with the women in our family.

But that was not me. It took me three hours to put the pillow over your head. Three long hours during which I argued with everyone from Alex to God and back to Aunt Evelyn, who wagged her finger in judgment at me.

"Mommy? I just threw up in my bed." Brandy stopped me. I'd not heard so much as a floorboard creak, and there she was, standing in the doorway, watching me as I hovered over you.

I moved to help her when she vomited again.

I forgot you. Laying in your bed, tucked in for the night, your mother's pillow over your face. When I fell asleep the next night I realized you had put it back on my bed for me.

I didn't buy the ax until you were nearly twelve. I saw it in the hardware store, the head smooth yet deadly. As I walked past I heard the weapon call my name. *Joan,* it whispered, *I am here. You're going to need me soon. It's almost time.*

And that's when I finally woke up. The stupid sloughed off me as I put the wooden handle in my hand, felt how well it molded into my grip.

My dreams that first night were of chickens, thousands of headless chickens and my arm the blade that destroyed them.

Chapter 9

Lucy

I did a very bad thing when the snow first hit.

Tippy actually demanded I do it. Just looking at the determination on her face, I couldn't deny her. She stood guard while I quietly pulled open my window and stole the snow that piled outside it. Following her instruction I gathered several containers, then brushed over the bare spot I had created.

We had a glorious night. Tippy and I had spent so much time together we no longer needed to speak. I could hear her voice loud and clear in my head, and from her expression knew that she shared my thoughts as well. We hunkered down at the end of the bed and watched the moon grace the falling snow, our bellies chilled with the flakes I had gathered.

We discussed Brandy and where she might be right now. How convenient it was, finding our old Easter baskets in my closet to use as bowls for the snow. How fun Mom had always made holidays, never having to work since the bank was closed, the three girls and Tippy always going for a picnic or to a church gathering, sometimes even the water park during the summer months.

Then Tippy got down to business. The snow went from dandruff flakes to avalanche conditions in just a few hours. She reminded me how important our water supply was becoming, especially since Mom didn't let us out every day anymore.

I refilled the baskets—a couple of times. Neither of us had realized how thirsty we were and relished the moisture. Tippy instructed me to fill every shoe and bag that could hold water, all of my plastic pencil boxes, my backpack, our stash of empty bottles under the bed. Even though I was freezing, she had me strip down to my skivvies and wash myself.

How alive that made me feel! The moon kept her eyes on me, my pale skin beaming back to her. Goose bumps climbed my arms as I washed, the snow not enough to relieve my stench but pleasant all the same. I turned from Tippy and dropped my bra to the floor, ran my wet hands over my chest, covering my nipples when they became hard.

"Having fun there?" Tippy asked.

I told her to leave me alone.

"It's a shame you can't save enough to wash your hair."

My good feeling faded as I contemplated how horrid I must look. I pinched a clump of hair and ran my fingers through the oily mess. I knew at least a week had gone by since Mom last let me wash it.

The flurry continued and Tippy, drunk on snow, insisted on going outside.

"You'll fall off the roof!" I warned her.

"You're too cautious. If you had any balls at all, we wouldn't be locked in this room."

I took my top sheet and tied it around her body, snug behind her front legs.

"Don't blame me if you get hurt."

I eased open the window again and helped her outside. Her ears perked with the breeze, her smile immediate. Tippy didn't move for several minutes. She appreciated the ambiance, the luxury of fresh air, no matter how chilling.

Once Tippy worried her way across the snow she relieved herself.

"Don't infect our water supply!" I silently screamed.

I tied the sheet to my bed frame and acted on Tippy's orders. With an old pair of underwear I scraped her dried piles off my floor and flung them like softballs into the back yard. My dog watched with amusement as I drained my wastebasket by tossing the contents as far as I could, knowing the downfall would cover my trail.

We didn't sleep until dawn.

When Mother fetched us Tippy and I were both terrified she had discovered our antics and would steal our loot from the night before.

"God, you reek. Get in the bath. I don't have to work today so I thought you could clean your room."

Just like that I was free. And worthy of her conversation.

Mom let Tippy out in the yard. Over the running water in the bathroom, I could hear her excited yipping. She could hear me purring as I crawled into the hot suds, soaping away the strain of the past week.

I laughed at the thought. My life had been reduced to a constant quest for water. And here I was, rolling in it.

"I made you breakfast," Mom hollered when I stepped out of the bath.

I streaked to the laundry room and found some fresh clothes to wear. Gathering an armload of clean outfits, I hurried them to my room and flipped the pile of nasty ones into the washer.

"Pancakes?" I was shocked. My voice came out as creaky as an old hinge.

"With sausage. It was quite the storm last night. We got almost a foot of snow."

Old Mom returned. I recognized her words immediately, her tone tinged with sweetness and a hesitant kind of love.

"And you don't have to work? That's great!"

Mom allowed me to change my bedding, borrow her mop for the hardwood floor, attack the walls with Murphy's Oil Soap. I also rummaged through Brandy's books and found her jigsaw puzzles, a treasure for someone with few activities and too many hours to fill.

Mom fed Tippy hot dogs and we played Yahtzee while my bedroom door stayed open, air circulating through all its nooks and crannies. The dog rolled across the linoleum, her antics enough to make Mom and me burst into hysterics.

Although laughing so hard sent me straight into a coughing fit. Mom ignored my discomfort, tossed Tippy more treats.

I couldn't help but wonder if this was Christmas.

We had a glorious dinner of turkey roast and mashed potatoes. Always a good girl, I cleaned the table, did the dishes, put the food away—except for the bits I shoved in my pocket and slipped to Tippy while Mom read in her recliner.

"I appreciate you doing all of the work," she said as she turned another page.

"I love being in the kitchen," I said, just in case she wanted me to resume my old position as lead cook.

We sat together until midnight, when Mom proclaimed she was hitting the sack.

I hoped that she would forget about the dead bolt on my door. Tippy screamed in my head that she was going to go bonkers if she had to spend any more time in my room, but, being bigger than she, I carried her and held her when Mom shut the door behind me.

"I had a good day with you," she said from the free zone outside my room. "I'm sorry it has to be this way."

"I love you, Mom," I said loudly as the lock turned.

Tippy immediately let loose a string of curses.

Mom stood stiff on the other side of my door. I put my hand against the wood and imagined her doing the same thing.

"Goodnight, Lucy."

When I went to the window the moon was gone. Fog settled in, obscuring her. Tippy nipped at my ankle and jumped on the bed. I followed her, exhausted. But finally clean.

* * *

My thoughts paraded around the room, random but as comfortable as an old pair of sweat pants.

Applesauce.

Bananas.

Hot blackberry cobbler, the deep purple of its heart washed clean with rivulets of melted vanilla.

Rolling snow man parts with Brandy in the side yard. Our scarves crocheted and colorful. Tippy, jumping with excitement beside us, her tail slicing arcs into the fluff, better than any trail of breadcrumbs to follow home.

The early onset of evening. Candles gathered in groups throughout the house, caroling, a silent chorus warming all our hearts.

Harvest spice. Winter wind. Speech class, the albatross of every freshman. Making the required three-minute commercial that was always the first-semester final exam.

My sister, teaching me to first lurch like Frankenstein, then mimic her ballerina twists and twirls as we explored the land behind Mr. Varnell's half-collapsed barn. Our hair, nests filled with leaves. Mom cackling—Old Mom cackling—as she tried so hard to comb out the mess.

Shopping with our allowance. Saturday morning bike rides to town. Stickers at the Hallmark store. Nickel candy at the old hotel where the creepy men who had never quite made it back mentally from the war lived. Buying socks for the old folks at the nursing home. Dancing for them. Brandy kissing all the forgotten women the nurses said never had visitors.

Trying our roller skates on the road out front, but unable to stand up with all the rocks in the way. Brandy showing me how to ride my bike with them tied around my neck. A balancing act. Swinging back and forth on the basketball court outside the YMCA, our hands intertwined, screaming with delight, the wheels so unencumbered on this surface, our bodies a vortex pulling all the joy in the world right into our center, into our hearts, entwining us, that moment, for all eternity.

Lines for the school play. The church Christmas program. Girl Scouts before Mom stopped letting me go. Before she turned off the phone. Wouldn't let me get the mail.

Jester, the cat we fed out back. His gold specks good fortune, Brandy told him.

My silly sister. Crawling into bed with me. Putting her ice cube toes into the backs of my knees. Tickling my sides. Telling me stories about her father, the dad who never looked me in the eye, a man who lived like a fairy tale in both our lives.

Scrabble.

School Olympics. The long jump, an event just for me. My gold medals. A whole day out of classes, at the university's football field, other kids' parents coming out to watch.

The homey, warm smell of chlorine. The heat of summer dissipated with one leap from the diving board. Learning to float in swimming lessons when we were too young to be in school. Brandy sinking.

Bible camp. Canoeing. Brandy running off with Rick Remsburg, the counselors hunting for them, yelling as they walked through the woods, my nerves on edge, worried. Her voice whispering in my ear after all lights were out. Her first kiss. My jealousy. My sister, so beautiful, so brave, my smile her personal hostage.

Dancing while the whirlybirds coated the sky. Raking the leaf pile. Tearing it apart again with Tippy, the three of us jumping in and out, gathering up handfuls, useless leaf bombs we threw anyway. The rest of the world hidden from us by a mountain of our own creation.

* * *

I stopped the whole hash mark gig, preferring not to know how many days of captivity we had suffered.

Instead I took to drawing on my walls, making a mural with the colored pencils I had hidden weeks ago. I drew the deer from the cornfield, Brandy, a tree about six miles from here that was the biggest thing I'd ever seen. Of course I had scores of birds and even some fairies soaring through my landscape.

Tippy, however, followed her own muse. I could barely even look at her work, the content was so disturbing. Mom with a knife in her back. Mom hanging from the same tree, her eyes bulging and covered with flies. Shit piles. Also with flies. Flames and eyeballs, all watching me while I slept.

Tippy formed big block letters screaming FUCK YOU BITCH from the middle of the wall. Every night she filled the words in with her vicious rantings after I went to sleep. Her lexis was so twisted that I had long ago stopped reading.

My dog wouldn't discuss it. I empathized with her frustration, but her negativity wasn't going to get us anywhere. We were lucky Mom never came into our room. I couldn't imagine how she would have tormented Tippy over her "artwork."

"I blame you for this," Tippy told me, in one of her moods.

Like Mom, Tippy fluctuated all over the place. One day she was all about snuggling and having her back scratched, the next berating me for my weaknesses and inability to free us.

"You don't even try the door. Maybe you could break it down."

"Tip, I can barely get the window open. How would I manage the door?" My energy was so depleted anymore I had problems holding up a book to read.

"If you weren't such a coward you would find a way," she barked at me.

"Why don't you do it?" I yelled, thankful Mom was at work. I couldn't tell if the words came out of my mouth anymore or just festered in my head.

"That's the winning solution. Why don't you crawl out the window? You could slide off the roof and the snow would cushion your fall. The neighbors would surely come let me out, if you could tell them I'm stuck here...."

"It's always about you, Tippy. I thought dogs were loyal."

"I was. Until this. Shit, I put up with your quivering for years and never said anything. I felt pretty sorry for you. But I have to draw the line somewhere."

I didn't talk to Tippy for two days. Or at least it seemed like two days. The darkness was so familiar I couldn't tell when one ended and another began anymore.

She finally apologized but stayed on her side of the room.

"The hungrier I get, the tastier you look," she spouted while I hovered over the wastebasket.

"You are really starting to annoy me. How can I look tasty?"

"I was talking to the trash can."

"Jesus, that's sick!" But I couldn't help the giggles that set in.

Tippy smiled and joined me on the bed. Her apology this time was genuine, her tail practically bruising me with each ferocious wag. We cuddled and I could feel her tension ease.

"We need a plan, Lucy. If you don't do something soon, we'll both die in here."

"She's my mother, Tippy. I can't hurt her."

Chapter 10

Tippy

I have been here before. Years ago. Locked in a cage, sad and quiet. Lonely and waiting. Looking out the door, trying to have a conversation with every bird or human or scrap of paper that came near me. Amazed that I, then known as Winnie the Wiener Dog, was trapped and no one seemed to care.

When your pack abandons you, it's hard to recover.

I have always lived with high integrity. Pooped where they told me to poop. Didn't jump on the furniture. Didn't lick the kid's hands, even if they were coated in all kinds of delicious foods. Played and performed and pleased my pack.

Yet one morning they promised me ice cream. We got in the car. I got to watch the neighborhood roll by—and barked at Felix, the stupid cat next door—looked out the window, tolerated the kid, let everyone know how happy I was to be with them.

I could smell the place miles away. Death. Desolation. Depression. And they drove me to it anyway. Me, Winnie. My pack walked me in, walked back out. I thought of the times they'd dressed me up in that stupid hero cape and I hadn't even complained. Itched, yes. Complained, no. Hadn't I done what my humans wanted?

Cages sitting on cages. Cats. Mice, even. A dozen birds. Everyone hollering for attention. The cute ones getting it. Me, with my bad eye, getting ignored. Laughed at.

The eye wasn't even my fault. The kid did it, not long before they left me. Put a plastic sword in and pulled it out, his mom screaming at me when I yelped. Like I had done something wrong. Like I wasn't good enough because he had disfigured me. My scar, hot. The place my eye had been a physical longing that I could never fill.

By the time you came I was putting on my best ostrich routine. Paw over my face. Shivering. Backed in the corner. Out of my head. The cage metal my pack had rammed through my heart. Winnie the Weiner Dog, skewered. And on display.

Your speech was song to me. Liquid. Smooth, flowing, easy. I uncovered my face. Waited for your head to bounce back. Worried about the awful words you might call me.

"Hi, beautiful. What's your name?" you asked.

I could smell my own waste on myself. In my former life this elicited horrible feelings of shame. But you only drew closer. You didn't seem to notice the depths to which I'd fallen.

My gaze met yours. I didn't want to play games and hide from you. Better to just let you see the badness and then you could run.

"Can I pet you?" Your finger slid through the bars, across the tip of my snout. I scooted closer and let it run over my cheek. Fell into you. Put the scabby wound against your palm and let you siphon the pain right out of it.

We melted together. The spike came out. Memories of the old pack, gone. My good eye focused on your tender face, and I knew that you would be my girl. That this time, this crate, the eternity I had lived in this foul-smelling building were well spent if I could cuddle up and feel your arms wrap around my body.

You turned your chin to the side. Smiled. Kissed my snout when I pushed it between the bars. We were so close I could see it. Your eye, also sick. Your eye, with a circle blooming inside like a flower.

I sniffed it. Your wound gave off a scent like the basement of my old home. Moldy. Wet. Slightly sick.

Excitement overwhelmed all other thoughts. Another girl joined us, your sister. Then your mom. She paused when she looked at me, her attention on my deformation. What was it she saw and you didn't?

You saved me. Opened the door, let me jump into your arms. Freed me. Loved me.

We shared the same seat in the car. You called me Tippy and it fit. I was no longer a Wiener Dog wearing a cape and doing flips for chunks of biscuits. I was Tippy, Princess of the Tea Party. Tippy, the Mouse Stalker. Tippy, Cuddler Extraordinaire.

And you were my girl.

I have been through this before. The wind is cold. I do not miss the outside. I have enough room to stretch my legs and roam from wall to wall. My cage this time is enormous compared to the last.

But not you, my little one. Your cage is so much harder to bear. I see your humiliation and it is mine from old. Pissing where one shouldn't. The sickness creeping through your system. Your scent no longer that of girl but of that familiar mildew spread from your face to your fingertips, even the bottoms of your toes.

I was alone when my pack left me. Stranded. Isolated. Left without explanation. The cape removed, the biscuits hidden.

My world was nothing but darkness when you found me. Saved me. Looked at me with your own polluted vision and held me despite my ugliness.

Now our roles have switched. Your pack has dissolved, your alpha powerful but ruled by a different moon. Together we are held against our will. We may be hungry, but we are sisters and we have each other.

We can warm the sheets together. Chase spiders for protein. Tell stories while I fold into you and calm you with my heartbeat, the kisses I slather across your cheeks.

This time, my girl. This time I will save you.

I have a plan.

Chapter 11

Joan

Six months after Mom passed I got the FedEx box in the mail.

Aunt Evelyn's books. Sent from a storage company in Maine, with explicit instructions from Mom's estate to turn them over to me once she was gone.

I locked them in the closet. When we moved to Iowa they found their way into the attic. I had no use for them.

After all, the rest of the family was long gone. Evelyn, dead at the table that day when I was a young girl. My Grandma Sweeney hit by a car four years later while getting her mail. Cousin Jackie drowned on a canoe trip on her thirtieth birthday. Her twin daughters suffocated, locked in a refrigerator playing hide and seek a year later. The whole Lang family wiped out during a tornado on the Fourth of July. Mom, her hands sawed off less than an hour before she finally bled to death on my living-room floor.

I brought them down the winter of your eleventh birthday. By then your birthmark and I were quite familiar, as it liked to tease me more and more as you matured, coming out to join us for a snack when it was pitch black outside and we were playing Sorry! at the kitchen table or hovering in the morning air before it had scrambled for cover after you had just crawled from bed. I had gotten to know it so well we were almost on a first-name basis.

I took to my room that first night and struggled to draw myself back out after I started reading. Aunt Evelyn had been very thorough, attaching notebooks to ancient journals so her study could be interpreted with each original document.

Banking didn't lend itself to historical research. I spent my days selling mortgages and signing customers up for car loans that everyone knew they couldn't afford. What did I know of Portugal? Kharakhorum? Monkshood?

But I learned.

Every Sunday afternoon while you and Brandy played with the church youth group, I was at the university library, piling books to take home, delving deeper into the subjects Aunt Evelyn had already studied. You lived with me and demanded my love. The least I could do was learn about you. Know what I had shed the day you burst onto earth. What I had borne onto the world.

When I first opened the box, I stumbled upon the story of my distant cousin, born just after the turn of the century and living out the life of so many women before her. Cooking. Cleaning. Managing her household, the children, the farm. Feeding goats and mending socks. Building a world that centered around God, work, and family.

Evelyn had been so thorough as to list the midwives that assisted Ruby as she tore from her mother's body. She included the teachers, pastors, neighbors and childhood friends that had helped form Ruby's value system and exuberant personality. One page detailed the courtship that ended in her marriage to Robert Snell and their journey from Kansas to the farm he had purchased in Missouri.

Ruby had been terrified to leave her mother and sisters. But like every good woman, she kept her opinions to herself and followed her husband wherever he led them.

I skimmed these sections, not doubting for a second that Ruby was an honorable woman. I sought the details of Ruby's family circle, how their secrets were shared, how she was forewarned about our curse. Did she have an Aunt Evelyn? As I searched through the box, would I find a holy woman in each clan who kept the others in line?

One of my immediate questions was answered when I found the adoption certificate for Ruby's son, Jacob. For years I had held onto the fact that Ruby's daughter attacked her older brother—something

I hadn't thought possible, since no woman in our family had ever birthed a boy. Or at least one that had survived long enough to be named. I had seen it as a sign that maybe our blood was weakening, the legend showing its cracks—maybe by the time I had my own children the birth-marked babies would be extinct and I could live worry free after all.

According to Aunt Evelyn, Jacob was the son of Ruby's closest friend, who perished with her husband in a house fire. How ironic that he would also be put to death by fire. Did little Janie know this when she reached into the stove and pulled out a burning log? While her own hands blistered and she pushed the flame into her brother's face, her strength amazing for a four year old? When Janie yanked the pan with fresh bacon grease and doused her burning brother with it?

Ruby knew instantly. She heard the commotion, she hurried to the kitchen, saw her son aflame and the smirk of satisfaction on her daughter's mouth. The light of the fire sparked, and Ruby saw the shadow in Janie's eye. I wondered if she even tried to save her son. Did she see her daughter for the imp she was and immediately quell the problem, or did she fight for her son's deformed future while keeping her back to the wall in that small kitchen?

Evelyn didn't doubt her cousin at all. Her pages extolled Ruby's efficiency. The four year old commanded the situation, but her mother's will rebounded. She dragged the girl to the yard, the glass bursting from the windows as the house lit up behind them. Ruby held the beast down on the stump she used for beheading chickens, her hand clawing the child's sweaty neck as she grabbed for the ax. Not once did she wail that this was her progeny or that her entire world was collapsing as the flames roared up the trees surrounding the house.

Ruby got purchase on the wooden handle and yanked it from the ground. She did not hesitate. She did not falter. She severed the child's head and watched as it plopped off the stump, rolling to her feet, the sickening smile still attached to Janie's mouth.

Before Ruby lowered her arms she joined her daughter on the ground. Her husband, drawn by the flames, had ridden home with his rifle in hand. As he witnessed his wife slaughter their child, he took aim and fired.

The bewildered man told Evelyn just months before he passed that once Janie was dead the house stopped burning. He had lifted her head from beside her mother, and he swore that she spoke to him—giggled even—the bad eye dead and shriveling as he stood there. Terrified, he threw the head into the bushes and turned to his beautiful wife. He embraced her while she bled out, his apologies answered only by Ruby's whispered assurances that this had been her destiny.

Robert never discussed that day with anyone besides Evelyn. He went inside the house to find Jacob, still clinging to life, his skin melted in most places. The boy's eyes were hollowed out and Robert took solace in the fact that he couldn't see himself. He gripped his son's hand, told him he loved him, then helped him join his mother and sent a bullet through his brain. After piling the corpses in the bedroom, Robert relit the flame and took off on his horse, never returning to his property.

The old man told Aunt Evelyn that he could still smell the stench of evil that radiated from his daughter's head. It had driven him half mad. He wound up in the barren lands of the west, working odd jobs for cattle ranchers or the railroad, staying far from women and children and anyone whose laughter might conjure up Janie's giggling head.

What would Ruby do in my situation? I've asked myself that so many times. You have always been so well-behaved, so mannered and pleasing. Would Ruby be able to use the same weapon on you?

Am I that weak of a woman?

Or are you so powerful that you soften me? Eat at my corners like acid? Emit a magnetism that fogs my brain?

I wish Brandy could have stayed. She was always my center.

And if I had asked her to, your sister would have swung that ax without blinking an eye.

Chapter 12

Lucy

Time trudged past, a slug on a lazy day, picking up speed only after dinner when I could easily sleep. Mom sometimes let me linger, do dishes, sprawl out on the living room carpet, quietly promenade with Tippy in the downstairs hall. When she either gave me her annoyed glare or pointed to the stairs, we dashed to our room and waited for the lock to turn.

But sleeping then was so much easier. After the waiting was done for the day. Our stomachs were full. Our minds at rest.

The mornings weren't so awful, either. Tippy and I were usually awake long before the lock opened, listening to Mom shower, waiting with throbbing bladders for our turn in the bathroom. Renewing our lockdown with our hunger sated wasn't so difficult.

The afternoon was when I really had trouble.

Day after day, despair marched in, lined up against the walls, stared at me in awkward silence. I could only avoid it for so long. Closing my eyes didn't work, for sleep slipped out of my hands as though slathered in warm bacon grease.

As the sun shifted away, the inside of my room took on a bleakness as stark as my view out the window. Desolate. Frigid. Blocked off and blistered with regret.

These were the hours I could never abandon. I watched the unchanging countryside endure the harsh breath of winter and couldn't keep the cold from creeping into my heart.

I would never drive a car.

Be a homecoming queen.

Write another book report. Even though I wasn't sure if freshmen were still required to do such things.

I wanted to be a singer. Not opera. Not classical, really. I didn't even want to be on the radio. Or in a choir. Me and a piano. Or a guitar. Or nothing at all.

What was I missing? What were other girls my age doing? Did they have dates? Auditions? Were they babysitting? Selling stupid candy bars for the band fundraiser?

I had never been on a date. No pizza and breadsticks, no shared coke at the movies, no basketball games. No boy had ever tried to even hold my hand.

Mike Brevaro. My seventh grade biology lab partner. His dark hair flighty, half curled at the ends and creeping out of the stocking cap he wore in the winter. His smile was so intense my cheeks turned beet red whenever he looked at me. I would have dated him. Sometimes I even thought about other things I would do with him.

But that would never happen now.

Boys.

Brandy had kissed three or four. One she had made out with in the church basement, by the water heater, when we were having a lock in with the youth group. Tobias, the foreign exchange student. The guy was goofy looking, but he had had the hots for my sister. And did she enjoy that!

At least, if she were dead, she had experienced some of life. Unlike me.

The walls closed in, tighter. My throat rusted shut with the agony I could hardly swallow. Where was Brandy? Was she having fun?

And why hadn't she sent someone to help me?

We had never vacationed much. Mom had used her time off work for home repairs and gardening, not for travel. I had only seen six other states: Illinois, Missouri, Kansas, Wisconsin, Nebraska, and for a few minutes, Indiana. No big cities. No subway systems. No foreign museums. Missy Spencer's grandparents had taken her to

France. She had seen the Mona Lisa. And I was supposed to be living there!

I would never visit Africa. Work for the Peace Corps or on a mission in Haiti. See humpbacked whales while on a romantic cruise with my new husband. Hike across Europe. Find vampires nested in the old cities there.

No one would ever be proud of me. I would be lucky if people even remembered my name. My life was nothing, empty eggshells tossed after the cake was in the oven.

Tippy could crowd me all she wanted. Her nudging couldn't erase the horror that hovered around my bedroom door.

Locked. My life, at a standstill.

Would I grow taller while she kept me here? Or would I shrivel? My clothes had already started to hang on me.

The world outside my window was boundless. Fields stretched on forever. Was this what it was like to live on the tundra? A vast frozen land? How did the pioneers survive in this weather?

I tried to remember things. Funny commercials from when we still had television. Protozoa. Plankton. The preface from our old church hymnals with the dark burgundy covers. The recipe for lemon squares. Adverbs and adjectives.

The names of trees and the shapes of their leaves.

But as the hours stacked up, it ceased to matter.

None of it mattered. Nothing but the sound of her footsteps, coming toward my door. Letting me out. Letting me breathe.

Letting me live.

* * *

The rime built up on my window, frosted my bones. I had on layers and layers of clothing, from my too-small long johns saved from winters past to the thick wool sweater I had stolen from Brandy's room. Nothing helped.

"Where is she?" Tippy would ask on occasion, believing that we were foremost in Mother's mind. "Do you think she knows we're hungry?"

"Get under the blankies." I didn't want her to get sick, but I also wanted her warmth to keep me from shivering. "She'll be here eventually. When she's good and ready. We just have to hang on until then."

I kissed Tippy's head. Pulled her tight. Slowed my heart beat to match her own.

* * *

Wallpaper makes a better decoration than a late night snack.

Tippy had suggested I pull it down, peel the borders along the top of the walls. We consumed it with icicles and jewelry boxes full of snow. Even as I choked on the paper, I could feel the paste mocking my stomach, setting in motion two days of sickness that nearly destroyed my room.

In my weakness I called for Mother.

Banged on my door, wailed and begged to be let out. My gut cramped up, forcing me to drool as I rolled around on the bed, clutching my stomach.

When the diarrhea hit I knew we were doomed.

Tippy hid under the bed while I lost it all. I barely made it to the closet and did more damage to the walls than the wastebasket, the stench of my own waste causing me to hurl onto my floor. At one point I even slipped in the bile as I hurried back to my bed, my clothes discarded and used to wipe down my mess.

"Please, Mommy, I need the bathroom." I pounded the door as I lay on the floor beside it. "I'm really sick."

I no longer knew if she was working or at home. We had no routine, no regular meal times. The sun didn't even seem to have a pattern anymore. I felt entirely lost. How long had it been since I'd even seen Mother?

I fell asleep with my head against the wall. When I came to my hand ached, my fist coated in the same blood that stained my door. My stomach lurched, and I hurried to the closet to relieve myself.

"Let me out!" I kicked the door this time, which was an enormous mistake. Moving my leg so forcefully caused me to be ill on the spot. I was horrified by the mess I left.

After hours she finally relented. The lock gave, and seconds after pushing the door forward Mom caught sight of me and retched in the hallway.

I bolted for the toilet. Wept hysterically as my insides exploded and I sat facing my own reflection in the door mirror. Naked. Covered in shit. Vomit crusting my greasy hair. So thin even the cheerleaders at school would have commented on my appearance.

I could feel the wallpaper bound up, undigested, in my intestines. A giant ball, the paper fiber cemented by old paste. A desperate attempt at a meal that even Tippy refused to eat after her first taste.

Mom walked in, gagged, put pajamas on the sink. I understood this to be her peace offering of sorts. Later she filled the basin with magazines, towels, a thermos of soup.

My hunger was frantic, as frenzied as an addict without a fix in sight. The soup promised to satisfy my aching stomach, the smell of chicken overwhelming the noxious odors of the bathroom. I struggled to unscrew the lid from the thermos and almost cried with relief when it finally opened. Part of me wanted to cherish the soup, hide it somewhere, have it waiting in my room for the day my gut didn't hurt so bad and I could enjoy it.

But I couldn't help myself. I put the thermos against my dry lips, let the soup scald my throat as the delicious broth slid down, falling into the abyss that was once my healthy stomach.

Less than a minute later my feet were coated in noodles.

The violent thrust from my stomach made my ass explode as well. To my disgrace, Tippy stood in the doorway, watching me as I decorated the linoleum with several different liquids at once.

Slowly she got accustomed to the stench and eased her way into the room. Tippy didn't even make eye contact with me, but hurried over to my toes and inhaled the chunks of chicken sticking to them.

"I get it now." I nodded at my dog as she licked the broth off the bathroom floor.

"Get what?" Tippy stopped for a second and looked at me.

"You knew I'd get sick."

"I told you I had a plan. I knew she'd let us out for a while." She smiled, went back to chewing.

"Yeah. Good for you. I can't eat at all." My stomach rumbled and I almost hurled again.

"All the better for me," Tippy said, not the slightest bit ashamed as she polished off my vomit. "At least you get a bath. Sometimes it's hard staying in that room with you, you're so nasty looking."

"Thanks, Tip."

"Thanks for the soup. This is delicious. Mom gave me some ham downstairs, too. I've been fantasizing about eating meat again. That mouse we caught didn't do the trick."

I was insanely jealous of Tippy's new diet but couldn't help recalling the day we had spotted the pest running along the floorboards in my room. She had nudged me out of my late-morning coma, looked askance at the tiny animal and gave me her hunter's eye. My nod of approval was slight. Tippy leapt from our bed and was on the rodent in a flash, her teeth bearing into the mouse's neck.

That was the most excitement I'd had in weeks. Tippy, full of energy. Her mesmerizing display of power.

She shook the field mouse until it was lifeless and jumped back up to offer it to me. After rummaging through my drawers I came up with some toenail scissors, and together we dissected the rodent. Cut the poor guy's fur like we were stripping him of a suit and peeled it back from his body. A few months earlier, and Brandy and I would have squealed at such a thought. Funny how hunger made you immune to some things.

"I'm sure this would taste a lot better cooked." I made my apologies to Tippy as I split the small bits of meat between us.

"This is better than silverfish any day of the week!" Tippy took the corpse and downed the remains in less than a minute.

Talking of our hunt sustained us for a week, and we constantly watched for another easy meal. Mom no longer routinely let us out. Tippy and I joked that our diet would at least be more consistent if Hitler were our parent.

"Well, get over being sick. You need to fill our water and come downstairs so you can eat."

I thought of scrambled eggs, pancakes, slice after slice of bacon spread out on a plate. Orange juice. Tomatoes, green and fried like Brandy used to make. A beef roast simmered in the slow cooker from the time we left for school until dinner, the aroma an almost palpable treat.

A perfect memory of my sister rose and wouldn't let go. Brandy in the garden, picking her tomatoes. Turning to face me, the sun strong behind her head, bouncing off her hair like a halo. Her dark eyes lit with joy. My older sister, trying to convince me that cornmeal mixed beautifully with her favorite vegetable and would make a perfect side dish for the ham steak she planned to cook.

"Oh, no. I can see them. Here come the water works," Tippy moaned.

"Leave me alone." I flapped my hand in front of her, tried to get her to leave the bathroom.

"What's wrong now? Tummy still hurt?" She spoke in a softer tone.

"No. I was just thinking about Brandy. The old days."

"Yeah, and they're gone. You need to think about the here and now. I doubt Brandy's lying around crying about you."

"You don't have to throw it in my face!"

"Yes, I do. Otherwise you'll never see it. Now get cleaned up and come downstairs." Tippy hurried out of the room. I could hear her nails clacking on the wood as she made her way to the kitchen.

I could barely stand. My legs wobbled, the walls swaying a bit as I clung to the sink for balance. I turned the corner out of the bathroom and almost fell when I saw my room.

The door was outlined in knobby white globs tied together and draped on the wooden frame. Garlic. I could smell it, even standing across the hall.

How had I not noticed it, living just on the other side of the door?

Mom had drawn on the walls as well. I stared at her creation, an amazingly detailed charcoal rendering of a farm house and a field of chickens. Half of the poultry had no heads. I couldn't help myself and walked forward to touch her work. Outside of the house stood three children, also incomplete. Headless. Haunting the wall.

Her work must have taken hours. Days, even. Just the meticulous strokes used to form the feathers were daunting. I swayed, staring at her drawing. Never had I imagined that Mom had such talent, such an incredible flair. The chickens were everywhere. Now that my eyes were open I found them on every wall, crouched in corners, walking sideways along floorboards.

All of them watching me. Even the headless ones.

My sway became a swoon. I hadn't the strength to endure the truth. Tippy and I had been starving, locked away for days at a time, sitting silent in our room while the snow danced outside. Waiting for Mom to let us out. To save us. To forgive our transgressions.

But she had been here all the time. Outside my door. On the backside of my wall. Sketching. Making a coop of the upstairs hall. Working diligently, quietly, not even speaking to me when she was so close. How nice it would have been for me to have her company, even her negativity. She could have opened my door and talked about her masterpiece. Let Tippy out to run around. Had me help her while she worked.

A slow, burning hatred ignited in me.

She had spent all of this time outside my door, while Tippy and I went hungry. While we snuck onto the roof to scoop up snow. While my carefully planned days of exercise and reading had dwindled to naps and the occasional bout of walking from wall to wall. Mom had never even said hello, let alone offered us a snack.

Tippy was right to have a plan.

I had been a fool not to develop one of my own.

Chapter 13

Joan

As I get older I realize there are parts of myself I have never truly known.

I've always been very reliant on others. People say that since I'm a single mother and I've never really had a man around, I'm pretty independent.

Not so. I've spent the past fifteen years seeking my mother's approval, praying for Alex to give me guidance. It's been a pretty steady routine: go to work, come home energized and ready to conquer the laundry, step into the house and see you're still there, endure the agony of a meal shared with you, go to my room where I can concentrate and discuss my day with my dead husband. Easy.

But without Brandy to keep my stage set, I've been free to bounce around through all the acts. Not that anyone is applauding, but it's really opened my eyes. For instance, cooking. I've always hated standing in front of the stove. Measuring, timing, chopping things up. But recently it's been necessary for me to pick up the slack and do it myself. What I've been missing! Call me Julia, I love the kitchen. I even bought a sifter the other day.

Last Sunday I skipped church and went to a movie. Ate two barrels of popcorn. Even enjoyed a game of pinball in the lobby before I drove home.

I've called in sick to work for the first time in five years, forgot to return my library books, and went home with some stupid redneck who bought me drinks down at the Huckleberry Inn. Yes, I was blinded a bit by the booze, but you'd think I'd have to be. I've not touched a man in over fifteen years. Let alone stayed at his house for three straight days, Jezebelling myself into oblivion.

And then there's you.

God, to be rid of you. Even without looking at you, you ruin my good days. I can be whipping up a plate of brownies to share with the girls at work and then hear your footsteps overhead. An instant frown, the batter in the trash, a third glass of wine.

I don't understand you. The last time I opened the door—after days of listening to you freaking out up there—your devil's stench was so overwhelming I could feel it fire through my pores and try to attack my brain. You were a corpse with a little air in her lungs, floundering just to cross the hall and find the toilet.

And then I became someone I'm not. You always find my soft spots when you're ill. I'm pretty certain that you manipulate me that way, see my weakness and make it your strength, slowly maneuver your way into my system. Poison me.

Mom didn't answer. Alex wasn't around. I listened to you hurling and could do little but wring my hands, pace my room, wait for a third-party intervention.

But when I saw the dog my heart melted. Poor Tippy. I had wondered where she was hiding, forgot she stayed with you in that horrible pigsty you call a room. She bolted when I opened the back door for her, but lost steam pretty quickly. Took her bathroom break and then petered out on the grass, her breathing labored.

I went outside to pick her up. The old girl couldn't have weighed eight pounds, and I easily carried her into the kitchen. We shared some lunch meat while cuddling on the floor. After petting her ribs for what seemed like hours, I broke down and bawled. No animal should be treated this way. No dog should ever suffer like Tippy has.

"Mom." You broke my silence hours later. Your voice was so hoarse it took me several minutes to interpret what you said.

"Yes?" I answered. I wanted to offer you a chair. Your wobbling made me uncomfortable.

"I'm so sorry for whatever I've done. I...can't remember what I did to make you so angry with me. Please forgive me."

Since Alex wouldn't answer I looked to the dog for guidance. Her shoulder bones were evident, the skin sinking in around them. Tippy gave me a nod, understanding my dilemma. Her one good eye stared at me, unblinking.

"You can sleep in Brandy's room."

"Thank you. I love you, Mom." Your smile was pinched, the sores caking your lips cracking open.

"Would you like some water?" I put on my best hostess routine and turned on the tap.

Tippy brushed against my legs, and I gave her some, too.

I wanted the dog to live.

Chapter 14

Lucy

I gained five pounds.

I watched myself in the mirror, the carcass, as I inflated. Tippy told me it was water weight; I didn't care.

Once I was steadier Mom let me wash my room down. I stuffed Kleenex up my nose so I could work without getting sick again, put my bedding through the washer, mopped the walls. Mom had been so nice to me since my bad spell that I couldn't help but sing while I worked.

"How can you be so happy?" Tippy asked. She rolled around on my bare mattress, her hair falling out in clumps.

"The door is open. What could be better than that?"

"Uhm…gee, I don't know. Going to school? Knowing your sister is alive? How about being fourteen and NOT having to scrape your own crap off the closet door?" She barked for emphasis.

"Quiet down. You don't want to ruin a good thing."

"You call this a good thing? Really?"

"It's the best thing I've got going. Unlike you."

"And just what the Hell is that supposed to mean?"

"Let's just say that I don't have hot dogs for breakfast. I get toast."

We argued for most of the day. Tippy emphasized my ability to simply throw a dining room chair through the window and exit the house that way. I reminded her that I could barely walk from the kitchen to the bathroom, let alone the distance to the Hanley's house.

"People do all sorts of things when their survival is threatened," Tippy said while I smoothed over the naked patches on her coat. I didn't want her to freak out over her own health and quietly gathered the wads of fur she had left on my bed. "Haven't you ever heard about mothers who lift cars off their kids or people who cut off their own legs with a pocket knife to get out of a bad situation?"

"It's so cold outside. How could I walk that far and not freeze to death?"

"Are you naked? Do you not have clothes in the house? Didn't anyone teach you to layer?"

"I can't do it, Tippy. I seriously don't think I could even lift the chair." I felt terribly ashamed of my weakness.

"Then you must have lost all desire to live. If I were a human I would have broken out of here months ago."

"Fine. I'm a horrible person. But if you are so concerned about escaping, why don't you just run off when she lets you out to pee? You could also go to the neighbors."

"My name is not Lassie. And she's not trying to kill me. Why would I need to run off?" Tippy jumped off my lap and stood at my feet, her back to me.

"Because dogs save people's lives. Besides, she's not really trying to kill me."

"No? Then what is she doing?"

"I quit the swim team without telling her, remember? She's punishing me." I shrugged my shoulders as Tippy turned to face me.

"Sweetie, you are my best friend, but sometimes you're just too stupid for your own good. What is a suitable punishment for your swim team offense? Being grounded a week? Okay, your mom is super strict, so maybe three weeks? Let's review your situation. She beat you. Pulled you out of school. Locked you in the house, then in your room. For months. Deprived you of food, water, bathroom privileges. For months. "

"I realize she's gone off the deep end...."

"She's been off the deep end for quite some time now," Tippy interrupted.

"She hasn't whupped me in a while," I said, trying to be positive.

"Because she won't open the door to your room. Would you please face up?"

"You know what? I'll face up to the fact that I'm tired of you and all your negativity. Why don't you go lay on HER bed for a while?" I stood up and tried not to gasp for breath as I pushed Tippy out the door with my feet.

I shut the door myself, from the inside. Listened as her nails clacked on the wood going down the hallway. Lay against the door, exhausted.

I was asleep before I fell across my unmade bed.

When I woke the room was pitch black and fear sped through my veins, directly into my heart. I could feel it throb from toe to temple, a drum cadence to the only word my mind was screaming.

Locked! Locked! Locked! Locked!

My legs were noodles, my arms concrete. If Tippy had been with me I would have forced myself to stand so as not to disappoint her. But alone I was nothing. Alone the darkness consumed me, revealed the truth of Tippy's words.

Hours later I finally stood. Conquered my terror. Walked to the door.

It opened, with ease.

My friend was waiting for me on the other side.

We tiptoed down to Brandy's room and curled up in her bed.

"I'm sorry," Tippy said as she put her head under my chin, her back to my neck. "I forget how young you are sometimes."

"I missed you. Don't ever leave me." I kissed the top of her head and we both relaxed enough to fall back to sleep.

Chapter 15

Joan

1836.

Arkansas became a state. The Battle of the Alamo cemented itself in American lore. Samuel Colt developed the revolver.

And your cousin, at least eight times removed, devastated her Mexican village by poisoning the water supply.

Maria wasn't yet seventeen, was pregnant with her first child and married to a man her father had arranged for her to serve. As a girl, Maria had been well behaved. Her mother and sisters cherished her laughter, the dark features that made her a local beauty. Within a year of marriage, Maria grew harsh looking, the beatings she endured causing her face such visible damage that the same people who had once been so drawn to her now looked away each time she neared.

But of course she didn't complain. Maria was raised well. She simply survived.

Her husband, Eduardo, had accused Maria of cheating. Again. His repeated kicks to her belly sent Maria into an early labor, during which she lost her baby. This resulted in more violence. The rumor mill went into over drive after Eduardo dragged his wife through the main artery of their village, his filthy fingers like a vise around her hair, pulling her whether she was standing or not. He only took breaks to put his fist in her face. On one occasion it was said that he displayed her to the men in the tavern, let them take turns humiliating her as men are wont to do.

Aunt Evelyn took the time to report on the current atmosphere of this section of Mexico. Apparently the wind itself had set the hairs on Evelyn's arms on end. She could feel Maria hovering in the area; she could also detect that not much had changed in the hearts of the local men. Watching the women, she understood that they still suffered in their marriages, their eyes silent yet pleading for her to leave. No one appreciated her questions, the interpreter she had hired, the suitcase bringing her modern effects into their isolated home.

The photos depicted a land of scrub and sand, a dryness that extended to the people's hearts. The odd individual nodded in her direction. Most information was gathered by Evelyn's hired man, an elder who lived close enough that he was treated as a tolerated visitor and drunkenly shared stories with the men in town as they put back tequila and whiskey late into the night.

Maria was still regarded will ill repute, her name a curse among her people. The villagers despised her and those who held but a vague memory of her in their veins. Women, in their world, did not kill. They capitulated. Women surrendered their will, their passion, their very souls to the more brutal sex.

But not Maria. Since her act of unprecedented carnage, no female in her village was allowed to share her name. She was an outcast even among the women.

Men, much like her husband and father, felt she had wronged her husband when the baby died. They chortled as they discussed her punishments, first at the bar and later when Maria was locked in the outhouse and offered to anyone who used it.

When her confinement in the fly-infested shack had ended, Maria was no longer sane. Her mother came to help her bathe and prepare the house to please her husband. She encouraged her to conceive again, but Maria was unresponsive. Almost comatose. Except for the hatred in her eyes.

Later her mother would recall the tales passed through her family but would deny knowing that Maria was the marked woman.

Until the husband told survivors that as he butchered his once beautiful wife, her eyes changed, became possessed.

"One turned black," one man explained. "He told her to make it stop and when she wouldn't, took a rock to her face. The witch never stopped staring at him with that vile eye. After she died, he spit on her, told his friends that he wouldn't have treated a dog so badly."

As for Maria, she knew her demise was imminent. She was prepared. The woman knew exactly how to avenge her own death and cause many more.

"Mother dreamt of dark water. She wouldn't even tell us what had frightened her so much, she woke up screaming and spent the entire morning in church, wailing. When she came home she forbade us from drinking anything the animals wouldn't touch. Several of our goats died, because we stole all their water." Her sister later admitted. She was among the few who lived once the contaminant was in place. Maria's family and the men in the bar who had ravaged her. They neither used the local water to bathe nor drank it, preferring their liquor to quench a thirst that never ended.

The sister alone knew what Maria threw in the town's water supply, passing the information to her daughters one night when she had imbibed too much of the booze her husband bottled and sold to the old men in town. The toxin was fitting. A festering, rotten chunk of flesh that upon birth had resembled her own mother, right down to the spot in her eye that had infuriated Eduardo. Maria chucked her stillborn daughter into the water and let nature take its course, the bacteria building as the baby's body decayed, the well a source of death for the wives and children of the men who had touched her.

Aunt Evelyn made many notations on her report, including a three-page journal entry describing the women still living in the village. Forlorn, she called them. Their faces disfigured by scars and poorly healed bones. She understood that the only medical help any received came from the other women in town or their families, if they were even allowed to speak to them. A collection of battered women, who had witnessed their own mothers endure punishment after punishment at the hands of their husbands and sons, saw this life as their destiny, their silent acceptance keeping the abuse alive generation after generation.

Evelyn couldn't wait to escape the village. She had never married and was fiercely independent, unlike the women she encountered in Mexico. Their passivity almost incapacitated her. My aunt, the powerhouse of all women in our family, left her documentary trip and hid for three months in Europe, "redirecting her energy," as she wrote. She did not seek refuge in the arms of a lover, the cold stone walls of a cathedral, or even the vast libraries that she spent weeks exploring. Evelyn sought the earth, sitting for days on end watching waves repeat their steady trip to land, or hunkering down in the forests, her skin coated in mud to ward off infestations of mosquitoes. I loved reading her passages on wind and rain, how she equated thunderstorms to county fairs and preferred a downpour to sunshine any day of the week.

Evelyn had to heal. She held it all for us: our family's history, the explosive guilt and fascination that propelled her every day to solve the enigma of our women. She alone could stand up in front of God and defend our ancestors or help Him point the finger and send us all to the burning fires below. I could feel her heartbeat just by reading her words, recognize it in my own chest, the muscle matching the rhythms of the water, my body's energy ebbing and tiding with each gust of wind as it flowed over my skin while her papers sat still on my lap below.

In my adulthood, Evelyn had crawled back out of her grave, just to distract me. She crept from the photo I kept on my bedside table, rummaged through my dreams. For years she had just passed time, watching, sitting in the background of whatever scenario my REM sleep created. Occasionally pointing me in a direction I didn't even know existed.

But now I could sense Evelyn sitting beside me, her arms alive as she gestured and clapped and made little movie shows with her hands while relating her stories. Inevitably she turned to me, glared. Demanded to know when I was going to get off my ass and get my work done. Rambled on and on about how she had easily predicted that I would give birth to the final one, the destined child, and how I would never be able to take care of things myself.

I showed her pictures of my dead husband.

Raised my shirt and displayed my left breast, the scar a pale tattoo that forever reminded me of my past. Showed my Aunt how I had once been brave, but that I had given all my courage away in one fell swoop. That horrible night.

"Hmmph. Get over it. How many years are you going to milk that wound?" She waved her hand.

Her written words kept me rooted, gave me purpose. Aunt Evelyn's spoken words just plain hurt.

I shut the journal, put her to bed. Didn't bother answering her question as she disappeared beside me. Yes, I struggled with my chore. But at least I was brave enough to live. Evelyn had chased the past, escaping the future; even my dead mother had seen through her bravado and understood that by not marrying, and presumably dying a virgin, she never had the opportunity to spit out an ugly female child of her own that she would hold and love and then a few years later have to kill.

Better not to love them in the first place.

Chapter 16

Lucy

I was barely off oatmeal and bouillon when Mom woke me one morning, told me to take my shower and put my hair up in a bun before coming downstairs.

Tippy and I exchanged worried looks, but neither of us had a clue what she wanted. I hurried to avoid any accusations of dawdling, which would instantly send Mom into a rage that I didn't want to witness. My shower was momentary, my hair dried in three minutes flat. My bun was efficient and secured with two elastic bands, not a hair stylist's idea of beauty but quick and easy and mother-pleasing.

My legs had gotten steadier, but my hips hated the stairs, and I struggled with my balance while descending.

"Showered and bunned."

"Good. Have a seat." She pointed at the kitchen chair centered in the room.

"And take your sweater off. You won't be needing it."

I gave Tippy a sideways glance, for I had lost so much weight that I had stopped wearing a bra. Neither of us knew how Mom would react to my lack of undergarments.

But I did as told. I stripped off my heavy wool sweater, oozed into the wooden chair, wincing at the cold.

Although I was afraid Mother would think I was hiding something, I wrapped my arms around my bare chest anyway. I didn't want her to see me this way. Naked. My flesh vulnerable.

Mom walked to the counter by the sink. From my days cooking with Brandy, I recognized the smell of the sage before I saw it. She had mashed some in a bowl with a whitish paste and had a big bundle of it sitting in a pan near the stove.

"God hates you, Lucy."

My heart plummeted. Mothers, by definition, were supposed to be encouraging. Hopeful. Confidence builders.

Mothers weren't supposed to drop such shrapnel-laden bombs on their children, even if it were true. Even if God Himself had come to tell Mom that He despised me, she should have sugar-coated it. Taken His words and spun them toward the positive. Not dumped this news like it meant nothing.

"He's always hated you. Ever since you took your first breath." Mom knelt in front of me, the bowl on the floor at my feet. "Probably long before."

I gave way to the shakes as she put her hands on my kneecaps, bowing her head in prayer.

"God, please forgive my child. We have discussed her for years, and now her time has come to be cleansed. To open herself up to You. So that You will finally accept her as Your own."

When she stood, Mom scooped some of the sage from her bowl and rubbed it across my forehead, in what felt like a cross.

"Forgive her her sins." Another line of the herbal mixture coursed down my cheek. "And the sins of those before her."

I dared not move. Tippy sat silent, her eye wide. I imagined mine looked about the same, the fear I felt more from Mom's instability than her antics. Why wouldn't God love me? I had never been anything other than good. I had tried so hard to make her tolerate me that I wouldn't chance her affection for even a moment's glory of being bad.

Mom ranted on. Talked to her version of God, a deity that despised me, while decorating my skin with her balm. The smell was overwhelming, the sage crushed and close to my eyes and nose. I had no idea what else she was putting on my face, just that it burned slightly and made my eyes water.

My face covered, Mom moved on to my neck, arms, and shoulders. When she finished, she went to the bundle on the stove and turned on the burner.

I sat, perfectly still, although I desperately wanted to run. Kick out the windows and flee.

Jump off the chair and declare that God did not hate me. How could she say that? How could she believe that?

With the blue flames dancing around the burner, Mom lit the sage and fanned the heavy smoke it created. She held it like a cigar and for a second I was afraid she was going to make me smoke it.

"Forgive this child, Lord. Take her back under Your wing. Cleanse her soul. Make her pure again," Mom rattled while she blew against the smoldering herb and coated me with the miasma.

"Oh, this is bullshit!" I heard myself scream. I pulled up from the chair, but Mom flattened me with her hand.

"That's Satan talking. He lives under your skin, Lucy. Let him be as vulgar as he wants! He's suffering! Hearing him curse means it's working!" She puffed more sage and choked me with the smoke.

"He does not live inside me. If anyone houses him, it's YOU." I couldn't believe my own mouth. I had never spoken to her like this.

"You're possessed. God has always known this. That's why the devil tainted you. Devil-girl." Mom raised her hands to the ceiling. "I could feel his touch on you when you slid out of my body…."

Mother ran her hands up her thighs, over her crotch. She was speaking so loudly I thought that the Hanleys could probably hear her, but then I realized I was causing most of the racket. Panicking. Huffing out my tension. Yelling at her to keep away.

"…You were so hot, you slithered out of me like a snake covered in oil, and I could feel how he had already held you, I could smell his stench on you, a whore straight from my womb…."

"SHUT UP!"

"…That beastly red hair of yours…."

"WHY ARE YOU LIKE THIS? WHAT IS WRONG WITH YOU? WHY CAN'T YOU JUST LET ME LIVE LIKE A NORMAL TEENAGER?"

"…Just one look at you and I understood. All of those horrible cramps I'd had while pregnant with you were just God's hands trying to push you out…."

This time Tippy chimed in. She hustled over to nip at Mom's heels.

"I should have killed you then. Before you were born. Let them suck you out of me like venom, I would pay again and again for someone to cut me open and haul you out and throw you on a burning pile, but no! I had faith that God would forgive you! Harlot!"

I stopped yelling. I didn't even know what a harlot was.

How could I ever win this battle? Fight her disease and get Mom to see that she was utterly mad? What could she possibly want from me?

"I'm sorry. I didn't…realize I'd done those things. Will God ever forgive me?" I whispered, trying another tactic. When Mom had switched to talking about aborting me, I knew we were driving down an entirely different street. For a second my empathy swelled and I realized that her craziness had much deeper roots than Brandy and I had ever imagined. But then my spine stiffened. Had she really had this perception of me since I was a fetus?

No wonder she hated me. Mom had always been drawn to Brandy, had such ease around her, shared laughter with her like they were best friends at a slumber party. With me she was stiff. Controlled. Anything but comfortable.

My eyes watered as my face heated. Whatever substance Mom had used to smear the sage gave off fumes that made it almost painful to breathe. I used this and acted as humbled as I possibly could.

She embraced me. Mom welcomed my tears and met them with her own.

"We're going to do this together, Lucy. You and me. We're going to clean you up, let God see you in your pure form. Let Him understand your stupidity."

"Yes, Mommy."

I let her pull me up beside her, the sage starting to dry on my face. The herb itched, but that discomfort was nothing compared to my humiliation at being half naked and the victim of another of Mom's crusades.

When she opened the basement door, the panic instantly set in. Mom walked behind me, closing us in, this space in the house still much larger than the shed. I thought of my sweater left upstairs and how goosebumps were swarming my skin, the cold air almost tangible.

She was escorting me to my tomb.

"Keep moving." Mom poked me in the back with the herbs in her hand. I hadn't realized that I had stopped on the stairway. "Go over there, by the window."

I knew where she was taking me. Brandy and I hated this room. We hadn't opened the door in years. The last time we did Tippy slinked in and barked at the air, something she never did. The dog's reaction had terrified us.

But Mom had altered it some. The floor was no longer covered in coal dust, and two old comforters had been thrown inside. My quick assessment also revealed six jugs of water and what looked like a bucket in the corner.

She pushed me in. I expected her to slam the door shut, but Mom joined me. Tippy was nowhere to be seen. She always hovered beside me, and I was practically hyperventilating when I couldn't find her.

"Stop looking for your dog. I left her upstairs. This is about you and God, and that damned dog doesn't have any part in it."

I stood with my hands wrapped around my chest. Not knowing what to expect. Despite the cold, I had been sweating so hard I could smell my own body odor under the scent of sage.

Mom left me for a second and powered on a machine just outside the door. She didn't explain and I didn't ask, but I could instantly discern a change in the air. Somehow she was pumping heat into the coal room! I looked up and saw a hole cut into the woodwork above the door, a tube inserted from the other side.

She lit the sage again. Puffed smoke at me. Walked around the small space and seemed to light it afire, fanning the bundle at the walls and back again at me. I choked, and her eyes crackled with joy.

"I can see the devil in there, Lucy. In your soul. You must let him out." Her finger touched my chest, my heart freezing upon impact.

Mother danced in the cramped space, her hands clutching the herbs, the smoke spinning through the room. The vision itself was astounding. For a second I pictured her chanting around a bonfire, a witch doctor trying to heal my wounds, and realized that maybe she actually had good intentions. This didn't seem like punishment. More like a last ditch effort that Mom had concocted to save me.

"I will, Mom. But I don't know how." Thinking of Mother as someone trying to salvage me, I felt a huge weight lifted from my shoulders.

"None of us know how, sweetie. You have to find it within yourself. Let go of the devil and let God in. He will help you."

She worried the sage through the air again, touched the concoction stuck to my forehead, and left me alone in the coal room.

When the door shut I half expected demons to jump out at me. I imagined them as children playing hide and seek, watching me, giggling, waiting until I was unaware before they attacked.

But thankfully they never showed.

I let my eyes adjust to the darkness. In my bedroom, Tippy and I had every inch memorized and lived as easily in the pitch black as we did at high noon. But here, with no lights, and the window boarded up, I stumbled over the comforters as I moved away from the door. The heat was really pouring in and I was thankful, for the blankets were stiff with cold. I sandwiched myself between them, shivering, wishing that I not only had Tippy's companionship but her body heat as well.

I closed my eyes and thanked God that I wasn't stuck back in the shed. That time in my life had been maddening, and I couldn't fathom enduring this with a foot of snow on the ground and the cold metal walls closing in on me.

But my words didn't come back to me. If Mom was right and God for some reason hated me, why would I feel so comfortable talking to Him? As I always had? Wouldn't I feel ill attending church? Wouldn't something horrible strike me down if God loathed me and I entered His house? I prayed all of the time. I talked to God dozens of times a day. If He couldn't stand me to the point that He wanted to strike me down as a fetus, why would my words enter the world with such ease?

I curled up as tightly as I could. The blowing heat made for some company, the noise rather calming. Listening to it, I imagined waves and an ocean that I had never seen, except in pictures and movies. I closed my eyes. Approached the faraway water. Ran into it, my body soaking up the hot sun, my arms outreached toward Heaven.

Chapter 17

Joan

The dog slept with me for a change. We giggled a lot about you, locked downstairs in the dark. The door bolted shut. Sweating away your sins.

Could God ever forgive you?

I fed Tippy popcorn, took her on a car ride, even bought her a big bone from the butcher that was almost the same size as her body. We had a blast. A couple of times she pawed at the basement door, wanting you. I pushed her away with the broom and we went on, pretending you didn't exist.

I couldn't help but stare at her face. Her bad eye. The scar from the botched job at the cheap vet her first owners had taken her to still showed the marks from the stitches, made her look like a rag doll. When I tried to touch it, she jumped away.

We were doing fine until the morning, two days after your venture into the basement, that Aunt Evelyn joined me at the kitchen table. I hadn't seen her in so long I had almost forgotten how she seemed void of all things feminine. Her skirt was long and disguised the way she sat, slightly slumped in the wooden chair, legs spread wide like a man. I appreciated the length of her hair, the thick braid that adorned her back but looked as though she'd slept in it for a week without brushing it in between times. She looked rugged. Wizened. Old.

"I don't know why anyone would allow an animal to live inside the house. Dogs belong in the yard," My great aunt told me, her fingernails tapping the table. "What will you do next, spread feed for the chickens in the laundry room?"

"I don't have chickens."

"That's odd. I could swear I heard them clucking before I came downstairs. Do you have my tea?"

I served Evelyn the hot chamomile she loved. Remembered, after all these years, to put honey in the bottom of her mug and let the hot water do its trick.

We said little. I read the newspaper, actually took a bit longer dissecting it than normal, while Aunt Evelyn polished an ax.

"Must you do that at the table?" I asked. After all, it was my house.

"Someone has to be prepared." She ran her cloth over the sharp surface, and I became almost mesmerized with her methodical movements. If I had gripped the weapon like that, my fingers would be lying on the floor. But Evelyn didn't have to worry about such earthly problems. She folded her fingers around the edge of the blade, practically burned the metal sterile with her tight grasp and frenzied cleaning.

We exchanged short glares. I knew why she was here.

"I'm handling things." The newspaper folded, I took it to the pile by the fireplace.

"Oh, indeed you are. As I'm certain you tell your mother on a regular basis. How long did it take her to bleed out, an hour? Or much less?"

"Please. How rude."

"Just being honest, dear. You can't spite me for that." She pursed her lips, raised her eyebrows in that creepy way she had, and downed some of her tea. "Now, let's get to work, shall we?"

I did as instructed: cleaned the table, put a kettle on the burner, brought my aunt all of her files, including the new ones she had carried in with her, and put the dog in my room so she wouldn't be a nuisance while we studied.

"This one was always fascinating. She was a half-breed, long before it became fashionable. All of her children died as they pulled them from her womb. Six of them, flexing and stretching and apparently eager to join the world. Until their legs passed through. Then it was downhill fast. All of them dead within minutes."

"What a tragedy." I understood the woman's pain. The disappointment of longing for your own flesh and blood to appear and instead being handed a corpse.

My mind flashed to Alex. His laughter. How Brandy was just like him.

I tried desperately not to think of you.

"Stay on task." Evelyn said.

"But I've read these files over and over again. What else could I possibly learn?"

"What else? How about a lesson in standing tall? That it's not butchery but the preservation of the human species you're fighting for?"

"You're one to talk. When have you ever taken matters into your own hands? It's one thing to study something but an entirely different story when you have to do it yourself." I stared her down.

"Good God, child. Don't you know anything?"

Her astonishment stirred my curiosity.

"I thought I pretty much knew it all."

We both sipped our tea.

"Do you ever see my mother?" I missed her, even now. Fifteen years later, and I could still see her watching my tragedy unfold, the terror in her eyes, the helplessness she felt written across her face like someone had scrawled it in black magic marker.

The utter devastation I felt when he took her hands, the blood dripping onto my skin, and used them on me. While my mother continued to watch, knowing that soon she would die.

"That's an odd question. But yes, I have. Just not recently. I spend my time elsewhere."

"How was she?" I perked up. For just a second I could feel my mother's embrace. However fleeting, it brought me back to the innocence I used to have.

"As well as could be expected. She gets along without her hands, but it is quite challenging for her. Alex helps out."

My mug slipped from my grip and shattered on the floor. In the room upstairs I could hear the dog barking, afraid I was being attacked.

"You've seen Alex?"

Sitting across from my great aunt polishing her battle ax, I could smell him in the room. Even in my chair my legs started to give way and I had to push my back flat against the cushion in order not to fall off.

With my eyes closed, I could swear it was the early 80's and my husband was just returning home from work. I would watch the clock and wait for him every day. Alex would come in, pull me into him, his breath and sweat and long-since-applied after-shave meeting my nose and overwhelming me with a wave of absolute comfort and serenity.

That same scent met me in my chair. What would Alex think of me now? He was handsome and pure. When other women walked past us on the street, their eyes lingered on him, then flashed toward me with jealously and even a bit of outrage that he would have me and not them. Alex radiated energy.

But he was dead, too. Had I passed at the same moment? I'd been numb for so long that sometimes I had difficulty telling whether or not my veins held anything even slightly warm. What a misfortune that I hadn't been able to hold him as his flame was snuffed and instead could barely even scream beneath the gag in my mouth. Was it my fault he was gone? Had the family curse somehow brought it on?

"How was he?"

"It's not like we had a long conversation. I was checking on your mother, and he was helping her up from the couch. I said hello, he smiled and that was it."

That was it? Fifteen years later and this was all she'd give me?

"Listen, Joan, you need to pull yourself together. Think of your life as a business. These other people, your employees. Would you stand for their shenanigans? Would it be beneficial to your bottom line if you allowed personal feelings and personality to supersede execution, delivery, profit?"

"No." Aunt Evelyn had a valid point. "I wouldn't."

"There you go. It's a business. If you ran a bakery and had an infestation of mice, would you just lock the mice up in the basement and wait to see what happened or would you eradicate them?"

"I'd call an exterminator."

"But what if *you* are the exterminator?"

A point I'd never truly considered.

"But she isn't a mouse." I argued. "She's actually a pretty good girl."

This truth about you was one of the greatest secrets I hid, even from myself. As much as I deplored having you as a child, you would have made another mother happy.

"She's the devil's spawn! Why can't you see that?" The ax slipped from Evelyn's hand. I jumped back, the blade barely missing my foot, and watched with horror as it embedded itself in the linoleum, the handle sticking out of the floor like a rudimentary grave marker.

"I do see it. She's destroyed my life. She came to this world covered in the blood of my husband. But...." I couldn't finish. I didn't want Evelyn to badger me for my weakness.

"There is no room for your quivering! There are no *ifs*, *and*s or *but*s when it comes to family business!"

"But each time I've tried to...take care of her...it's like my mother steps in and stops me. My gut screams that it is the worst thing I could ever do. I look at Lucy and see nothing but a white light surrounding her and can't take that final step. What if you're wrong? What if she's good inside? What if this whole...legend...is nothing but that? Or if it is true, what if Lucy turns it around? Have you ever thought of that? Maybe she's the one to stop the evil and take the stand for righteousness!" I found myself rising at the end of my outburst, towering over my aunt, my fists against the table.

"Feel better now?" Evelyn dismissed me with a wave of her hand.

"A bit." The good thoughts of Alex and my mother were slipping away. The negativity was fogging back into my soul.

"Do you think that all the mothers before you were heartless fiends bent on killing their own children?"

"I don't know what to think." I was nothing if not honest.

"They loved their girls, too! Remember the Aussies. Both families. Do you think that mother wanted to give her daughter to the dingos? But when they were all sitting with her, and that little imp was smiling, giving the tell-tale sign with her eye, do you think that her mother said, 'Yay! Now I finally get to live out my dreams and get to slash the throat of my baby and let these wild dogs ravage her flesh'? Do you? Really?"

"No."

"And Easter Sunday in Norway? Seventeen people killed before the mother put an end to the horror? Do you think that while cooking the ham for dinner, she was mulling over how to destroy her own flesh?"

"No." I was getting burnt out on her lessons.

"But they did. All of these women did. All of them, proving their honor and faith and dedication to the blood line. Without hesitation."

"Lucy has never hurt a soul." Once again I defended you. Such an odd stance for me to take.

"Not yet. But her role is different, isn't it? She's not just a local scamp. She's not looking to bring down three or four bodies. Her death toll will be in the hundreds of thousands. Millions, even. That child of yours will bring down the whole human race, if given the chance. Why can't you see that?"

A vile image filled my mind. You, dancing with your little dog. The two of you in a fancy ballroom, packed with people from all over the world. Your gown was long and black and whipped violently as you twirled around. A cacophony of laughter panicked the room. When you turned to face me, your bad eye was ablaze, and despite their terror, the people fell to their knees before you, your crown of snakes slithering as you glared at me in triumph.

No, you wouldn't be content as one of many. You were born to rule. To relieve your father of his position and take control of Hell. Evelyn gestured to her cup, and I refilled it with boiling water.

From the basement we heard you laughing. Giggling hysterically, your voice razor blades that sliced the walls as it echoed through the room. You took over our conversation. Made me realize what a fool I'd been to stand up for you.

"I can see it."

I had to practically scream for Aunt Evelyn to hear me over your cackling.

Chapter 18

Lucy

Sleep kept me captive for a small eternity. I so wanted to escape my life that I just closed my eyes and let it all slip away. Forgot about Mother's thoughts on aborting me. Her determination to free me from the devil. The utter starkness that made up her insanity.

I woke up once, took off the rest of my clothes, laid back down on the comforters.

They were so wet from my sweat that I pondered wringing them out to save the moisture. The air scorched like hot pavement and I half expected scorpions and lizards to crawl out from under me, sand dunes to undulate the length of the room.

When I finally came to, I felt dizzy, confused, like I had been unleashed in the dark labyrinth of Mother's barmy thoughts. Nothing was stable. Everything was off-kilter. Even my skin seemed out of place, my fingers heavy clumps of wood, my lungs embers that glowed bright orange each time I took a breath.

Still, my thoughts returned, as always, to water. My senses honed in on it and wouldn't let go. I could hear it dripping, big heavy drops pinging against metal, all a fantasy that I couldn't convince my mind to disregard.

No matter how hard I tried to ignore it, my body obsessed. Closing my eyes only brought images of rain barrels and overflowing gutters to mind. My lips, cracked and torn, reminisced about the days when they had not yet uttered the word *dehydration*.

I didn't want to move, let alone crawl along the dark floor until I found the jugs of water. Had I been here for hours? Days? Was Tippy okay?

My heart cringed at the thought of my best friend. Alone. With Mother. Would she be safe? Did Mom have her chained somewhere, covered in gravy, waiting for the God of Hot Dog Eating Canines to descend and prove that Tippy wasn't an evil beast?

At least I didn't have to worry about her hunger level or how much of my water she might slop up when I wasn't looking.

I could barely contemplate standing. Just lying on the floor I felt like an unproven surfer, trying to balance amidst the waves, all wobbly legged and out of sorts. Something was very wrong with me.

How had I gotten to this place? In all of the great plans I had made for my future, none included being trapped in the coal room, naked and loopy.

For a while I couldn't stop laughing. But laughter quickly turned to hysterics. Without Tippy looking to me for strength, my emotions gave way. And the tears weren't just about my bad situation. They were for my sister, both because I missed her ferociously and because she had completely and utterly abandoned me, knowing Mom was nuts and that I wasn't safe with her. They kept running down my cheeks as I thought about all of the years I had striven to be a good girl, following Mom's and God's rules, living up to my responsibilities.

But this was where my best behavior brought me. Lying in the pitch black, weeping for a mother who had always hated me, for fathers both dead and divine. Lonely. Afraid.

Thirsty.

Crying just added more anguish to my sore throat. I calmed myself. Took deep breaths. Promised myself I had a resilience that others my age lacked. That God couldn't hate me.

Maybe I was the one who had gone mad. Maybe I was really lying on the beach somewhere, taking a mental vacation that had gone horribly awry, and had somehow become trapped inside my own mind.

Thinking of the ocean again led me right back to my current reality, where I was parched beyond reckoning and had no one to help me but myself. I willed Brandy to show up and fetch the water for me. Or at least to prop me up on her shoulder and help me get there.

The jugs were miles away. In the dark room, the walls were tilted, the floor at an odd angle I didn't think I could navigate. I inched forward, remembering back when our family was functional and Mom had taken us to the county fair. She had found a comfortable bench and was eating an elephant ear while Brandy and I braved one of the rickety rides. The metal base had rolled just like the coal room was doing now. We had screamed at the top of our lungs while we spun around, trying to get Mom's attention each time we whirled past, waving when we could pull our arms up.

What fun that had been.

But this was certainly a different story. A nightmare with no ending.

I had to stop. My insides threatened violence if I continued.

Yet images of water filled my mind . Chilling in a frosty mug. So cold that the ice cubes chunked up together, freezing into one big block. Even hot water. The bathtub, steam rising from its belly, bubbles coating the water's surface like an old man's beard.

A cup of hot tea. Spiced orange had always been my favorite.

And Brandy. Spraying me down with the hose in the dreadfully hot days during our summer vacations. Sometimes we even turned on the sprinkler while Mom was at the bank and spent our afternoons doing yard work, keeping ourselves cool while completing our daily chores.

My face itched, the drama of having a billion flesh eating ants consume my outer layers running a close second to my raging thirst. The sage and cream were caked to my skin and cracked like desert soil. I had clawed at it until I smelled fresh blood and even then couldn't stop myself from trying to get it off.

Which led back to a running faucet. How delicious would it be to turn on the hot water, douse a washcloth, and scrub the crust from my skin? The clean scent of Ivory soap fed my fantasy, and for just a second I could feel the sage loosening from my forehead, my reflection in the mirror that of a younger, healthier me.

I crossed over the edge of the comforter as though I had made it across state lines. I was on new terrain, the old cement floor, somewhat of a rough shock to my knees as I used up another brief surge of energy. My forehead met the slightly cooler surface of the floor, balancing my body as I took a break. Time was of no concern. If it took me six days to find the treasure on the other side of the room, then so be it.

Of course, I might be long dead by then.

Not that anyone would care.

Except for Tippy. She'd whine for me. Especially once she got whiff of my decaying corpse. That would be disastrous for her, that odor, wafting about the house while she tried to go on with her life. Mom probably wouldn't even notice it.

Another couple of inches.

But maybe this was Mom's dilemma. Maybe she was like Abraham, whom God told to kill his son....was this *her* test, and I just the pawn in the whole ordeal? If that was the case, the water would be poisoned. In the dark I wouldn't be able to see if it was clear or tainted green or had razor blades floating in it. When it came down to it, I really couldn't remember what it should taste like anymore. Mom could have filled the bottles with battery acid, and as long as it was liquid, I wouldn't know the difference.

I must have been in the basement for six weeks to be so devoid of all moisture. My tongue hung outside of my mouth. My eyeballs felt like they were going to pop from my skull like ping-pong balls, and for just a second I wished they would, hoping that their release would ease some of the tension.

When I finally reached the far wall, my heart thumped wildly. My fingers met the groove at the bottom of the concrete and followed it along the edge. I had seen the jugs here, right before Mother locked me in. My eyes had flashed on them like cameras, emblazing their image forever in my mind. The water was my safety net. My security blanket.

My salvation.

But I couldn't find them.

I hurried as best I could, panicked, my first thought that I would go utterly insane if my fingers didn't find the liquid cache soon, my second that my heart was just about to challenge my soul to a drag race and end this quest before I locked on target.

Then the world changed.

An explorer would have been jealous. An architect, inspired. A very damaged, dehydrated teenager on the verge of lunacy—ecstatic with the taste of freedom.

The walls didn't end.

I fumbled, hands pushed against the cement, a blind cave fish bumping into the room's boundaries with every movement. My breathing evened. My heart registered its concern, but mellowed enough for me to keep working. For a brief spell the dizziness that kept me roller-coastering while perched on all fours subsided.

And where the corner always stood, the world kept going.

The modification was so slight, no wonder Brandy and I had never discovered it during our basement explorations. A hallway of sorts, smaller than the rest of the room, barely big enough for me to squeeze through. I crawled the wall with my fingertips, pulled myself tall and thin, and wedged myself into the skinny space.

The air there was cool and delicious. I sucked it in and felt my skin spark alive again, shivering with the change of temperature.

Trembling with excitement at my turn of luck. Like a key, upright one second, twisted to the right the next.

I shifted into feather form, something I never knew I could do. So light I could traverse the teeniest space. Just float around without a care in the world. Maneuver better than the mice that had scouted this area years before me.

My mind was so focused that I could watch my thoughts string across the walls like fresh spider webs. My body slinking. Each drop of blood in my veins consumed by this brazen escape, my quest for the ever-elusive water that had somehow beaten me out of the coal room. How had I not noticed it leaving this hot space we shared?

Where was it?

For that matter, where was I? And how did this maze extend past our house without anyone noticing?

I smelled it before my brain clicked in. Gritty. Loamy, the scent so strong now I could almost feel the moss climbing into my nostrils.

The cornfield.

This ancient path, my new-found salvation, wove beneath the Hanley's farm.

The deeper I inched through the darkness, the closer my head came to the roof, the black soil crumbling as I brushed against it.

Tendrils reached through the earth, pulsing with the faintest light, allowing me to finally see as I continued to work through the buried path. Was this part of the underground railroad? Some hidden torture chamber the sicko who built this house had designed? Had I become part of a freaky science experiment Brandy had created, a rat trapped in her maze?

Desperation had pushed me this far, and fear of suffocating between the tight walls kept me going.

That and my precious memories of the stream frozen at the edge of the field. The water in it pure. Cold. Mine. Would it drip underground? Wet the walls? Could I suck it straight from the soil? Because, at this point, I would.

All I wanted was water. The sense of freedom I was experiencing was so secondary to the siren song of hydration that I would have gladly signed away my years of adult independence for the promise of never again having lips that cracked like old cement.

The space narrowed more. The ceiling dropped. As slowly as my body moved, the earthen opening swallowed me at a rapid pace, walls screaming past like stampeding freight cars, their shrill warning cries not enough to deter me.

But the oxygen was sucked straight from my lungs, my swollen tongue the troll keeping air from passing back through. Vines crept in ringlets above me, their delicate touch reassuring as I collapsed, tucked so tightly into my dirt coffin that I couldn't even lie down.

When I stopped I realized what a fool I'd been. How Mom had duped me. Teased me with the gallon jugs of water, led me like one of those old cartoon donkeys following a carrot, and I had simply obeyed, thinking somehow it would be easy, drinking, gorging on the liquid gold, sucking down every sip, a pool party for my mouth.

Tears didn't even come this time. My body was too dry. I pictured my sister, her eyes glowing, her face alive with laughter, and said my mental goodbyes. She hadn't returned for me. And now she'd never be able to find me. Mom had won. Drawn me to this grave. Was probably cuddling with Tippy, laughing while I wheezed below her.

Tippy. My baby. I wished her the best. Hoped Mom wouldn't boil her one day and feed her to the coyotes. Prayed that dogs really had long-term memory and that she'd always remember my kisses. My scent. My love for her.

I was ready. A seedling planted deep in the earth. Ready to shed my shell and emerge, glorious, into sunlight.

My eyes closed, I waited for God to take me. Or, if Mom was right, for the devil to pull me down to an eternity worse than this life I'd already lived.

The tug came from above. I felt it squirm past my face like enormous tapeworms, thick and strong and bent on survival. At first the roots slipped by one or two at a time, then built in force. They wrapped me in their strong arms, wove around my head like a wedding halo, curled around my shoulders, down to my toes, growing thicker each second. I began to fight with my last tinge of strength, but then they hummed, swaddling me like a thousand nurturing hands, until I just melted into them.

The corn. Buzz-cut in the field but strong in the soil. Protecting me.

It sucked me up like a tiny piece of ice through a child's straw. Catapulted me through layers of dirt and halfway across the field, where I fell into the snow, cool at last, surrounded by frozen water.

My body hurt too much to move. But my mouth opened wide, sucked up the moisture, shook uncontrollably as my teeth suddenly grew as cold as my skin.

Tippy would be so proud of me. Somehow, in ways I could never explain, I had finally gotten out.

Alive.

But practically paralyzed from my ordeal.

I knew I wouldn't last long in the weather. Shirtless, shoeless, half-mad. I didn't even recognize where I was. The house wasn't visible. The Hanley's out of sight. Just me, the corn, the blessed snow.

Chapter 19

Evelyn

My entire life I've been surrounded by fools. Idiots content to suffer their days in a blind stupor rationalized by the spoils of their income and oft-quoted blurbs from whatever book they draw forth their gods.

Like my sister. Building a life flat on her back. Her lofty childhood goal to find a husband, procreate, keep his britches pressed and his offspring clean, wile away the years following his orders and never having her own mind. Which, of course, she executed with pride.

Not a very dignifying existence. But she was taught well by our mother. And her mother before her. And all the others at the front of the line.

Imbeciles. Their thoughts merely rancid flatulence in the webbing that is our world. Their days a pile of well-penciled calendars, diaries brimming with useless drivel that would leave the most faithful of nuns comatose, their minds blackened with boredom.

And yet, somehow, we are connected. This line of cooks and luxe queens, so kitschy in their home-made aprons and holiday brooches. As a child, I ambled through life wearing my father's shoes. I couldn't bear watching my sister better her posture by walking the house with books on her head, let alone participate in such inane activities. My strong back came from the rifle I toted, the heavy texts I kept in a bag at my side.

I still have difficulty reconciling my relationship with these fixies, the women in my family, pushing their way through life with voices as shrill as their nails, with high-riding bosoms and hair so permeated with spray even the bugs couldn't unglue themselves to get out. That Doris and I were born of the same woman is ridiculous. That we shared blood and burden, our youths fermented in the same rooms, that we heard identical words but with such different connotations—all borders on the blasphemous.

And they thought me the odd one.

Dad didn't mind my ideas. In fact, he often chuckled while I emptied his pocketbook playing poker, listening to me rant like the traveling preachers Mom would always drag us to hear. I was the son he never had. I was the off-spring with promise, the one who could figure his books, tend to the fields, challenge his friends to any philosophical conversation and leave them slack-jawed.

Never marry. A woman should not be shackled. I wasn't. I managed my father's money, played with it on the market until we achieved a lifetime's comfort, then set about the world on a tour that kept me going for decades.

Forget children. Let someone else carry them, clean their bottoms, navigate life around their petty needs, listen to their relentless whining. Such a life was not for me. Instead of baby teeth and birthday cards, I wanted to collect turquoise and the ivory carvings that I bought off tribesmen during my visits to Africa.

After living with my father, I never needed another man. My hands grew black with oil when my automobile needed repairs. My shoulders, muscular from yard work and keeping wood ready for the fire. I felt no fear walking into a man's club, joining them on the leather sofas, cigar and scotch in hand. Nor did I get a bad reaction. They accepted me as their own.

Which opened many doors. In my twenties I was virtuous and kept my stockings free from runs. No matter my life's path, I respected my mother and her beliefs, chose not to bring any blackness to her house.

But what a change a decade brings. At thirty-three I had adopted pants, which were much better suited for hunting trips and long rides across rough terrain. I was on my third excursion through Europe, a lone traveler, gathering information, charting my lineage in an effort to understand how my sister's offspring would infest the world. Many a lover had met my bed, but none moved me enough to get an invitation to stay.

Until my train trip to Madrid, and those first steps I took onto the platform before seeking my hired hand.

She was delicate, a raven so fragile I longed to cup her in my hands, and protect her from the ferocity of the wind. As soon as I laid eyes on Josephina, time ceased all motion. I struggled to inhale a mere breath. To remember that we were of the same species, inhabiting the same planet. That perhaps, if I stood close enough to her, the air she exhaled would pass her body and become one with mine.

After my father died, I never needed another man.

But I certainly began to understand them. The wanting. The ego that pulled them along, crushing everyone and everything in their path. The absolute craving of such porcelain beauty, the desire to possess and own it, to trade all in one's life for three seconds of lips locked to a breast, a hand running along the spine of someone as exquisite as Josephina.

Something I could never have.

Oh, but I did.

Chapter 20

Lucy

My body grew so numb that I could no longer differentiate it from the soil. A last-ditch effort to raise myself failed. The long red locks that had always been my pride had frozen to the ground, holding me prisoner.

Snow began to fall, the massive flakes camouflaging me. I thought of God, standing over me, His tears turning to mush in this winter weather long before they fell to Earth. He didn't hate me. Mother was wrong. Already He mourned my loss.

I tried to let go. Hurry the inevitable along. What had I read in books? That when you were freezing to death, the worst thing you could do was go to sleep? As desperately as I tried, my mind wouldn't shut down. My eyes stayed open, the snow caking in my lashes, my shallow breaths wrapping smoke around my head.

Which is the only reason I saw them.

An oasis, I thought. If I were disoriented and stumbling through the desert, this is what I would see. My mind would play tricks like this. Just as if I had survived weeks lost at sea and kept seeing coastlines and far-off ships that weren't really there.

I knew the deer were imaginary. An eleventh-hour effort on behalf of my body, fueling me to get up and move, find warmth, water. Freedom.

They closed in, and I marveled at how real they seemed. Timid at first, the beasts came at me from all angles, but I could only watch the ones that walked directly toward me. I guessed their numbers at twenty, if not more. A huge male followed behind the others, stood poised at the edge of my vision. His antlers rose from the snowy mist as though he were a warrior on horseback, arms raised and ready for battle. My heart warmed at the sight of him.

The buck snorted and the others parted. He stayed on the outskirts of the herd, his dominance understood by all of us. From my position on the ground, I was able to maintain direct eye contact with him. No words had to pass between us. Just from his posturing, I instantly understood his decades of wisdom, his power, unrivaled in these back woods, and that, like a father, he had come to protect me. For the first time in months I felt a modicum of security.

The smell of their fur overwhelmed my senses. Each animal gave off its own scent, but I translated it into fields, overgrown and riddled with the witchgrass and foxtail that irritated the area farmers.

Hot breath hit me. The herd, melting my snow blanket, closed in, licked the thin sheet of ice I called my skin. A few nudged me. Even though the excitement had just begun, I could feel myself edging into sleep and wondered if they were trying to keep me awake.

In my mind's eye, I had already found shelter. A cottage, a raging campfire, heavy blankets, and hot tea roiled through my thoughts. Like I was being carried on a tune, floating to some extent, but streaming along, my body supported by the thick base chords, the wooden posts supplied by the oboes.

None of it made sense.

But nothing had in a long, long time.

My toes twitched. I felt their flashy movements, wanted the rest of my body to follow suit. The deer found it a good sign and began backing away from me, their absence allowing the frigid wind back in. My throat was still too rusty to scream, but mentally I begged them to close the distance, to take away the wicked weather.

Then he pushed forward.

Their leader, the massive buck, who came to me like Santa Claus, a stranger bearing goodwill, the gift of Christmases to come.

He put his nostrils directly against my face. Sniffed me. Moved his head forward and drew the scent from my eye, a move Tippy had made many times, but in this situation seemed like a test I needed to pass. I tried not to fidget as he inspected me, then put his cheek against my own in an attempt I instinctively knew was meant to lend me comfort.

The rest of his movements were fast. Using his antlers, the buck scraped me off the frozen ground as though I were a cookie trapped on a baking sheet. When my skin was freed he lifted me with his massive rack, gently placing me on the back of a younger male, where I miraculously stayed without even a fear of falling off.

They escorted me to a thicket that guarded us from the night wind. The snow hadn't fallen nearly as hard in this area, and the buck lowered himself to the ground once we were safely hidden. I could feel more bodies close in on us, pushing us to the center of the group, where the does came to greet me. Their touch was instantly healing, nurturing, full of warmth.

Several necks stretched over my back, my thighs, the tips of my toes. Their heat enlivened my blood, but I was too weak to move. I reached over to rub the side of one of my new friends and instantly knew her story.

She showed me her favorite areas to run, and I felt her youth explode like flames through my limbs, could savor the thrill of bolting through tall prairie grass, taste the summer heat through my nostrils, the joy in my eyes similar to that of the friends bounding beside me.

Then shadows rose, subtle at first, tainting her memories like an oncoming storm cloud. The smells hit me, the absence of all things pure, the oily, black ugliness of humans. A house jutted up, then three, then new roads, a school. The woods and fields forever shrinking.

The next doe was older, wiser. Her emotions slid under my hand as smoothly as her coat. From her I gathered her grandmother's story, and the timeline passed down to her. Through her eyes the grasses were ancient, the land untouched, the herd enormous and healthy. She protected her own. Listened to the howls of night and swift movements in the tall grass and fought to keep her children safe, to protect the future of their species.

I felt the pull of the moon, the wind, the seasons. Drifted from favorite feeding spots to watering holes and hunkered down to rest with the always shrinking numbers of my family. Witnessed my children shredded by semi-trucks, my parents gunned down and hauled off by laughing humans who threw them mercilessly into the backs of pickups. Stampeded through the blades of old corn plants, my every organ pounding with stress, the combine a threat I couldn't handle.

Less to eat. Tainted water. Algae clogging everything, plastic trash pretending to be food, a thousand acres whittled to an alleyway between housing tracts. The stars faded from being a blazing map in the sky to barely a memory, their beauty hidden by city lights.

The first doe brushed up against me and took me back to her favorite field. We ran together this time, side by side like sisters, crossing back and forth across each other's paths, teasing, jumping, thrilling at the feel of the earth under our hooves.

Just as we leapt over a rotting log, my new friend turned her head to me and smiled. I recognized the road as we neared; my neighborhood. The closer we came, the faster the weather changed. From late summer to the frigid clasp of winter, we worked our way into my yard. Stared up at my window. At the angel in my room, waving down at us, her inner light falling on the field.

We were gone just as fast as we arrived.

Back in the thicket, back in the cold.

I couldn't keep my eyes open. They had saved me, after all, but it wasn't enough. Wrapped in the warmth of the deers' compassion, all I wanted to do was fall asleep. Give myself to a dream world where I really could run with them. Where my mother was Earth, my family these beasts, my future just as strong as the legs that propelled me into tomorrow.

* * *

I woke, swaddled in my pathetic bed, my skin so warm that I could feel the sun beaming onto my back.

But of course, in the coal room, the sky wasn't visible, and I was back to my original state, hot and thirsty but more lucid.

My water supply wouldn't stop nattering, calling me to it in a voice that sounded amazingly like Brandy's. The liquid was hot but a blessing. I dragged a jug to my bed on the floor and almost lost control of my bowels when I tripped over the man lying on my blankets.

In the distance I could hear Tippy barking. Faint but sweet, protecting me.

In the here and now, I could hear myself hollering, the man laughing at my fear.

"Oh, please, stop." I could feel his presence more than see him. His body gave off a chill, like he was an ice cube in my basement Hell. "It's not like I'm going to hurt you anymore than your mother already does."

How did he get into the coal room without me noticing? Wouldn't there have been a light when the door was opened? Had Mom let him in?

"Who are you?" I finally whispered.

"For that matter, who are you, Lucy?"

I couldn't answer. My mind took to the situation like a frog being chased by a group of children, jumping so willy-nilly that my thoughts couldn't sit straight. His question made no sense.

Distraction did another dance when I remembered my birthday suit. Here I was, fresh from the jaunt with my outside friends, my body so devoid of moisture that I was certain I had just bathed in fire, my teeth feeling like they were going to explode out of my shriveled gums like popcorn kernels—that thought a relief when fantasizing about how the blood-flow from that event would coat my throat with liquid, no matter how unpleasant, claw marks ravaging my skin as if rodents had attacked the sage concoction because they had no other fodder in this dank room. My appearance was disturbing, and I was naked to boot.

With an unknown man. In the basement, which might look like a cave but most certainly resembled a frying pan. Naked.

"Have some water, Lucy. It's okay to drink."

I couldn't answer. He handed me a cup, filled to the brim with water, floating chips of ice promising to make it an almost surreal treat.

My manners fell to the wayside. Never mind my birthday suit, the water was more urgent. Once the beverage was in my hand I could no longer control myself and let it slide down my throat with all the daintiness of a rodeo clown. Water rushed from my cup and out the corners of my mouth, leaving clean trails on my otherwise filthy face.

"Wow. You certainly are thirsty." The man laughed while I continued to relish in the cold water.

No matter how much I drank, I could not get enough. My throat became a waterfall, my stomach threatening to drive everything back up again.

"Maybe you should give it a rest. Put it down. You can always have more later," he said. "Here, have a seat."

Suddenly my mind ping-ponged back to the issue of my nudity. I dropped the cup and tried to cover my special spots with my hands.

"Oh, my, such modesty. And after I've been staring at you naked for quite some time now."

The stranger was certainly no light bulb, and although my eyes had adjusted to the dark a bit, I could not see my clothes.

"Can I please get under the blanket?" My tongue felt encased in glue. The words were difficult to form and clunked out of my mouth like rusted metal from the junkyard.

"Just sit down and don't worry about it, Lucy. You have a very nice body, but right now you're way too thin for even my tastes. No one likes a starving girl. Which is why I brought you this!"

The man produced a plate, complete with all my favorites: meatloaf, mashed potatoes with gravy, and two pieces of homemade bread, butter liquefying on top.

"I also brought you an iced tea to go with it," he said as he tapped his fingers against the comforter.

A slight breeze ruffled the cobwebs in my head, just enough that my thoughts reassembled with astounding clarity. How had I not noticed this food before? The smell permeated everything, made my stomach break out in a Sousa march like the ones my band performed in the Fourth of July parade, practically crippled me with the need to eat. The steam was still rising from its dish, the bread so warm that I saw the butter trickle down the sides and drip off the plate onto my companion's hand.

With a quick shake of my head, the hint of light that had allowed me to see the meatloaf died and all was dark again. My nostrils picked up the decay that had once been the meat, the image of a rotting cow tainting my thoughts, maggots squirming through its corpse while the birds pecked away at its eyes. Even the bread sent flashes screaming through my head of concentration camps and the sawdust-filled loaves used to keep the workers barely alive.

"No thank you." This time my words sounded like my own.

Just like that the meal disappeared.

"Well, fine. Be that way."

My body was exhausted, my hands tired of covering my nipples. I found the edge of my bedding with my toes and managed to slip underneath the top comforter, surprised to find myself alone.

"Who are you?" I asked again.

No one was left to answer.

* * *

He came back the next morning, wrapped in sunshine.

"Haven't you slept enough, little girl?" The man's head glowed. I couldn't find the source of light and, after several awkward moments of silence, gave up trying.

"I don't exactly have much else to do."

"Ah, but you're forgetting the obvious. Why did your mom lock you down here?"

If he had tied my mouth shut with jute, I couldn't have grown quieter.

"I can't even remember. It has something to do with the swim team." I closed my eyes, willed myself back to sleep.

"It has nothing to do with the swim team. You know that, Lucy. So, tell me. What possible reason could she have for putting you in the basement?"

"Let's see...she hates me. God hates me. She wants me to somehow find a way for Him to love me again. Nothing major." I rolled over, tried to hide my eyes from him.

"And you think she's crazy?"

"Wouldn't you?"

"Nah. I probably know Joan a lot better than you do. We have a little...history between us." The man chuckled.

"You know Mom?" I didn't really have to ask. Obviously she had let him down here with me, so she had to know him. Otherwise how would he have gotten in?

"I'm pretty close to Brandy, too. Although I have to admit I haven't seen her in a long while. Well, since before you were born. Your mother never mentioned me?"

The stranger produced the glass of water again. I counted six ice cubes, still holding their own, the liquid cold enough that they weren't even melting.

He sat it in front of me.

Laid two glazed donuts on a white napkin just beside it.

"No. What's your name again?"

The room got darker. My will power shattered and scattered into the corners like a hundred roaches bolting for cover. I kept my eyes averted from his and pulled a donut to my dry lips.

Bliss.

He rambled on in the background, talking about my family, I presumed, while I donned a pink ball gown and joined in the waltz. Curled around the dance floor, swinging to the music, long white satin gloves pulled all the way over my elbows.

I stumbled back to reality when he shook the glass in front of me, and the ice clanked so loudly I worried it would alert Mother upstairs.

"Please don't do that," I whispered between bites. For a second I felt guilty about getting my gloves all sticky but shook off the fantasy as I continued to chew.

"Here I am, telling you how I met your grandmother, and you can't even pay attention."

"You're right. I'm sorry. It's just that I'm so….hungry."

My smile was a sad attempt at an apology, but I gave it my best effort.

"When you get back upstairs, don't forget to tell your mother that I said hi. She'll know who I am."

I was confused. He was leaving? Did I want him to?

"But I don't. You've never told me your name. What should I tell her?"

"That your dad stopped by for a visit. I'm your father. Don't you remember me at all, Lucy?"

Chapter 21

Joan

Without Aunt Evelyn guiding my thoughts, I might have totally forgotten you in the basement.

We were having breakfast when the dog went haywire.

She jumped to her tiny feet, turned in circles, barked violently. Checked the back door. Came to me for some sort of reassurance, I suppose, then went back to her post guarding the basement door.

"For goodness sake, can't you shut that beast up?" Evelyn said.

I had just gotten to my feet when you opened the door. I must admit, I jumped a little in my skin when the handle turned. The three of us stared at it, expectantly, not knowing what was behind it. Certainly not anticipating you.

But there you were. In all your glory. Stark naked, all angles, elbows and kneecaps and shoulder bones threatening to take out the plaster as you leaned heavily against the wall.

For a moment I thought you were dead. How else would you have moved? The coal-room door had a dead bolt. I had installed it. I had even personally moved the tool cabinet directly in front of it, blocking any chance you had of moving the door forward. That thing weighed an absolute ton.

You pulled yourself through the threshold. Stood at the top of the stairs. Your face was hideous, blackened with coal dust, the vapor rub I had smeared on your cheeks causing a skin infection that looked like boils. Rancid, seeping ulcers with blood crusting their every edge.

Tippy must have thought you were a zombie. She sniffed your legs, woofed, backed away. The instinct to curl her lips and snarl at you fought desperately with her confusion at seeing you again. We had all assumed you were pretty close to dead by now.

"Get the Goddamned ax." My great aunt was standing. Shocked at the sight of you.

You had to drag your right leg with your hands, hooking them behind your knee and pulling it forward to keep your balance. Which was awful to begin with. You leaned so far to the right I didn't understand how you stayed on your feet at all.

When you finally made it to the middle of the room, where I stood, your hair looked clumped, black, almost like it was full of soil. For an instant I thought you were mad. A lunatic. Your eyes certainly looked like you had given them to the moon.

"How...did you get out?" I asked, backing up, afraid you'd touch me.

Your pause was dramatic. When you tilted your head, I worried that you didn't understand me, had somehow lost control of the English language. But then your lips, broken and repulsive, curled into a smile.

My spine tingled. All the years I had held you when I so desperately wanted to push you down the garbage disposal, all the prayers I had said, begging God to rid me of you, for my own Mother, drenched in blood, watching my life rot in front of her, they were nothing. Nothing to be feared. Nothing to remember. Nothing to be hostile about. Mom's death? In the past.

The sight in front of me was something else entirely. Beyond frightening. Powerful, even in your weakened state.

You had become a monster. Deranged. A psychopath. A nightmare to usurp all of the other treacheries that had invaded my life.

"That nice man you sent to talk to me." You raised your head just enough that the kitchen light hit your face, bounced off your bad eye. Like a beacon, it lit up everything in the room.

My heart jackhammered in my chest. "What man?"

Evelyn stammered in the background. The dog whined, turned in circles. I put my foot into her ribs and pushed her toward the hall.

"The one who's hair was a light. He didn't tell me his name."

I cringed when the ax hit the wall. Aunt Evelyn was standing, gesticulating wildly, calling me a coward. Your words were hard enough to understand without all of the background noise covering them up. Deciphering your speech was like trying to discover the aria in two pieces of grinding metal.

"Lucinda Shay Tew, you'd better tell me right now who let you out of that room. You weren't done in there yet."

You were still alive.

"He said you knew him." A beetle crawled between your fingers, headed up your right hand. Your eye pulsed when you brought it to your mouth. I almost screamed when you placed the bug on your tongue, when its exoskeleton crunched between your teeth.

"I sent no man." I wanted to slap the defiance out of you but was rendered motionless by the sight of your snack coursing down your throat.

"He called himself my father. When he opened the door, he said to tell you that we are at peace."

I backed against the counter, gripped it with all my strength.

When I turned to Evelyn for some sort of guidance, she was gone. The wall showed no sign of her weapon. Her mug of tea sat untouched.

I was absolutely breathless.

"Really, Lucy? He did?"

"I'm really tired, Mom. Can I sit down?"

I pulled the chair out for you, scooted the chamomile closer in case you wanted to drink it. Where seconds ago I had been repulsed by your presence, I wanted nothing more than to pull you tight and cradle you in my arms.

"God came and opened the door for you?"

Chapter 22

Lucy

Bad graces.

Good graces.

Tippy. Trippy. Snippy. Lippy.

Back in bed, the door open. Grape juice. Iced tea. Hot tea. Milk.

Oatmeal. French bread. Apple butter. Cream of chicken soup.

A mother, reading stories. My mother, reading stories. The words rounded out of her mouth and spiraled across the room. Sing-song. Pages turned, teeth clipped important letters, my good friend the dog snuggled against my side, her tail thumping.

The three of us together.

I wanted Brandy. Could almost hear her, in the woodwork, memories of her stalking me through my recovery.

Mom must have killed her. I envisioned her body, sleek like a deer, churned up by tractors, a spray of red and her history had crossed the finish line, the only lingering bits of her chunking off the equipment as it rolled through the field. My sister loved me. She wouldn't have left me like this.

But now I was the good one. Touched by God. Forgiven. My existence profound.

Mom catered to me. We had been going like this for days, most of them a blur of sleep and sickness. I had flashes of her bathing me, cutting my hair when she couldn't get the knots out, putting salve on my lips and hands. She rubbed my legs, tucked me in, made a point of propping the door open at night when she left for her own room. Pulled the spoon from the bowl and wiped my lips with it when soup slipped out of my mouth.

Part of me enjoyed it. Finally achieving that good-girl status. My only fears the ones that jumped out in my dreams. Having Tippy back.

Tippy. Drippy. Flippy. Clippy.

My thoughts attacked me in swift staccatos, then died away for hours after their brief burst of energy. Tippy would breathe against my cheek, and suddenly the buck would jump into the room, keeping me in check, his one-second presence enough to remind me of what he had done to save me. Then my dog would move ever so slightly, and the buck would leave as though he'd never even been beside me, as though our moments had never intertwined.

I grabbed an inner tube and went floating down rivers while Mom kept her vigil beside me. Her words wrapped the room in crisp, pretty paper. I cherished the times she picked up my hand, held the tips of my fingers, sat with me in silence. One night she did my nails in light-purple polish, even applying a second coat.

She asked me over and over about God. What had it been like, being in His presence?

I didn't know what to say. That, in retrospect, He had tempted me with meatloaf and somehow I had passed the test? I remembered the water that never needed refilling in the glass He gave me. A miracle.

We went over the Old Testament, the other miracles shared over the course of thousands of years. My voice was becoming stronger. Mom let me read directly from her Bible. From the old *Guidepost* magazines she had accumulated through the years. Of course, after two paragraphs my throat shut down, but this time Mom was very understanding. When my coughing started, she would roll me over on my side and let me sip tea from the glass when the spasm had passed.

Mucous crusted around my eyes, the rim of my nose. Like infection was oozing out every place it could find. Mom cleaned me with a warm washcloth, and every time she worked on my face I thought of the moment, in the basement, when I had longed so desperately to wash myself like this and clean off the sage and paste.

Tippy looked like her old self. Her coat, patchy but growing back, gleamed again. Her eye was full of confidence. How much time had passed since we were separated? Enough that she no longer hovered on the brink of death.

But we both knew that I was far from out of the woods. We just never discussed it.

Tippy couldn't have cared less about God. She didn't ask me about Him, about the mysterious meatloaf meal, or how He had unlocked the door for me. We didn't even have to conspire about drinking water or what to do with our waste anymore, and Tippy barely acknowledged that we had shared this time in our lives. I clung to her unabashedly, but was strangely alienated from her at the same time.

As my strength increased, so did my alertness. I noticed oddities. Like how Mom never went to work. I tried to keep track of days, to investigate this phenomenon without ever leaving my bed. But my thoughts were hard to master. From what I could tell, she never left the house anymore.

Neither of us did.

And then there were, of course, the hens. I was flabbergasted when the first one ventured into my bedroom without so much as an invitation. The bird was quiet, curious, but certainly not threatened by me or Tippy. I could understand finding me a pretty worthless opponent, but even with gentle prodding Tippy had no interest in chasing the chicken and allowed her to take over the room like it was her own.

Later, when I awoke, that same hen was having a heyday in the corner, six or seven of her friends bobbing their heads back and forth in rapid conversation. Mom dozed in her chair, her hand lying limply beside her, two of the chickens rubbing their feathers against her.

When I tried to ask Mom about them, she told me I had been dreaming. But I could hear them clucking from the hallway, so loudly it sounded like Mom had dozens of them walking our floors.

I dropped it when she started getting edgy. "Why does everyone always accuse me of keeping chickens in the house?"

Like she never saw the drawings on her way to the bathroom. Or the pile of heads accumulating by the top of the stairs. Maybe it just took me so long to navigate my path to the toilet that I let these sights distract me.

Of course, the greater question was who else had asked her about the chickens? No one had set foot in our house since before Easter, when one of the women from church dropped off some fresh eggs for us to prepare for the hunt we did every year on the rectory lawn.

I mostly talked to Tippy, priding myself on the fact that I had finally escaped something, even if it was only the coal room.

"You did great, kiddo," she told me before slathering me with kisses. "I was rooting for you the whole time."

"Do you think she'll let me go back to school soon?" I couldn't help but ask.

"Don't push your luck. Take things one day at a time. You're out of the fire right now, but the frying pan's still pretty hot to the touch."

Tippy.

Rippy. Zippy. Jippy. Shippy.

* * *

We left the movies, the laughter from the flick we had seen lingering between us as we headed down the street.

The world was remarkably quiet. The just-warm-enough air of a late spring night blew around us softly, giving Mike an easy reason to put his arm over my shoulder and pull me tight against him while we walked downtown.

Now and then a car drove past, the water on the road carried on its tires, but barely discernible over the story Mike was telling me about Joe Buxley, a kid on his wrestling team who fell asleep on the bus and started kicking his leg like a dog. A couple stood smoking in front of a coffee shop on the next block, but as we neared they went back inside to enjoy the atmosphere and get a shot of caffeine.

Brandy and I had splurged for hot chocolate there once, and the taste filled my mouth as we passed the front door. I almost suggested to Mike that it would be a great treat, the whipped cream piled with chocolate ribbons, but I didn't want to do anything that might interrupt this time we had together.

Alone.

He held my hand and my blood surged through my veins, making my entire body alert and so excited I thought for sure I might explode.

We went to the park. The trees were just starting to leaf, but the crocuses were out *en masse* and watching us from under the street lights. Mike put his mouth to my ear, whispering things I'd only heard in dreams, the proximity of his lips and breath causing me to shiver.

Brandy said it could be this way. When you were with a boy. She had shared all of her kisses with me, but when I look back on it, I think she left a lot out, as well. One time, in the locker room, the older girls had joked about some of the things my sister had done behind the gymnasium during her lunch hour. I was appalled at the words they used, really didn't understand what they were telling me. When I asked

Brandy later that night, when Mom was far out of earshot, Brandy's face had lit up and she told me that some things were too personal to share.

Now I think I might be having one of those moments. Mike told me he wanted to kiss me, and he did. He was so much taller than me that he had to bend over while I curled up on my tippy toes and met him part way. I had waited for this for years and didn't want to approach it like a coward.

Our lips met and what was left of the world melted away. The cars were gone, the trees and grass and even the small threat of being caught after dark in the park, which wasn't allowed. I cherished the taste of his breath and chased it with my tongue. Loved the feel of his fingers, pressed into my back, pulling me into him.

We strolled to the swings and shared one for a while, Mike sitting on the hard plastic while I faced him and slid onto his lap. For just a second guilt sliced through me. If Mother had any idea what I was doing, she would kill me.

But I liked it too much. Way too much to stop.

Night came in full force, cloaking us, allowing us a bit more privacy. Mike wrapped his jacket around me, then put his arms inside my shirt to keep them warm.

My body was on such a high I thought I might pass out. His fingers feathered over my belly and lower back, causing me to jump up.

"Ticklish?" He asked, grinning.

Before he could touch me again, I took off, giggling. The grass was slick, and I tripped just as Mike grabbed me from behind. We did a backward dance toward the covered slide while kissing and laughing. I tried to tickle him back, but his hands were strong and gripped mine fiercely. He pulled me onto the cold metal, and we scooted until our legs were well hidden inside.

The time for conversation was over. Mike snuggled into me, his hands freezing, his breath hot but steamy just the same. I tried to crawl on top of him, but he moved me back to the bottom, insisting it was only fair since I had the coat.

"Let me warm you up," I said in a voice I barely recognized as my own, opening the jacket as Mike pressed himself completely against me.

We were a twist of hands and mouths. A symphony of lips and tongues. Cold, but boiling underneath the wet wind.

I ran a mental checklist while my limbs melted: my armpits were freshly shaven, we had no monthly visitations to worry about, and, like a good girl, I had on my nicest, cleanest pair of underwear. My body had no intention of stopping and I didn't think my heart did, either.

Mike touched me in places I didn't know existed. Put my hands on parts I found disgusting but pertinent all the same. Concentrated on my bra and the contents within.

We were probably visible at the bottom of the slide when I moved my head to the side, his mouth glued to my neck, Mike's rhythm the baseline that propelled me along. I throbbed. My entire being, head to toe, caressed, loved, totally on fire, so stunning I could hardly breathe, let alone open my eyes, was so wrapped up in my moment that I barely noticed when the man above me changed.

Or did he?

When I turned to face him, to open my eyes and savor his handsome beauty, he was on me, laughing.

My Father. The man with the backlit head. The one who had stood in front of the door and opened it, magically, pulling me up from the floor when I wasn't able to help myself.

"Wow! Someone is certainly feeling better!"

Chapter 23

Tippy

I hated our separation. My job was to protect you, keep you herded onto the right path, give you my heart so that you would grow and be able to give others the same. This was very hard to do when I couldn't get to you.

I could smell you, yes. Not that I wanted to. Your odor had gone from my girl to my girl with that sickness in her eye to a stench that invaded the whole house, like that rotting skunk that reeked in the backyard last summer. Enchantingly mysterious, yes, but frightening at the same time.

At times I trembled. Didn't know what to do, really. My mom taught me about living with humans, following their rules, pooping outside. She was well rehearsed. Knew all the lines. Told me that you played, you entertained, you guarded, but most of all you steered your master with a pure heart. Let her think she's in charge, when all along you are leading her on a strong path.

Dolly was her name. Her scent always made me think of breakfast foods. Many times when you and your sister ate before going to school I'd be under the table, sharing a memory, knowing that I would never see her again.

My mother was wise. A flower, really. Beautiful. And the magnet that pulled all other creatures to her. Always unfolding, alive with information.

When Mom fed us, she would rest on her side and tell us stories of the world while we suckled. Some of my siblings pushed and shoved and didn't much listen. But I did. I wanted to know. To understand how I would navigate my life was more profound to me than getting three extra drops of milk.

She told of dogs and a life, like hers, spent cherished in the warmth of nighttime cuddling and slices of bacon thrown directly from the pan. Or those sad cousins who were outside, fenced or chained or even humanless, their hearts heavy. Times change, she warned. You can have glory and the next moment shame, a home and then isolation, food and then terror. But above all, she urged me never to reduce myself to the circumstance. If my master was mean, then he was mean to me and I accepted that and gave him nothing but love.

This, however, was different.

For this I had no lesson.

One master, hurting the other. My girl, dying. My girl, hurting in ways I couldn't begin to understand. Locked away. Kept from me. Close enough I could discern your presence, far enough I couldn't find you.

I followed my mother's words to the best of my ability. Sent you my love. Could you feel it? Standing in the kitchen, knowing you were somewhere underneath, smelling the suffering on you, I would close my good eye and will you my affection. Picture you in my head. Picture myself back in my superhero cape. Put us together.

Dolly. My mother. Obsessed with integrity, her value system unrivaled. When I needed her the most, all I could find were snippets of our past conversations.

Joan. Your mother. She gives me hot dogs. Speaks to me as though we are chasing the same dream. And that dream is to not find you.

I eat. At first I could not, not with you gone. Then she appeared before me, my own mother, her scent flooding the room. Showed me how thin you were. How sick.

"Who will help her, Tippy?" Mom asked me. "This is your girl. She has no one else but you."

Which was exactly why I had stopped eating. How could I keep emptying the kibble bowl when you were so wretched? When you had nothing?

"Tippy, who will help her if she can't help herself? If you are too weak to move, if you don't keep up your strength, who will save this poor child?"

Her point so valid.

A dog's role, a good dog's role, is to always protect the young ones.

So I eat. Cuddle with the enemy, get to know her weaknesses. Pass time waiting for my moment to shine.

Yet things still change. The air in the house keeps my hair on edge. I find myself unfocused, concentrating on the corners, not quite able to put my paw on things that creep past. Both you and your mother talk to people who aren't here, see things that I can't see, lie to each other while telling the truth. I don't know what to think anymore.

But the outside is more disturbing.

I remember my house before yours. The boy who took my eye. His toys, soldiers, army men, big fighting cars that he rolled all over the living room. He would line them up for battle. A wall of weapons. A procession down the center of the room. A stronghold.

I see that here. In the mornings, when she lets me into the yard, your mother doesn't even notice. Past the metal building, past the car and the trash cans. So far out I can barely see them.

But who couldn't smell them?

It hits me, their unity, the mass of them, when the wind blows against my face. Like I've barreled into a closed door. How can she not notice?

They are lining up where there once was corn. So much stronger than me. So much larger.

But mine, just the same. Someone had to take charge. Merge the inner team with the one outside. I like that I am not alone, but I want to be their friend long before they spy me with her and think I am on the wrong side.

I called to them. Hiding behind the shed, where your mother couldn't see me, I put on my most professional voice and howled as desperately as I could. When I focused, I was shocked to see one of them already so close we could almost touch noses. Then my eye hunkered down and another, well blended with the trees, moved her head. Let me know she understood. And her friend moved as well. Tiny nods, hidden from humans, and I caught the flicker of dozens more.

We acknowledged our singular role. Worked our separate languages into one.

Set our goals. Our boundaries. Shared information.

We meet every morning, in the cold, in the dark. Swap updates. Prepare ourselves.

They are gathering, Lucy.

I may eat when you do not, but that is because I must. I am your eyes and ears, and cannot succumb to sickness. I must always be at the very top of my game. Because you won't be. She forces you to wither. Even though right now, today, she lets you eat, who knows what tomorrow will bring?

But I promise you this, my girl. I will be the strong one. When you are too weak, I shall carry you. Get you to safety. Defend you.

When the time comes, I have an army.

We will win this war.

I have a plan.

Chapter 24

Joan

Was it possible that I'd always loved you?

Flesh of my flesh.

What kind of sign was it that God Himself let you out of the basement? And Evelyn had left?

Surely that meant I didn't have to kill you.

I prayed. Called out to my mother. If she were in Heaven, wouldn't she already know? Was that why I hesitated to use the ax?

If God loved you so much that He took the time out of His busy day to open the door and send you to me with messages of peace, did that mean it was all over?

How would I ever know what to do? Maybe He was tempting you. Like Eve. You could either be good or sacrifice the future of humanity while you put on your devil suit and seared us all with your hatred. I couldn't figure it out.

The damned dog never left your side anymore. Wasn't that also an indication? Would she be so loyal to someone inherently evil?

I moved the ax back into my bedroom closet. *Fool!* It chided me in Aunt Evelyn's voice. *Coward!*

But when I stood my great-aunt next to God, He won hands down every time. Your basement visitor had changed the entire game.

What a relief for me. So much so that I couldn't help but worry about Brandy. Could she come home now? How would I find her? What would I say? Hey, pumpkin, I kicked you out because I was doomed to destroy this other one, but now that's no longer important?

I didn't know how to continue. We had walked to the edge, you and me, leaving all behind, and now here we were, a team again. Or, really, for the first time. The two of us. Amazing. I'd never not been wary of you. Never not despised you.

Never allowed myself to let down my guard and love you. Like a mother should.

Despite your brutal beginnings.

I did the only thing I could think of.

Braved the basement. Turned off the heating system blazing through the coal room. Fetched the Christmas tree and all of our ornaments.

A family, devoted to the same God, celebrated the birth of His son. We would, too.

Chapter 25

Lucy

Time meant nothing to me anymore. I slept like Mom had slipped me cold medicine, which I wouldn't put past her. Sometimes my mini-comas seemed to last days, but my internal clock was so tangled they might have only been minutes.

When I snuck a peek outside, I guessed we were still in December. The Hanley's farmhouse was edged in colored lights that I could barely make out from so far away, but I remembered their family always being diligent about removing them on time.

The world hadn't yet taken on the pale frigidness that spoke of January days, either. The cold that gripped Iowa and froze the ground solid had not yet arrived. In December, the snow was wetter, the soil more malleable. Once the New Year turned, that quickly went to the wayside. Even with the curtain blocking my view, the yard looked like it was still 1999.

Mom did nothing anymore but surprise me. She helped me dress, propped me up and fed me real meals that she had cooked herself, brought me books from the library.

One morning she let me lean against her while we worked our way downstairs. My body was filling out, but my equilibrium protested every step I took. In my care to walk without falling, I didn't even notice how Mom had rearranged the furniture to accommodate our Christmas tree.

My mind snapped the second I saw the boxes of decorations. This meant we had passed through November, for Mom never allowed us to set the tree before the Thanksgiving weekend had been and gone.

So it definitely was December.

What a relief to know. My captivity, which seemed to have lasted decades, was relatively short-lived. At school we would be nearing the end of the semester. Marching band would have wrapped up, the choir would be rehearsing for the seasonal show. Our youth group at church would be singing at nursing homes and gearing up to adopt a couple of needy families for the holiday.

Last year we had outfitted three children with coats, boots, gloves, and toys. Just twelve months ago.

"What day is it?"

"Well, that's a strange question," Mom answered, pulling the angel tree-topper out of a box and putting it on the coffee table. "Why would anyone want to know that?"

I had forgotten her illness. In my weakened state, I had given her back her rationality when it wasn't yet deserved.

"You're right. It doesn't matter. I was just worried about making you a present and wondered how much time I had."

Which was, strangely, the right answer. Mom pressed her forehead against my own, a move she'd often made with Brandy. She held my hands. Swayed back and forth just a tad.

"Lucy, honey, you don't need to get me anything. The whole basement-door thing? You could never top it. How lucky I am that God found you worth saving."

We stood together until I was about to collapse. I dared not move, no matter how uncomfortable I was.

Mom took over the ritual of the tree. Did her annual chores while I slowly hung ornaments, wheezing when I got tired, sitting when I had to rest.

She floored me when she took out an old CD, found the player that had been locked away for several years, and put on music while we worked. I tried to sing but couldn't hang ornaments and breathe at the same time. Still, I appreciated Mom's voice as she belted out my favorite carols.

At one point, even Tippy joined us in song, her howl both mighty and small.

"This year there really is magic to the season!" Mom proclaimed as she placed tinsel at the end of each branch. "Doesn't it all seem so much brighter to you?"

It did. For the first time I felt welcome in my own home. The walls seemed to shine.

* * *

"Your grandmother was a ball of fire." Mom put down her book and smiled.

"Your mom or Dad's?" I asked. In my fourteen years, Mom had rarely discussed our dead relatives except when she told Brandy stories, conversations they shared privately.

"Mine. I never met his parents. They passed when he was a child."

"What was she like?"

"Hilarious. She loved to sit around the kitchen table and play cards. Someone was always over, the neighbors or friends from church, and had a game going while they talked. I miss that. A house full of people. That...friendliness."

I wonder what has happened to my mother. To make her so standoffish, so alone in life that she was envious of such casual relationships.

I certainly knew why I was.

"Sounds fun. Did she work?"

I was weaving pot holders. Mom had located my old plastic loom when she took the empty tree box back down to the basement, a trip I was thankfully too weak to maneuver. Amazingly, an entire bag of remnants was stored with it. I figured this gave me hours of activity, if I went slowly. Which I was bound to do.

"Not for years. When I graduated from high school, she got a job typing for a local attorney. Mom loved the gossip, and since she couldn't really tell anyone about all the tidbits that passed her way, every time I saw her I became her secret confidante and learned all the details about everyone in town."

I tried to picture Mom as this person. Young, loving, listening intently to her own mother's every word.

"She knew how to handle everything. When my dad died, she was sad for a moment, but then we went to the funeral home and she organized everything, wrote the obituary, stood by his casket and greeted everyone at the showing, went to the bank and dealt with all of the papers, the insurance. Not until days after her work was done did she allow herself to fall apart. And even that was…stoic. She told me to go to my friend Marjorie's house and stay there for a while. A couple of days later Mrs. Newcastle told me that Mom had called me home. When I returned, the place was spotless. She was wearing an apron and her cleaning gloves. Had a huge smile on her face, red lipstick on. I was just amazed, because all of this time I had been waiting for us to cry together. To sit on the couch with our photo albums and talk about Dad. But Mom wasn't like that."

"I'm sorry." I didn't know what to say. It felt like Mom was reaching out to me, and I had no idea what she wanted. I didn't want to take a false step. Or trip over my own feet and do a face-plant in front of her.

"But she was great. Every year that I was in school she would get lonely. Sometimes she'd jump in bed with me in the morning, declare that I was incurably ill, call the office at school and tell them I had a fever, and we'd spend the day baking cookies or playing board games."

"Sounds like fun!"

"It was. She was a wonderful mother. I really miss her."

"How did she die?"

The question fell between us like a bomb.

"Just who the fuck do you think you are?" Mom spat. Her eyes narrowed and her mouth twisted, her face instantly molding into the Mom with whom I was most familiar.

"I…." My stammering was instantaneous. "I…I…I'm…."

"Get away from me! Go upstairs!"

I tried to stand up, but it took too long. She yanked my elbow and threw me off balance, sending me straight to the floor.

"Mom!" I yelled, hoping she'd snap out of it. Jump back into the skin of the mother who had so recently forgiven me.

"Don't you *Mom* me!"

Her shoe hit my hip. A minor pain compared to the fists that pounded my face while she bent over me.

"How dare you! You know how she died! You were there, watching! Weren't you?"

* * *

Strangely, this time my comfort came from the chickens.

They came to me when I had finally made it into bed. Fluttered onto the comforter. Surrounded me, the headless ones, their concern so tender that I almost forgot the blistering aches that accompanied my every move.

I petted them, just as I would Tippy. But I longed to cling to them as I would have my sister. These birds that I had never really met before, but merely passed in the hall. These eyeless, faceless creatures that seemed as forlorn as I.

Eventually one hen let me cradle her.

We swayed, back and forth on the bed, her neck touching just under my chin. I was thankful for the feathers that covered her neck, where her head would have connected. I didn't want to gaze down at an open wound. Or even be reminded of the horror that took off her head.

The room pulsed with Brandy. I gasped her name and watched birds rush to comfort me, their fluffs and struts and constant chattering surrounding me, musical, almost as though they were singing to calm me down. I longed to cling to them as I would to Brandy. I took a breath. I could smell my sister. Fill my lungs with her.

Yet every time I opened my eyes I was greeted by quizzical heads, bent sideways as if wondering about my mental state. Bits of feathers flying. The headless one, still nestled in the crook of my arm, lending me all the warmth in her heart.

I named her Sissy. Held her and longed for the post-beating attention that my sister always gave me. Her attempts at minor first aid. A handful of Band-Aids, the ice pack, my hair brushed and braided. Testing my bones to see if they were broken, in her authoritative pretend-doctor way, asking, "Can you move it? Can you bend it? Does it hurt if I do this?"

Spilling a rush of sweet words to help me get past Mom's emotional betrayal.

Funny that I had never had to reciprocate. Brandy had taken a few swats, even a couple of memorable punishments, but never to the extent that I did. Mom hadn't beat her with the belt. An extension cord. Brutal words that flew around the room, ready to peck out my eyes and coat the walls with laughter while I bled on the floor.

Sissy rustled in my arms.

I lapsed into good thoughts. If I had learned anything in church, it was to cling to the white lights that spotted my life and thank God for these moments.

Finding Tippy. How lucky was I to have her?

Winning the spelling bee in seventh grade. Not just on a local level, but I had taken crown of the entire county. Mom and Brandy had driven me to Des Moines for the state competition, where I placed sixteenth. Not the best, but not bad, either. No one from our school had ever gotten so far before. The newspaper even printed an article about me.

Mr. Mitchell, the choir teacher, had often told me I had the best voice he'd heard in years. A songbird. A soprano with a maturity he found stunning. Last Christmas he'd let me sing "Ave Maria" at the school performance, and I'd gotten a standing ovation. From everyone except Mom, of course. My sweeping eyes couldn't even locate her in the audience.

Good times to balance out the bad.

Mom's quick turn to craziness. A chicken in my arms.

No school, no friends, no freedom. God personally coming to my aid in the basement.

My body, so weak now I didn't stand a chance at survival if Mom closed her eyes to me again. My dog curled up against my hip, oblivious to the fowl surrounding us.

Later I would wake to a room full of them. They kept time like living, ticking clocks, constantly making light chirping noises, punctuating each moment with just a bit of sound. They nested on my furniture, had taken residence in the corners. My bed was dotted with them.

But when I rose in the morning, they were all gone. Sissy, her friends, any trace of feathers.

Chapter 26

Evelyn

The episode with Josephina ignited a decade of delight for me.

She might have been the first, but she will also forever remain the best. Her beauty, for years, went unrivaled. The utter thrill of tasting her, controlling her, reaching my claws in to rip out her spine, was never surpassed in all of my travels.

I don't even have to close my eyes to remember the night she became mine. The memories color my every thought, even as I walk strange streets or conduct business with men who look at me as if I would honor the lurid details of their bedroom fantasies.

How would they feel, knowing that my ideas so easily put theirs to shame?

I stopped Josephina on the street that night as she worked her way home from her job cooking for a wealthy family on the outskirts of her village. Pretended ignorance. Feigned difficulty with the language and layout of the few streets in town. Acted helpless, a lesson I had learned well from watching my sister grow up.

Josephina's smile lit up the night. She understood my confusion, altered her route to escort me down the murky streets to my rooming house.

That's when I felt him. The Devil, creeping up my thighs as I watched her walk. Her hips, graceful, perfectly formed, the tip of her braid bouncing as she turned to make sure I was following, all a lure baiting me to consume her.

She reached out her hand, thinking I was shy. Grabbing me in camaraderie, hurrying me a bit in the late hour, protecting me from the unknown. Perhaps she had caught a sulfurous whiff of him, too.

What a poor move on her behalf. I hadn't found her with a plan. I hadn't schemed or devised any exact method of extracting her soul. But when her fingers clutched my own, they sent shockwaves of electricity through my whole body.

And it reacted.

I had met her in the dark, yes. Acted befuddled, yes. Josephina had stirred my insides, had tempted me, yes.

But I did not know my own capabilities.

She touched my hand, put her skin against mine, and we were at once the same. Flesh. Combined.

I dug my nails into her arm, hooks she couldn't escape. Pulled her into me so rapidly her breath was lost. Joined our lips and swallowed her meager screams before they became a public warning.

And I never let go.

He helped me, that devil. While I had always detested the look and feel of a man's skin, when he jumped into my own, I was thankful for the power that accompanied it.

But Josephina certainly wasn't.

I chewed on her tongue. In our position I could track the horror in her eyes, the terror as it shut her fragile body down. This excited me in ways no man could. My thighs pounded with glee, the throbbing livened each cell of my body.

My nails turned into talons. In one fast movement I shredded her dress, leaving her slip half attached, her left breast vulnerable to attack. For some reason I liked it better as it dripped with her fear, her blood. Which got me so inflamed I ran my left claw down her belly, opening her abdomen, the shriek of pain my new friend released only sending chills of pleasure down my spine.

Which reminded me of hers.

I bent my sweet Josephina backward, keeping our lips locked in a lover's kiss. Her struggle was flowing out of her with the blood that pooled around our feet, but she still had some vigor left. She tried to flee, to push me away, which was foolish.

I put my right hand at the base of her neck. Trailed my devil's nails down her back, tracing her curves, over her hips and up her side.

One swift movement, and I had her spine in my hand. Talons in, talons out. The strength of fifty men helped me as I yanked, pulling it free of her body.

I swallowed her final breath.

Dropped her bones to the ground.

Licked her sweet blood from my hands.

Felt him leave me, the Devil.

Sneaking down the alley I found a neat pile of men's clothing, folded, lain out like a housewife had put them on a dresser, pants on the bottom and underwear on top.

I transformed. Used water set out for someone's dogs to clean my hands and face. Donned my new outfit. Put my dress in my satchel. Walked back to the rooming house, where I thrust it in the fire and watched the fabric burn before I fell into bed.

The next morning I found the train again and headed to Belgium, tracking the story of yet another bit of my lineage that had fallen into cahoots with him, the Devil.

Soon I would start a second journal. A first person account of a woman from my family grown to adulthood, cognizant of the curse. And living it with merriment.

Chapter 27

Lucy

Tippy attacked the closet door, her growl gutting my sleep.

Despite our weak condition, she threw her body against the wood with frenetic energy. I slithered across the bed, put it between me and the closet, pressed my back against the wall. My survival instincts had faded to a pale yellow. I realized way too late that the door was still unlocked and that I could have bolted as soon as Tippy indicated danger.

We were both gasping with fear as the handle began to jiggle. Tippy doubled her efforts, tackling the door, pawing at it when that didn't work, her bark so threatening that I expected Mom to scream up the stairway at any moment, telling us to quiet down, or at least ask what was going on.

But of course she didn't.

She didn't care about our safety. If we had a burglar hiding in my bedroom, Mom would give him a gun and tell him to have at it. To save her the trouble. Get us to that finish line once and for all.

The door finally burst open, the foul air I could never clean immediately filling the room and reminding me of the horrible days when I was so ill. Shame overwhelmed me, but I was so intent upon the creature causing such turmoil in my room that I kept it at bay.

I screamed when He fell into the room. Let my lungs open wide until I realized who He was, and even then it took me a while to quiet down.

Tippy, however, would not stop. She went after His knees, nipping and clawing with a ferocity I had never seen.

When God leaned over and pulled her into His arms, her quiet was sharp and instantaneous. For a second I thought she had died of shock or joy or just plain weariness. But when our eyes caught, Tippy practically collapsed, paralyzed by fear, silently begging me to come fetch her and keep her safe.

Which I did.

"Sorry about that," I apologized. "Tippy is very protective of me." I put my hands out and almost had to wrestle her from God's arms when He didn't relinquish her.

"Boy, she's feisty. The wrong person might really hurt her if she does something like that again."

"She'll be good. I promise."

I found myself back in familiar territory, sitting on my bed, on the edges of my room so no one would see me in the window.

Did I need to tell Him about the house rules? Did He know how much trouble I'd get in if Mom or one of the neighbors saw movement in my room?

I decided not to tell Him. I put Tippy in my lap and slowly stroked her back, stopping only to rub her ears. Her quivering unnerved me.

"I thought I'd come check up on you."

God raised His eyebrows at me, and my stomach flip flopped as I remembered my dream, and the dirty things we had done together. I blushed and looked at my feet, willing Him to forget about my lustfulness, if He even knew.

"I'm doing better. Thanks again for helping me."

Without moving He crossed the room and was right in front of me. He lifted my chin, forced me to meet His gaze.

"You don't look so good, Lucy. Your color is better and you're walking a straighter line, but she's still not being nice to you, is she?"

I appreciated His concern. My thoughts jumped straight to my sister and how she could have sent someone to check up on me, could have easily told someone our story, gotten our family help. Instead, God was taking pity on me.

Or maybe He was just a figment of my imagination. Maybe this whole scenario was just a black hole that had opened up in my mind. Maybe my mother loved me like no other, and the horror of the last few months was just a plot thought up by an alternate personality, maybe she and Brandy visited me daily in my hospital room and my sanity was so far gone that I never noticed they were there.

Maybe.

"It's been a lot better, really. The door is open. Well, this door, anyway. Tippy gets to go outside and that's enough for me. I'm just getting the whole walking thing down again, my legs are all funny." I shrugged my shoulders, felt shamed again because I was acting way too familiar with my Lord.

Why did He have so much interest in me? He couldn't be real, could He? Would God have really chosen me as His pet project?

"You can't lie to me, Lucy. I know *everything* about you." His smile took on a sinister feel as He emphasized the word *everything*. I noticed that He had bad teeth, thin and yellowed and sharp.

The air in the room changed. An electrical charge entered my personal space, pulled at the ends of my hair like I was suddenly surrounded by an aura of static cling. Creeps crawled up my back, settled into my scalp. My skin felt like it was betraying me.

I started to hyperventilate when He dropped His eyes to my chest and slowly pulled them back up again. Grinned that old-man, razor-toothed smile. His face changed shape subtly, reminding me of a wolf for a split second, then morphed back to His regular look.

Tippy whined—a sad, sorrowful moan that in any other circumstance would indicate she was in grave pain. I clung to her, hoping my heart beat would keep her calm.

"What's wrong with you two? Have you been away from other people so long that I frighten you?"

I pulled my dog in even tighter and looked at the comforter.

"I guess it's humbling for us to be in Your presence." I was at a complete loss for words.

"How sweet. But I think we're way past that, aren't we, Lucy?" Like a whisper God had moved onto the bed with me, His words hot against my neck. "Think of all we've done together. Our conversations when you were so weak downstairs. I held you in my arms and carried you through the basement, when you were so lifeless that only my breath kept you alive. And then, well...I don't have to remind you of anything else, do I, Lucy?"

His lips touched my ear. Tippy bolted off my legs and screamed as she hid under the bed, her whimpering dissonant, a metal-upon-metal accompaniment to my new nightmare.

I wanted to join her on the cold floor. Wanted to holler for Mom to come meet God and help me out of my predicament. But He and I both knew she'd never answer.

God wrapped His arms around me, His body pressed against my back. I shivered as He joined his hands in a fist right between my breasts.

"You know I'm in here, don't you?" His forehead tapped my skull. I knew very well that He was in my thoughts. My dreams.

My nightmares.

"And you know I'm in here, too, right?" God uncurled His fingers and pressed two against my heart.

I nodded my head. He wrapped His arms even tighter around me. I wanted to push away but knew how rude it would be. What person in their right mind would ever do that to God?

"Can you guess where I'll be next? Because I think you already know."

Which I did.

Images flipped through my mind, naughty thoughts like the ones in my dream, only worse. God and me in my bed, in Mom's bed, outside, all arms and legs and naked backsides. I felt a mixture of terror and bliss, but I couldn't see His face, only feel it, like teeth sinking into my skin, the fire of infection quickly following it.

"You've always been such a good girl, Lucy," God told me before His tongue slid down my neck.

I became a tree, rigid and unmoving. Thought of the deer, our colors blending together, the wind cooling us both while the sun scorched the land. My fingertips expanded and turned green, my toes burrowed further and further into the soil. My body was round and healthy, reaching forever toward the sky, wanting the sun, yearning for the water that bathed me and kept me strong.

"Tell your mother I said hi. I'll be back for her. She's been waiting for me for a very long time."

I was still outside, arms reaching toward my siblings, my children, our hair alive with the sounds of the forest, the beasts who relied on our bodies for their own home. I could hear His voice but it spun past me, could feel the scrape of His fingernails against my nipples but chose to ignore it.

With a tap against my shoulder, God was gone. He didn't need to escape through the closet, the front door, even out the window. I turned my cheek and the room was encompassed in an odor so foul I thought maybe He'd left some of the dead to keep me company.

I got off the bed, bent to find Tippy hiding underneath it.

She had crapped herself and not even moved. Poop covered her backside, the floor, the underside of my box springs.

We finished a surreal night with baths. I cleaned my good friend before Mom caught sight or smell of her, kissed her head, tried to get Tippy to respond to me again. The shivering that had caught hold of her while God was in our room didn't let go for hours.

Not that I felt much better. I stayed under the hot water and dragged the soap over my skin, humiliated. My body felt dirty, my mind deceived. The worst part was knowing that He could see me, naked again, my skin crawling from His touch, nothing able to take that nasty feeling away.

We slept in Brandy's bed.

* * *

I tried not to let any bad ideas creep into my head. Nothing sinful, but nothing rude, either. God could obviously hear these ideas as clearly as the prayers He vetted every day.

But my thought-diet didn't last for long.

I had never really imagined what being around God would entail. My visions of Him were of a giant Santa Claus with viciously strict rules, who welcomed you with open arms if you survived the gauntlet of wicked choices He threw your way. He would look at a list and know my personal habits, whether naughty or nice, give me a lecture or two on honoring thy mother, maybe a pat on the back if He felt I'd done well on any of the morality tests He'd given me.

Being a good girl, I'd always felt safe. Like God wouldn't bat an eye at letting me into Heaven if I died the next day. That no matter what Mom said, He'd know my true heart.

But somehow God had gotten word that I was a slut. And He was cool with that, even wanted to take advantage of my bad-girl status.

Maybe He was just like all men. I'd heard the girls talk about them, their boyfriends and their sexual expectations, the male teachers who were always trying to get a glimpse of their boobs, men they babysat for and the ways they came onto them during the drive home.

When Mrs. Ray, my Sunday School teacher, explained God she described Him as love. I had always figured this as the love I felt for Tippy—a loyal, heart-filling devotion that could be seen as nothing but goodness, nothing but light.

I had never even considered that God's love was sexual. That 'giving myself to God,' as people had often told me to do, meant losing my virginity to Him.

But the possibilities existed. How many men, religious leaders even, had proclaimed that God told them to have sex with certain women? We had discussed them in school. They were always hot topics whenever one crept into the news. But maybe instead of pariahs, these men were truly living God's word.

Maybe David Koresh had been onto something. Because God, to me, was just as crazy as people made Koresh sound.

Tippy and I couldn't discuss it. How could you bad-mouth God? If He was the ultimate power, how could we even think about His actions as deplorable? And we both knew He would hear us.

I tried to wipe my thought-slate clean.

What I really wanted to do was find Mom in her room, curl up with her in her bed, and have her hold me while I explained my God-fears to her.

She would never understand.

He was in my head, yes. In my heart, for certain.

And Tippy and I both knew where He would be next.

When I started to cry, Sissy jumped off the bed and joined me on the floor. She didn't even try to tell me where she had been, just nudged me and pushed herself under my arm, forced her way into my heart.

Chapter 28

Joan

I woke to a shotgun blast of terror. Threw back the covers, dropped to the floor.

Someone with a heavy footfall stepped into my bedroom.

I contemplated hiding under the mattresses, the only place I could squeeze quickly and quietly. The bedskirt offered some protection, would make him bend over and raise it before he saw me. Just enough of a pause that I could scoot to the other side, make a run for the door.

My mind flashed to Brandy, the nightlight in her room that would expose her sleeping body. Had he already gotten to her?

I couldn't hear him move, but I had to take action. My daughter's life was at stake. I pulled up the fabric, ready to slide under the bed.

But he was already there. Waiting, a smile on his face.

"Alex!" I couldn't help but scream. Only after I alerted my husband did I remember he was dead, not part of my current nightmare.

That the Brandy I invoked was grown now, out of the house.

My legs moved of their own accord.

The man with red hair roared with joy. "Joan? Joanie? Don't you want to play?"

As I reached the bedroom door, he popped in front of me, blocking my exit.

My body started to convulse. For over a decade this man had lain dormant under my skin, a giant snake ready to strike. I always knew he'd be back. Knew I could never escape him.

"It's been a while, hasn't it?"

The beast moved forward and I backed up quickly, whimpering as I walked, already ashamed. Ashamed of my weakness. Of what he had done to me in the past. Of the horror that lingered in the air between us.

My legs brushed against the comforter. I didn't want to be by the bed. The mere thought of it sent another wave of terror through my system. I hedged to the right, toward the window.

Stupidly thinking I might be able to get out.

"Oh, Joanie, you're so funny. Still trying to get away."

He reached his clawed hand out and spun me around. We stood so close to the window that I could almost touch it, except for the new barbed wire coating the woodwork, thwarting any chance of escape.

The razor-wire glistened, the Venus Flytrap of prison yard metal. Beckoned. Yearned for my blood.

I could hear it laughing at my plight, but in my mind I still weighed the options. If I jumped into the window, it wouldn't faze him. He would work the wire like a puppet, let his creation slice me until I was but bone and dangling strips of flesh.

And then he would start in. He would love it; the excruciating pain, the panic as it crescendoed past terror and into the electrifying white light of realization that death would be such a relief, so welcome—if only he would permit it.

Which he wouldn't.

My eyes shut. Tight. I had survived this once before. If I followed his direction, if I didn't fight and just forced myself to relax, I could endure it again.

"You probably could, Joanie, but this time you're not going to get knocked up. I don't have much reason to keep you alive."

His jaw opened around the back of my neck. The pain was immediate and severe. I found myself screaming, the wound secondary to the red hot alarm screeching through my brain, that he had read my thoughts—he had known what I was thinking—I could actually feel his hands inside my head, rummaging around my brain, plucking away at my gray matter, tossing things aside, pushing new things in.

Before he threw me on the bed, he waved his arm as if a ringmaster during a big presentation, and exposed our audience.

Alex, tied to the chair, squirming and fighting his restraints. He was yelling, but no sound passed his lips. I had never seen him so angry. His face was contorted with rage, every vein in his body taut and on the verge of bursting.

My skin ripped as the intruder pulled at my nightgown. I stood in front of my husband, exposed from head to toe, this other man telling him the nasty things he was going to do to me.

But for just a second, everything went still. Motionless. I managed to push out my hand and could almost touch Alex, my husband, the only man I had ever loved. My fingers were within an inch of his leg, the dark hair that covered his entire body.

This time the shotgun blast wasn't terror.

This time it hit my husband straight in the nose, his blood and brain matter spattering all over my face, my hair, even landing in my mouth as I bent forward, screaming, the redhead entering me from behind, hollering like a bunch of drunken frat boys that have successfully completed some campus prank.

"Joanie! Boy, I've missed you!"

Claws raked down my back.

Ripped down my front.

My dead husband watching. Again.

"Mom? Are you okay?"

You pushed open the door, entered my room. My first thought was that I couldn't believe your audacity, as my bedroom is strictly off limits. But at the same time I was so relieved I could barely speak.

"I heard you screaming."

I was back in bed, the blankets tucked under my chin. "I was having a bad dream."

One that never ended. You turned on the light, and all I saw was him, the intruder, the redheaded disaster that destroyed my life and put you in my arms. A daily reminder of the night Alex was taken away. Of what my life could have been.

"Get the fuck away from me! Go! Get out of here!" I hated looking at you. Just the sight of your hair, that horrid color, sent my blood pressure zooming. "I want you to leave!"

But you didn't move.

Had you developed your father's power? Were you going to laugh at me, taunt me, come at me with your claws?

"What's on your wall, Mom?" Your mouth dropped open.

I saw it for the first time. A blood splatter, fresh and seeping down the white paint.

You looked at me, puppy-dog eyes filled with fear, and again at the wall.

Oh, Alex. My God, how I loved you.

I couldn't stop the tears. Figured you would devour them raw from my cheeks, cackling like your father, feasting on the agony that lived just under my skin.

But instead you crawled under the covers with me, put your arms around my shoulders, and kissed the top of my head. As if I were the child.

"I've been having some bad dreams myself lately," you told me.

What an odd thought. Could demons feel fear? How did they suffer?

Then I remembered God. Fetching you just before you started rotting. He had to have seen something worthwhile in you, something that I couldn't.

We clung to each other, our eyes glued to the nastiness on the wall. I didn't dare tell you about it, didn't allow you that power over me, to know that your father had siphoned my soul straight from my body.

Oh, Alex. My heart lurched at the thought of him. I wish his death had been as quick the first time.

"Do you want me to help clean it?" you asked. If it had been Brandy, she would have demanded to know how a dream could have physically damaged the walls. You accepted it without pause.

We got the oil soap and two buckets, lit up the house so nothing could jump out of the corners at us.

"You might want to change nightgowns, Mom. That one has a big rip up the backside. I can see your underwear."

Chapter 29

Lucy

We worked together for hours, side by side, barely speaking.

I never knew beheading chickens could be so bloody. Or why Mom would possibly want to do it inside the house, let alone in her bedroom. The corpses on the floor outside her door were piling up fast, and I had tripped over the newest batch when coming to see if she was okay after her screaming woke me up. Their story was smeared across the wall by her window, had somehow travelled the length of her ceiling, even dotted the area around her dresser.

I hoped we wouldn't be eating them anytime soon. The unsanitary way we stored them unrefrigerated in our hallway didn't seem quite right to me.

But nothing in our house did.

We had to change Mom's sheets, all of her bedding, even get out the steam cleaner to try to remove the stains from the beige carpet.

Was this part of her craziness? No sane person would take up butchering her house chickens, late at night, right beside her own bed. But it wasn't my place to ask questions. I knew I could never sleep after having seen the goo coating her walls, so I didn't mind helping Mom get her room back in order.

Tippy ditched us both, preferring to stay in the kitchen while we washed walls. I felt a strange closeness to Mom that I couldn't explain, except that she seemed oddly vulnerable, in need of my companionship.

"Tell me about God," she requested after I had dumped our dirty cleaner down the kitchen sink and brought the buckets back full of fresh water.

Her shoulders were hunched, and for just a second Mom looked old, withered, wearing a shroud of patheticalness that I had never seen on her before.

I had nothing good to say.

"When I was downstairs He talked about how well He knew you." And Brandy. But I didn't want to mention her name.

"Really? He's heard my prayers?"

"I assume. He said that years ago you spent a lot of time together. Before I was born."

She stood stiff as a board and closed her eyes, hand paused on the wall, the kitchen towel sopped with hot water that practically poured out of the cloth while she lingered, immobile.

"Yes. He helped me through a very difficult time. How wonderful that He remembers me."

My lips stayed sealed. I watched Mom as she regained her composure, worked through whatever caused her to stop cleaning.

"I didn't know chickens had red blood. I mean, I guess I did from cooking and stuff, but not THIS red. In the packages from the store it usually seems somewhat yellowish-red, I think."

"Chicken blood?" Mom asked. She picked some bits of flesh off her nightstand and threw them in her bucket. "What are you talking about?"

We faced each other, confused. I searched her eyes for some signal, whether she was Old or New Mom or Some Different Mom that I hadn't met yet.

"I just thought that this was...." I stammered.

Mom said nothing but looked at me like I was speaking in riddles.

"God came to visit me earlier tonight," I confided, wanting to change the subject, but not really wanting to talk at all anymore.

"Oh, Lucy, that's wonderful. Tell me all about it."

Mom smiled, a fake display of happiness that could not compete with her discomfort. I had the feeling she wanted me to talk just to fill the air with sound other than our rags wiping against the paint. Mom never had interest in my life.

But then again, who wouldn't want to know about my personal relationship with a God that made house calls?

"He actually scared me, at first. And Tippy. Boy, did He frighten her!"

Mom tilted her head, quizzically. For a split second she looked just like one of the birds in my bedroom and I almost broke out into hysterics.

"He came in through the closet while we were sleeping," I explained. "Tippy barked her head off at Him. Of course, she had never met Him before, and it was very confusing for her."

"What did He say to you?"

"Not much. He wanted to make sure I was feeling better."

"That's it?"

I didn't know if Mom doubted me, or if I had been too simplistic and roused her suspicion. But then again, maybe my exhaustion was clouding my mind. I hadn't worked this hard in a long time, could barely stay on my feet anymore.

"Well, we talked about how I need to give myself to Him completely."

"Now, that's what I would expect God to say. How did you respond?"

Could I tell her that Tippy had an explosive reaction to God's conversation or that it was all I could do not to hurl when He touched me?

"Very politely." Did all women have sex with God? If Mom found it absolutely normal that God wanted me to join Him physically, did that make it right? Or since she was batty, did that make the idea absolutely insane?

I couldn't ask her about it. Brandy had never warned me of God's intentions. Tippy wanted to be left alone and pretend that our encounter with Him never occurred.

"Sometimes, He scares me." I let my thoughts grow wild.

"I can certainly understand that. How wonderful is He? How powerful? I would probably cower in His presence."

"He certainly makes me tremble when He's around."

But I couldn't help but wonder, if God had had sex with so many women, how had He only had one son? What was the likelihood that throughout all of time, the billions upon billions of women that He had overseen and convinced to give themselves to Him, and He would only get one of them pregnant?

I blushed. What if that was my role? Was that why He found me worthy of His attention?

We finished her room. I started the washing machine, helped Mom put away the ladder, and checked on my dachshund. My body was ready to collapse.

"Thank you for helping me, Lucy. I know that wasn't an easy chore."

We stood on opposite sides of the hall, neither of us wanting to go back to bed.

"Can I get my glass of water? I forgot it in your room," I asked. Mom hated having me in her personal space, and even though I had just come from her room, I knew better than to walk in without asking.

"Sure."

I hurried to her dresser. Spied God, shirtless, waiting under the blankets for Mom to come back. He patted the empty side of her bed and smiled at me.

"You'll sleep better now, Mom."

"I will?"

"God's in there, waiting for you. He'll watch over you tonight. He must have known you were having a hard time."

She bent forward and kissed my forehead, but never batted an eye when Tippy and I headed to Brandy's room so we could go back to sleep.

* * *

In the morning, after she had returned from the store, Mom made me join her in the kitchen.

"Get on the chair!"

Our camaraderie from the night before was long forgotten.

"Take off your shirt."

Tippy and I exchanged worried glances. I didn't spy any sage on the counter. Or cream.

"Now, Lucy."

My eyes moved toward the door, but unfortunately Mom caught me looking.

"I said *now!*" As her hand caught my cheek, I thought of the chickens outside her bedroom. They were gone when I got up this morning, the pile of bodies removed without so much as a trace.

My stomach fell when I thought about her butchery. Could she have been slaughtering them for their blood, not their bodies? Was she going to purify me that way now?

My shirt landed on the floor. I had figured it out. Knew what she was going to do to me. What else would you use chicken blood for but some kind of ritual? And what better to symbolize your fertility than blood?

She was going to coat me in all that gore to prepare me for my pairing with God!

Did that mean He would come after me today?

Dread filled my heart. I didn't want to do it. But how could I defy Him, when everyone I had ever met worshipped God as truth and love?

"I'm sick and tired of looking at that mop of yours." Mom surprised me.

I looked up, saw the small box in her hand.

"From now on you're going to have chestnut hair, like your sister."

She put on the plastic gloves and starting oozing dye into my scalp. With her rolled-up sleeves so close to my head, I could see the scratch marks the chickens had left all over her forearms. They must have put up quite a struggle. Mom's skin was a scabby mess.

If she had been the same woman I'd worked with last night, I would have asked her if she wanted me to clean the wounds for her. As it was, I kept my mouth shut and decided to let her worry about them.

While we waited for the color to set Mom retreated to her room and I stayed in the kitchen. The timer ticked away as I silently inspected the refrigerator. No big containers of blood filled the shelves. No chicken meat, no gizzards, no indication of what Mom had done with the bodies from last night.

From across the room I tried to inspect the yard. Daylight flooded the kitchen and I had a fantastic view of the back, the fenced in area that Tippy used, even the shed.

I figured that's where she'd put them. Knowing that I couldn't go outside and that, even if I could, the metal building was the last place I'd ever visit. What a perfect place to hide them.

I could see them there. Close my eyes and envision the metal bar on the back wall, the one she'd tied me to when she locked me in. The hens were hanging there. Legs tied together and strung up to drain the blood from their headless necks. In the grasp of winter, they'd probably be just as cold as if Mom had put them in our freezer.

I got goose bumps just thinking about eating them. Would she make me pluck the feathers? I wouldn't even have the slightest idea how to go about it.

Something jumped from behind the shed, and I had to cover my mouth to keep from screaming.

A deer, sneaking forward to let me see her.

I waved, sent her my best thoughts. Let her know I was feeling much better. That I was walking pretty normally again. Thanked her for her loyalty.

We stared at each other until Mom came back to finish my dye job. As soon as she entered the kitchen, the deer slipped out of sight, almost magically, her movements so swift and silent that even Tippy didn't react to her disappearance.

Mom pulled me toward the sink and rinsed the color from my hair.

"Much better!" she declared after I'd dried off and modeled my look for her.

I became a brand new person. If Brandy were still around, we'd finally look like sisters. I couldn't help but stare in the mirror, excited over my new locks. Hoping that maybe, just maybe, He wouldn't recognize me when He came.

* * *

Tippy and I developed OCD.

Our routine, which we executed at least twenty times a day, started with a quick inspection of the hallway in the mornings.

We rolled out of bed, checked the hall for any sign of chickens, feathers, even poop—which we had never seen. Tippy could go on for hours about how everybody poops, even my 'imaginary' chickens, as she called them, since she had never really seen them. But these chickens never did.

"Sometimes I get a funny feeling and think I see something out of the corner of my eye, but at least I'm not crazy like you are!" She chastised me when I asked her about the fowl Mom kept upstairs. "I don't have them crawling all over me on the bed at night!"

I started to pay more attention to Mom's drawings. When I had first noticed them, I was so furious with her for keeping me locked away and not letting me eat that I didn't do much more than glance at the walls when I walked past. With the stacks of corpses in the hall, I was often so concerned about stepping on them that I watched my feet more than the charcoal renderings.

But the more stir-crazy I became, the more attention I paid to all the little details.

For instance, the sideways chickens. Poised to strut up the wall. What was their purpose?

Tippy and I could sit at the end of the hall, backs to the linen closet, and watch them move. Up the side of the door to Mom's room, over the top, down again. A parade that never progressed. Were they protecting her? Keeping an eye out for strangers who might enter her room? Waiting for me?

I named each one of them. Plucky, Picky, Pokey, Petals. Tippy played my game, if only to pass time, and selected E names for the ones on the west wall closest to Brandy's room. Esther, Eliza, Eggy, Elaine. They pecked for food but did little else.

The headless gals were hardest to pinpoint, as Tippy and I didn't know a lot of decapitated folks to name them after. But given time we came up with a list, and called them Anne, Margaret, Catherine, Ms. Antoinette, Lady Jane, and Beatrice.

We ignored the humans for days but eventually determined that if we were going to give the hens their own monikers, we'd better name the people, too. But we never said these out loud. I got the willies thinking about them chasing me with their bloody axes and didn't want to rouse their attention with direct conversation. I even avoided eye contact. Which wasn't hard, considering they didn't have faces themselves.

Funny how headless sorts can see just fine when they need to. Like Sissy, finding my bed at night, or always sensing when I needed a hug.

"Holly, Barbie, Cathy, Betsy," I yelled out the names of some of my favorite dolls, many of which were slumbering in our attic, finally noticing that most of the hens with heads were grouped together in fours.

"But I swear that last week there were six of them on this wall," I pointed out to Tippy.

So we began to watch.

We got up in the mornings, did our bathroom chores, ate breakfast, performed any odd duty Mom assigned, then made our way into the hall.

I could read while we waited, but many days I found it too difficult to focus on the words. Instead I just sat on the hardwood floor, my dog in my lap, and waited for their world to come alive.

Hens over Mom's door. The people by mine, stock still, never moving. But as the days unfolded, watching Mom's artwork became as thrilling as a soap opera, the greatest entertainment Tippy and I had had in months.

Of course, I had to narrate it all to my dog. She had no desire to see the chickens, but once the story got rolling, she loved to listen to me talk.

The birds with beaks hated the headless bunch and would often chase them, forcing them into the less detailed land by the bathroom door. Lady Jane and Ms. Antoinette were inseparable and stood up to the other gals, but Eliza could run them off just by fluffing her feathers.

They had cliques and their own status within those cliques, just like the girls at school. Plucky played with Holly, but the others didn't want her on their turf and would peck at her for coming near. Cathy chastised Holly every time she brought Plucky over, her wings spread and eyes blazing with fury.

The groups snuck around, stealing food. A few of them even laid eggs and tried desperately to hide them from the others, often beside the banister or in the corner by my room.

Mom preferred that we made no noise, and we moved around upstairs as quietly as falling leaves, watching our girls, checking on all the indicators that told us of the outside world.

Every night we checked the Hanley house for Christmas lights. About fifty times. Knowing December hadn't passed kept Tippy sated. She loved getting gifts and felt elated at the whole idea of Mom faking Santa Claus for us this year, having a special day where we all got along and had endless piles of food and cookies to comfort us.

We monitored our water bottles. Collected odds-and-ends, snacks that we could hide away. Listened to Mom's movements, her routines, the times she slid out of them, ruffling our feathers, as Tippy and I never knew what she kept up her sleeve.

I followed the moon, but Tippy claimed she could feel her pull in her every bone and didn't need to witness her path through the sky. Sometimes I quizzed her on whether our friend was waning or waxing, but my dog would have none of that.

"That is so trivial. Why would you even ask?" Tippy often crawled up on her high horse, and sometimes it took days for her to come down.

I couldn't fall asleep if my toothbrush was facing toward the toilet and got up about fifteen times to check it. Always moving around silently, on tippy toes, trying not to wake Mother.

Or put the farmyard on high alert. I couldn't imagine the beating I would take if the chickens noted my presence and roused Mom with their vigilante clucking act.

Tippy refused to let our door be closed. I didn't really blame her, but she pushed at it a hundred times a day, ensuring she had a path just the size of her body to squeeze through, that the latch never had the opportunity to find purchase, to lock us back in.

After meals I checked the refrigerator, just to make sure it was well stocked and that Mom hadn't pulled any of our feathered friends out of the shed yet. I was getting too attached to our chickens to start gorging on them.

Not that I would ever turn my head at a good meal. Neither of us would do that. I just wanted to make sure she wasn't feeding me my own friends. Random chickens from someone else's house, yes. *My* chickens, no.

Although I knew that someday it would come to that.

Better the chickens than Tippy.

If she ever tried to hurt my dog, I'd have to kill her.

Chapter 30

Evelyn

After warming my gullet with a hearty drink, I often found myself in whatever boarding room I'd taken, sitting in front of the mirror, analyzing myself. My totally unencumbered and rather bizarre life. How I'd spent my best years chasing a story that climaxed with my own transformation into the star of the ancient plot.

I couldn't have cared less anymore about the long-lost idiot relative of mine who had somehow found her way to Japan, infected the world with her children, then suffered her own death at the hands of her middle daughter, the one destined to kill three of her neighbors while they slept at night. Or that wench in Maine who worked in an infirmary and sealed the fate of twenty-six patients, all dying of some lung ailment that would have taken them eventually, anyway.

The only reason I kept researching was the cloak travel offered. Who would suspect a woman brave enough to voyage the world—alone even, a scholar whose purse knew no dearth? Who would look at my handsome face and make any comparison to the monsters that inhabited my extended bloodline?

What freedom came with my lack of address. My ability to jump onto a train, a boat, or simply toot my horn and pull back onto the road that lead further into the countryside, through the wilderness, to the edge of the world where the days were skirted by nothing but ice and the darkness of the forever sea?

The familiar black eternity that hardened into the volcanic stone I called my heart.

No, even if I were caught blood-covered with my talons out, people would not point fingers. They were the same in every city I dropped my dimes, filthy with their hands held out in expectation, a mob rendered silent by their stupidity and stunned by the fact that I carried my own books. I at once hated the humans that shared my earth and envied their pain, the sultriness of their tears, that I could take them to an entirely different plane with the use of my straight razor, a lick of fire, or by simply draining all of the fluid from their eyes.

Which I was wont to do.

I devoured a child in Hong Kong, five hours after I had slaughtered her in my bathtub.

Plied the fingernails out of an old man's hands while he wept his apologies for touching me earlier in the bar. No one ever discovered his remains.

In east Texas I purchased a young woman and kept her with me for three weeks but tired of her whining and left her scalp on a fence post when I drove out of town.

The other women in my family were pathetic. Weaklings. Amateurs. The only ones I held the slightest respect for were those who had felt him like I had. The ones consumed by the devil. Those that had risen to the occasion and experienced the lust brought on by a fresh kill.

He and I had grown quite close. I could feel him grow inside me, take over my skin, empower me to collect souls without any weapon other than my own hands, and turn to him for conversation while I did so. That he could reside within me and stare at me from his own body at the same time struck me as incredibly profound, so overwhelming it left me breathless, almost ashamed of my human vulnerabilities, my inability to perform such amazing feats without his assistance.

Like my father, this entity joined me late at night. I had sworn off men after my discovery of female flesh, but he was like no other. I would wake to his hands, heavy on my thighs, fall victim to the lure of his teeth, his heat, the shared experience of having just peeled the skin off the innkeeper's wife's face.

What intoxication. How I craved him, his passion, the way my entire body ached when he had finished with me.

I watched myself in mirrors. When I stood before one, the first few minutes I was still Evelyn, the tall, drab stranger who walked like a man, braid curled around my head, collar tight around my neck.

Then the change began. My dress diminished, exposing my curves, the bite marks covering my skin, the bruises my lover had left in the darkest of places. My hair fell to my hips, as thick as in my youth, back when my father wrapped it around his hand like rope after we had ridden the back acreage of our farm.

Thoughts of Dad led straight to my present-day partner, his hands tearing at my body, his thrusts so powerful that I never knew if I would survive his lust or if I would bleed to death after he had shredded me with his need.

The mirror told all. I could see myself, the degradation my devil imposed on me, and I loved myself, that wickedness, that power, the horror I welcomed with open arms. My eyes reflected back a woman with her own dark spot, the birthmark, the indicator that I was one of his chosen few. A woman cursed.

A woman in love.

My mother was the first to notice. On my yearly trip home, after the trivial hellos and hugs from the group that had gathered, she came to my room just after midnight.

"Who is he?" She crossed her arms, already judgmental.

"He who?" I played coy, but quite frankly she had caught me off guard.

"The man you're seeing. I can tell by the way you walk it's a bit more than just *sight* now, isn't it, Evie?"

I cringed at the name. I was so far removed from that child that I almost threw the bedside lamp at Mother.

"I would say that that is none of your business." I turned away, furious. How dare she?

"You can say that all you want, but I am your mother. And you've never exactly been...well, wise with your decisions. As they regard the men in your life."

We had a stare-down. I understood her implications and was astonished that she knew how my relationship with the husband she all but ignored had flourished during my childhood.

"Shut the door on your way out," I ordered, knowing I would not stay long at home.

Nor would I return for Mother's funeral, six weeks later, when she passed after being struck by lightning during a freak late-February storm.

My lover and I were too busy for me to take a holiday back to the old farmhouse. We were exploring. Thinking of different ways to feed our hungers, physical and sexual. Together we travelled the jungle, wearing thick fur and vicious fangs, making late night visits to the natives that hunted there. We swam out of the ocean and onto passenger ships, found ourselves savaging the vile street vendors of Russia, entering farm houses in the remote lands of Montana and feasting on entire families in one night.

He pushed my every boundary. Just when I was about to collapse from his touch, three of his friends would appear and ravage me for days on end. While my lover commanded my every move, held me down when needed, took my very own belt and welted my skin with it.

I couldn't bear his absence. What was I, alone, but just another wretched female, another copy of my sister, waiting for him to arrive, willing to do anything to make him return faster, to stay by my side, to never leave again? How I hated myself. For being weak.

For being a woman.

But those moments of loneliness, of utter raving desperation, were when I started my own book. If I couldn't be beside him, then I could relive our adventures on page, document our destruction, let the world know that this woman they called frumpy could satisfy the ultimate male hunger.

I sat. In front of mirrors. Wearing my scholar's skin. Divulging my greatest secrets. Waiting for him to return to me. Writing. Realizing.

I was the oldest specimen of the family curse. The last one living, my eye-inside-an-eye visible only to myself, and here we were, not too far from the next millennium. My atrocities far exceeded any committed by the family members before me. The devil himself had taken a personal interest in the development of my more salacious interests.

No crystal ball was needed here.

I was the woman poised to take over his role.

Chapter 31

Lucy

I dreamed of water.

Floating, drifting, swaying with the waves. A gentle dance. The moon spotlighting my journey, dragging me deeper into the boundless ocean, to a spot where no human would ever find me.

Black air encased me. How bizarre to be alone, with no lights, no other people, no indication of where wind met water.

Lips met my legs. Tiny mouths, nibbling along my skin, tasting me. I thought of seaweed, reaching up to grab my feet. The beasts that waited and watched, wondering if I was a meal or someone they should fear.

I had no raft, no life-preserver, no clothes.

Just the legend of the night sky, telling my story.

My skin savored the salty water. The slight trickle rolling over my shoulders. The occasional splash against my cheeks, when I closed my eyes and luxuriated in the rhythmic bobbing of being adrift.

The stars set their stage, the sky exploding with applause as they came alive to play out their drama.

Other creatures, I'm certain, found the dialogue indecipherable.

But for me it was written. For me it made perfect sense.

One star in the sky and from there came many.

Crashing, burning, some even settling. Years wrapped in decades covered with centuries, all bound together by a millennia made of mountains. Drop outs, bullies, even excavators. Cleaning, pushing, covering up.

The boiling beauty of one giant hot spot.

Screaming at me from above like a giant eye.

The Moon. Pulling me with nothing but her love, her honor, the music that flowed from her like a waterfall.

In the sky, all was clear. I had no doubts. The truth cemented itself in my heart, but in the hush that followed I heard all the animals gasping.

The Moon. Singing to me on the endless sea. Calling, dragging, whispering of what wonderment I will bring.

The Moon. Standing in the sky, a warrior queen, a mystic, her hair long and black, reaching all the way to the water.

I gripped her tresses and hauled myself out of the ocean.

She wanted me, after all. The Moon.

My mother.

I would come to her.

* * *

"How are the ladies at the bank?" I asked Mom while we shared lunch at the kitchen table.

"Obviously, Lucy, I haven't seen them in a while."

I knew that, but I had only questioned her because I was curious about her employment. The longer she allowed me to eat properly and live confined to the entire house, the more I settled back into my skin. I worried that if Mom didn't work, we wouldn't be able to pay our bills. The food supply would shrivel.

But then again, if the bank seized our house, maybe someone would find me.

Release me.

The tragedy of Mom's life broke my heart. How horrible to lose your grasp on sanity. To be the one in charge, with children relying on you, while you fell apart and couldn't comprehend the world you created while you crumbled.

"Why would you even ask?"

"I was just making conversation."

"Well, don't bother. When I want you to know things, I'll tell you about them. Eat your soup and go back upstairs."

So I did.

Upstairs was quickly becoming my favorite place to be. Away from Mom, with the bathroom and its constant flow of accessible water. I started to think of it as my own personal Disneyworld.

* * *

"Who does she think she's kidding?" God asked.

He had appeared from behind my bedroom curtain, strutted forward like it wouldn't matter if the Hanleys saw movement from my bedroom.

"Please don't stand by the window. I'll get in a lot of trouble if Mom finds out!"

I reddened when I realized that I had just chastised God. What kind of heathen had I become?

"Lucy, why would I ever care about that? What bothers me right now is that she tried to disguise you."

I didn't follow.

"I hated it when she cut off your pretty hair, but it had gotten disgusting down in the basement. I forgave Joan for that. Most mothers would have done the same."

He put His hand against my head.

I remembered my colored hair. Felt shamed because God and I had the same natural color, and Mom hated it.

"I need to fix things. Now, this might hurt a bit but it will end fairly quickly. Hang on to me if you need to, Lucy."

God ran His fingers through my short hair, then stood massaging my scalp. I was starting to wonder what He was up to when He began to pull.

Pain didn't describe it.

Pain was just a small word, very rudimentary, ineffectual.

God yanked. Stretched. Pulled my hair out of my scalp.

The effect was white hot. A branding iron to my brain. Like the sun had come directly into my room and scorched out my eyeballs.

I felt my jaw drop but could not scream. As He continued, moving from bangs to the back of my head, I was completely blinded and reached out to Him for strength.

My hands landed on God's hips.

"Women are always clinging to me when they're in pain. They'll do anything to get it to stop."

I dropped my hands.

His work ended quickly.

"Much better!" God declared, tossing my long hair behind my shoulders.

I pulled a few pieces back in front of my face. Even though He had finished, my head continued to throb. Even my vision wobbled.

But I could tell the color was gone. Either my blood pressure had crowded out my vision and everything was showing up red, or God had changed me back to my natural shade.

"What will I ever tell Mother?" I wondered out loud.

But my words fell on empty air. God was already gone.

Chapter 32

Joan

Nine more days.

You acted oblivious, but I could see through your game. How much longer until Christmas, Mom? What day of the week is it? Did you go to church today? Why else would you ask me these questions?

Nine more days. So we were both counting. I just wasn't throwing it in your face.

Would it happen immediately? When midnight struck on the year 2000, would you grow horns and wreak devastation over all of His creation?

I kept the ax under the bed. Tried to channel Aunt Evelyn and gather the strength to use it. If I allowed you to meet the deadline, what then? Could I still bring the weapon down and end this nightmare?

My world became a small wooden box that you nailed shut. I didn't care about going to the grocery store, paying bills, attending any of the holiday parties going on in town. All I wanted was for this to end. Our existence together. The curse that had been put on my shoulders all those years before.

Evelyn was right. My weakness was transparent. I could barely even get out of bed anymore, other than to use the bathroom or let the dog out to piddle. This battle should have been fought and won years ago.

If he had survived your conception, Alex would have been on your side. But he hadn't known the powerhouse I called Mother. Not the woman who lived behind the sweet smile and sunny disposition, but the tiger crouching in her bright eyes.

She would have saved the day. Mother always protected me; she would have taken this situation out of my hands and carved it into her own treasure. You wouldn't have lived through your first three months. Not with that red hair and the way you were brought to this earth.

And now, here we are, with nine days left.

Could you feel a change in the air? Did you know what would happen? Had he told you, your true father, how the world would change when you took over?

Evelyn had warned me. And still, I had done nothing. But what if you changed things? What if you replaced your father, and your devil skin wasn't so atrocious? People thought you were an angel. But then again, so was your father, once. Before he tired of serving in Heaven.

"Actually, Joanie, dear, that's just a story people like to tell."

Just a simple thought of him, and he slammed back into my life to haunt me.

"I never served anyone. They served me."

He was upon me like a hoard of starving rats. Teeth shredded my every cell. Struggling only made it worse, but I was so horrified, so disgusted by his touch that I couldn't do anything but try to get away.

"Let's do it all over again, Joan, shall we? It's always been one of my favorites. What with your mom watching and everything. Or, should I say, giving me a hand?"

We jumped back to the bad day.

And there was Alex, alive, my beautiful husband. I couldn't help but tremble in his presence, even though the suffering of all the years after hung in the air like paper lanterns, lit up but ready to catch fire at any second.

I had known it was coming. That morning, when he left to rent the moving van and I was making Brandy her oatmeal, I tasted bitterness and couldn't get it to go away. It traveled into my nasal passages, so that all I could taste or smell was fouled. Whatever had settled upon me was bad, and I knew it was there to stay.

We had packed all week, gone over to the new house to get the walls and floor scrubbed and ready for the transformation that would make it our new palace. When Alex came home and backed the U-Haul into the drive, I helped load the small stuff but left the furniture for the college kids he had hired to help out.

My main concern was keeping Brandy out of the way, saying goodbye to the backyard and all of the birds we had fed over the years. I was trying to get pregnant and didn't want to lift a thing.

But when the man with red hair joined the group, I all but fell apart.

How could I explain to Alex that this fellow, working harder than all of the others, made my skin feel like it was on fire? That his stench made me want to vomit? That I felt the life completely drain from my body when he looked at me?

The bitter smell became stronger.

I stayed at the old house while they unloaded. Met Mom when she came to help with Brandy, relieved to have someone else with me while I was so queasy.

"Do you think you're pregnant?" She asked, when I told her of the strange scent. "I was so sensitive to smells when I was in my first trimester that for a while I couldn't cook anything but pork. Your father had to take over in the kitchen when he wanted any variety in our diet."

The four of us went out to dinner. Alex, always charming, was worn out from his day arranging rooms with the moving crew. Brandy couldn't wait to sleep in her new room, her patience already being tested by the fact that we had to put on sheets before her bed was ready. Mom was proud of us and was going to do some rudimentary unpacking when we got home so we could sleep and have a glass of water in relative comfort.

Watching from the future, I was shocked at how happy I was, right at that moment, right before the horror. My hand reached instinctively to my belly, rubbing it, cherishing whatever might or might not have taken root inside me, hoping to fill the extra bedrooms in our new house very quickly.

Alex had left the outside light on, and although we all had to carry in a few bags, it felt like we had lived there forever.

Except for that smell.

He unlocked the door, and Brandy shot off like lightening, heading for her new room, which was three times the size of her old one. We had painted it light purple and decorated the walls with butterflies, one of her favorite things.

Just as I was about to corral my boisterous daughter, I was flattened to the floor, my neck bouncing off something rock hard, as though I had run into a clothesline while driving at high speed.

The house was dark when I reopened my eyes. We were in the living room, I could tell by the carpet, and while I could see my husband's feet and my mother's, I had no idea where Brandy had gone. Was she in her bedroom? On the couch? I couldn't turn my head that far.

When I went to holler her name, my mouth wouldn't open.

"Save that for later. I want to hear you scream all night long, so don't waste any of it now. You wouldn't want to disappoint me."

His mouth was right beside my ear. When he stopped speaking he bit into the crook of my neck, latching on like an alligator. This time the sound passed my lips and my screeching filled the room with terror.

Alex was on the chair. Right inside the window, thrashing against constraints. I had no idea what held him; I couldn't concentrate enough to even think about such things, not with the creature latched onto my back and digging his hands into my flesh.

I still couldn't see our daughter.

But my mother was watching. Her eyes bulged, her fear apparent as she watched the red-headed man grope me. I wanted to mouth some words of comfort to her, but couldn't do anything but scream.

The assault lasted hours. It could have been days, but portions of it passed while I was living somewhere else besides in my head, and I lost all sense of time. When I didn't give him the reaction he wanted, when my tears weren't enough, or I had gotten so hoarse I could barely eke out a scream, he would start in on my family.

A punch to the head for my husband. His words, obscene, discussing my body and how he was going to ravage me. More than he already had.

And my mother. My poor, poor mother. I never wanted her to witness my weakness. To see me battered and bleeding, sprawled on the floor in front of her, forced to perform the lewdest of acts while she suffered, was bad enough. But when he touched her, too, I came unglued.

"Oh, you've been expecting me, haven't you?" The man tore open my mother's shirt and embedded his exceptionally long fingernails into her breasts. "Don't tell me you gave up on me? Did I take too long?"

When I reached for his foot, he stomped my hand.

"Really, Joan. Learn your place. I'll do what I want, when I want. And don't think it bothers me that she's so old. Do you think your precious Mommy has ever had it up the ass?"

I whined and brought his attention back to me.

We put on a show. For our audience. I was amazed, after all the blood soaked into the carpet, that I had any left in my veins at all. How had he not yet done me in?

Although I wished for years afterward that he had.

Alex was the first to go.

After hours of witnessing my personal tragedy, he was exhausted, his cheeks coated in tears.

"Have you seen enough yet, Alex, my man?" the intruder asked. "Tired of watching?"

At first I was terrified that the man would assault him as well. Untie Alex, flip him over, and wreck him just as he had me. But when the redhead walked to the corner and came back with our shotgun, we all knew Alex's life was over.

Before he died, before the last second we shared together, Alex sent me all of his love with a barely discernible nod. Just the slightest dip of his forehead, and we were frozen in that moment, our silent farewell.

My heart exploded with the blast that took off his face. The man held me over Alex's fresh corpse, his fingers forcing my eyelids open, the scene paralyzing me with sorrow and fear. My mouth opened, but the scream I desperately wanted to unleash refused to budge from my throat. Blood turned my new curtains into gothic art. Bits of

Alex's brain fell from the walls, the drapery rod. As his body slumped, the chair toppled. Alex landed on the floor, his skull a white watermelon husk, the pink meat staring at me as my captor grabbed my arm and twirled me around to face him.

"Well, it's just the girls now, isn't it? Should we get this party started?"

Hours upon hours upon hours. The things he did to me so shameful I didn't know how I'd ever be able to face the world again. The things he made me do to my mother so atrocious I knew our relationship would forever be so fragile we'd never know another day but this one.

"Do you think you've had enough yet, Joanie? Because you know why I'm here, don't you? We're going to have a baby together!"

Did I pass out then?

"I don't know. Could you ever have enough? Let's see if your mom will give us a hand."

He laughed as he tied her forearms to the chair, then pulled the handsaw out of a moving box piled in the corner of the room.

"You should be more careful who you hire for odd jobs around the house, Joanie. Remember that in the future. I don't want my daughter to ever get in trouble like you have!"

The first cut was horrific. Mom's cries were guttural, mind-churning horror. They filled the room, sliding down the walls with the drips of blood as it sprayed from the cheap saw-blade.

How I loved her. I could barely comprehend that Alex was gone, but at least it had been sudden and he hadn't suffered. Too much.

But this man was evil personified. Her pain was his glory. When she closed her eyes, he kicked her in the knee so hard I could hear the bone shatter. He wanted her to watch.

The sawing took forever. Our attacker savored his work, went about it like an artist. When Mom's wrist hung from her bone, connected only by the muscles underneath, he flipped it, mocking her, cackling through her pain.

When the first hand was severed, he paraded around the room with it, making bloody handprints on the wall, dipping her fingers in her bloody stump and drawing curly-qs, wavy lines, anything that caught his fancy.

"This is so much fun! Let's do it again!"

By the time he had removed her other hand, Mom was all but gone. Her head rolled limply against her shoulders, but he pulled it back up by her hair and slapped her to consciousness.

The blood pooled at her feet, soaked into the carpet. I imagined the pad underneath sucking it up, drinking it like a sailor, taking Mom's life and making it a Bloody Mary to last throughout eternity.

I was happy she would soon die. To end her suffering. To get her out of this room, out of this house, away from my torturer.

But he had one last thing planned.

"Wake up, Mom. You'll want to see this!"

He took her hands and used them on me. Started with my mouth, pushed a finger between my lips and made me suck. Then became cruder. The man pushed his fingers inside Mom's severed skin, wore her hands like gloves, and squeezed my breasts while I yelped beneath him.

"Do you see that, Gladys? I think Joanie likes it." When Mom didn't respond appropriately, he bludgeoned her other knee, the pain forcing her eyes wide open.

Her hands developed a life of their own. I was barely alive myself, and knew I had to be hallucinating, but when I looked over at the chair where my husband had toppled, the redhead sat holding my daughter.

He pointed at my crotch, my splayed legs.

Mother's fist entered my body. Brandy giggled while I bucked on the floor, Mom's fingers reaching into my very womb, checking, I was almost certain, that I was ripe to carry on the family curse and that his seed had been planted.

Brandy watched while her grandmother bled out. While her severed hands roamed my sacred spots, while I writhed beneath them. The devil laughed and pointed, tickling my little girl, telling her horrible things about me.

"Your Mom is such a slut. Look at what a whore she is!"

Brandy threw back her head triumphantly, joined him in laughter.

"But guess what? She's going to have a baby. You're going to have a little sister."

"I am! A little sister! How do you know?" Her excitement filled the room. For a second, I was so elated that she wasn't in fear, that

Brandy seemed oblivious that her dead father lay right beside her chair.

For a second.

"Because I put her there. But you've got to promise me something, Brandy."

"What?"

"You're going to have to look out for her. Your Mommy is going to be sick for quite a while, and you're going to have to treat that baby like she's your own."

"Mommy's sick?" Brandy finally looked at me, her eyes absorbing the situation. "Are you sick, Mommy?"

"Promise me, Brandy. Tell me what you're going to do." His hands ran up her legs as he talked, and what strength I had left dissolved as I thought about what he might do to my child.

"We're going to have a baby! I'm going to have a little sister! And I'm going to have to take care of her, because my mommy is so sick!"

The past faded.

The curtain came down.

But when I reopened my eyes, he came right back at me, teeth yellowed and dripping blood.

On the pillow my mother's hand flinched.

I would never survive this another time.

At least, if I managed to die, I wouldn't have to live with you again.

Nine days left.

Nine days, and then I was done.

Chapter 33

Lucy

The horizon stretched out like long strips of cotton candy, layered one flavor on top of another, pink, yellow, peach, and pinker still, until it gave way to the blueberry taffy that made up the sky.

As night neared, it all darkened. The fuchsia contrasting to the black that made up all the landmarks.

They rose from the ground like miniatures. The farmsteads that dotted the countryside, trees reaching up in prayer, all dramatic, outlined against the colorful sky. From my perch against Brandy's window, I could make out barns and silos and the homes of people who used to flavor my life.

The Millers lived a mile to the west of us. Their house sat, black, empty while they finished their second-shift jobs at the Walmart twenty miles away. I couldn't imagine how busy their store was, so close to Christmas.

Four grain elevators abutted the gravel road that eventually connected to the highway, running south. Birds jumped from spot to spot, foraging for seed in the cold. From so far away they looked like the fleas that infested Tippy's tummy in the summer.

Mr. Wyckoli had been a widower for six years now. Brandy and I used to bake him pies and big loaves of bread and bike them down to his house. He was a sweet man. I could see his light on in the kitchen, this one bright flag breaking up the night, and knew he was sitting at the table, probably in his undershirt, watching the little television mounted on top of his microwave. Smoking his loneliness away.

It hit me hard. Mr. Wyckoli's depression. After his wife passed, he rarely left the house. Just wiled away his hours watching game shows and playing solitaire. His house was filthy. Mom had sent us down several times to clean it for him, and I was always ashamed to touch his dirty clothes, feed them into the washing machine. I couldn't imagine how he felt inside, watching us do it for him, seeing us scrub his toilet and or scrape the old food off the dishes that stretched the entire length of his kitchen counter.

A couple of times a year Brandy would visit him, open up his barn, and take out his riding mower to run over his yard. I picked up the sticks for her, made piles in his side yard. Took the rake and tried to tame some of the vines that grew wild around his hedges.

Did he think of us? Miss our holiday cookies? Did our lack of attention this year send him into a deeper cave, emotionally?

Poor man. Alone, and I couldn't do anything to make him feel better. We had tried to convince him to get a dog. He loved Tippy, even babysat her once for me when we had to travel overnight for a mission event with church. But he didn't want one of his own. He didn't want to abandon it when he finally died and met his wife, when, he said, they would be united for all eternity.

I touched the window pane. Sent him a bit of good cheer, all that I had in me. How odd that my life would become like his: passing time watching my chickens parade around the walls, talking to a sister that didn't live here anymore, waiting for the day Mom would finally kill me and bury me in the backyard.

From the edge of my vision, I saw movement. Ants running across the field. When I narrowed my eyes and concentrated, I realized that the deer were streaking through my neighbors' yards.

I dared to move the curtain. Twenty, maybe thirty, stretched like a garland across the horizon. I wouldn't yell to them but screamed in my head so loudly my eardrums pounded, and I about fell over when they stopped as a unit and turned to face me.

My fingers wiggled in a pathetic wave.

The buck stepped forward. Raised his head. Bowed to me.

I could feel our connection. Just seeing him made my heart beat stronger, my will strengthen. As if he were inside me, bolstering my confidence.

I nodded.

He lowered his head, his eyes remaining fixed on me.

The herd ran into the trees, where the branches pulled them in like children, protecting them from outside eyes.

I wondered if Mr. Wyckoli would outlive me.

* * *

I liked it better when Mom had just muttered through the night.

Now, her bad dreams kept us all awake. I wanted to go to her, rouse her, do anything to get the agonizing screams to stop, but I was afraid.

What would she say about my hair?

When Mom started begging for someone to kill her, Tippy and I decided we were being petty. She needed help. What did my hair matter in the whole scheme of things?

My hands shook so violently that I could barely turn the knob, and I had to use both of them to twist it far enough to unlatch the door.

Tippy and I both sighed with relief that it wasn't locked. God must have closed it completely when He left us. My dog and I no longer shut the door all the way.

But the second my eyes adjusted to the mayhem in the hallway, I slammed it closed.

"What the fuck was that?" Tippy backed away.

"I don't know."

Mom's screams were piercing.

"Don't you dare open that door again!" Tippy hollered when I reached for the knob.

"She's in trouble, Tip. She needs me."

"Oh, screw that. She's never needed you. She couldn't give a rat's ass if you lived or died. Why do you care about her?"

"Because she's my mother." I found enough strength to pull the door open again.

The hallway was gone.

The stairs, non-existent.

I couldn't tell if the house was on fire, but I felt caged by flames. Nothing was burnt, but everything was scorching hot. My fingers sizzled when I caught the door frame, gripping it fiercely to avoid falling into the abyss that stood between me and Mom.

Her wall chickens had gone into hiding. They no longer protected her room. Even through all the darkness I could see new friends pulling free from the paint and dropping into the swelter down below.

She had taken in snakes.

Hundreds of them, big and small. They festooned her doorway, as if they had come to embellish the house for Christmas, only in less traditional colors.

I remembered my own madness. Cherished the fact that I still had enough of my wit about me to realize that I had gone crazy. How else could this happen?

The board beneath my feet started to crumble so quickly that I was certain I'd fall straight through to the basement. And what would await me there? The corn?

Any corn that could grow in this madness wouldn't be a plant I'd like to meet.

Mom screamed again.

"MOM! I can't get to you!"

I retreated to my room. Shut the door. Put my hands over my ears. Tried to block out her horror.

Tippy paced. Her nervous grumblings were punctuated with florid curses, exploding out of her mouth like a bowling ball hitting the pins.

Mom didn't hold back. Whatever was happening to her, she couldn't swallow the pain. Her agony sounded like she was being skinned alive, lemon juice poured onto her open wounds.

"What are we going to do, Tippy?" I sat on the edge of the bed for a split second, hid my face in my hands.

I darted back to the door and peeked out, hoping I'd only imagined the crazy scene I'd seen earlier.

But the snakes were still there. Falling, almost dripping out of Mom's walls.

Where were the chickens when I needed them? They could chase some of the smaller serpents. Peck at them.

"You mean, what are *you* going to do, Lucy." Tippy's eye took on a menacing look. "What *you* should have done all along. There's the window."

Tippy pointed her snout at the only escape route.

"Leave. Get help. For all of us."

I stared at the window. For so many months I had longed to jump and sprint to the Hanley's house but hadn't had the strength or the nerve.

"Get over to the fucking window, Lucy, and open it." Tippy commanded.

I was frozen.

"Turn. Walk. Open."

Mom's cries curdled in the air.

"Whatever is devouring her will find us next. I personally don't want to be a tasty meal for the next panther that comes through here." Tippy backed away from the door, headed for the closed window.

"No panther is coming to get us, Tip."

"Then what the Hell is making her scream like that?"

We listened. Watched the door rattle. Wished, for just a fleeting second, that the lock was in place and no one—or thing—could climb in with us.

"Tip, I love you," I told my dog, just in case I didn't get another chance.

"Love me enough to save me."

"It's more complicated than that."

The house shook, and my clock fell off the wall.

"Go. Now."

For some reason I looked at the hour hand and remembered that my batteries had died about two years ago; I had been too lazy to change them. Three o'clock. The right time, twice a day.

Shivers crept up my thighs.

"If I refused to move, you'd slap a leash on me and drag me against my will. I can't do that for you. You need to go, Lucy."

"She needs help, Tip."

"Open the door."

I did as told. The floor was still gone.

"Close the door," Tippy instructed.

Mom's screeching sounded like a flock of birds racing away from danger.

"Go to the window."

I managed to inch forward. Was this the end? The end of us, our family? The end of our house? How would I ever get downstairs?

When I made it across the room, I stood and stared out at the blackness.

"You're not waiting until daylight. I know you're afraid, but man up for a change."

Tippy walked behind me, her little body a tripping hazard if I dared back up.

I could feel her fur against my heels. I wondered if she would bite me if I didn't go forward.

My hands struggled with the window. I lifted it up but couldn't get it to stay in place long enough to take out the screen.

"Use your books. You can stack them and hold it that way."

Before all of this trouble with Mom, Tippy had been a quiet dog. Never the diva she was now, bossy, and all put out if things didn't go her way.

"How will I get off the roof?"

"You're the human. Remember? You have a much bigger brain than I do. You figure it out."

I perched on the window sill like an enormous bird, terrified to jump, especially when I still wasn't too healthy. I didn't want to hear my bones snapping.

"Dear God, please, Lucy. Just do it already!"

I stood up on the roof, moved carefully to the ledge.

"And just what do you think you're doing?"

His voice was sudden and unexpected and almost sent me tumbling over the edge.

"I need to get out. I need to get help."

"Help for what, Lucy?" God grabbed my wrist and pulled me back toward the window. I loved that He provided me the safety net I'd wanted but felt my heart deflate as I lost my opportunity at freedom.

"Mom. She's been screaming all night and I can't get to her room to see if she's okay."

"Really? What's going on with her?" I knew He already had all the answers and didn't know if I was supposed to respond. I had no idea what was going on.

"I don't know. But she's been hollering like she was dying. Tippy and I can't stand it anymore."

"So why not ask her yourself?" God kept hold of my wrist while He climbed through the window.

Tippy bolted for the bed again. She was silent this time as she hid under the box springs.

"I tried, but the hallway floor was gone."

God chuckled.

"Are you dehydrated again, Lucy? What do you mean, the floor was gone?"

"It just wasn't there. I almost fell into the basement when I started out of my room."

He helped me from the roof back onto solid flooring.

"That sounds pretty serious. Let's take a look-see, shall we?" God grinned at me and His teeth made me shudder. His eyes dropped to my chest again.

I couldn't help but squirm.

We crossed the room together, His hand firmly grasping mine. God did not even hesitate when He opened the door.

And of course, there was the floor. Perfectly intact. Making me look like a fool.

"Do you sleepwalk, Lucy?" God smiled again, poking His toe on the wooden planks in the hall. They squeaked, and I realized that this was the only sound in the house. Mom had finished dreaming, or being boiled alive, or whatever had made her so distraught only a few minutes ago.

"No."

"Well, let me tell you a story. Let's have a seat, shall we?"

God escorted me to my bed, the only place in my room for us to sit down. My tummy flip-flopped, anticipating the worst.

"What do you think will happen if you try to jump off the roof?"

I preferred hearing a story, but being interrogated about my behavior won hands-down over the other things I feared God would do to me.

"I might break my leg. Or get hurt somehow." I felt six years old.

"Lucy, I know exactly what will happen to you. You have two alternatives: stick out this bad period with your Mom, which will end, eventually. Or climb out the window." God put His arm around me, pulled me so close that I could smell His body odor. I wondered if He had to shower. His hair didn't look greasy, but His skin reeked of something like cigar smoke.

"If you climb out the window, it won't be pretty. There's not enough snow left to break your fall, and quite frankly, your body is in a hideous state. You've been ill for months and your bones will not hold up well. You're an awkward child. If I hadn't intervened just now, you would be lying on the ground with a compound fracture in your left leg and a broken hip."

"You can see that?"

He didn't answer.

"Now, think about this. Your mother has never really proven herself a supportive parent. Do you think she'd take you to the doctor after that? To the hospital? How would she explain that the daughter she had sent away, who hasn't been here for months, supposedly, fell off the roof? She wouldn't. She'd either use the shotgun on you or put you back in the basement and leave you there until you died."

What a horrid thought. I couldn't imagine living through that again, with all those injuries to boot. Surviving the darkness. Without Tippy. Without any hope this time. Just waiting to die.

"Now, if you can just restrain yourself, Lucy, I promise that you will outlive your mother."

"Is she dying? She certainly sounds like it."

Of course, Mom had quieted down now that God was on the premises.

"Promise me that you won't go out the window."

I hoped Tippy heard Him. I didn't want to defy God, and I was certainly tired of my dog prodding me to jump off the roof.

"I want to hear it from you, Lucy. Promise me."

"Okay. I promise. But...what if I can get out from a downstairs window?"

God stiffened His back. His hand moved to my thigh, where He tightened His grip.

"This is the safest place for you. In the house. With your mother. You'll know when the time is right for you to move on. And you won't have to break out any glass to do so."

I dared look God in the eye. As soon as I made contact, He quit talking and had me plastered against the bed before I even noticed we had moved.

"I just love good girls. Your pure little hearts. The sweetness that surrounds you like a whirlwind of sugar." His lips pressed against my own. "I bet you even have on white cotton panties. No, not panties. Bloomers."

He undid my jeans and pulled them halfway down my legs in a second flat.

"See! You do! Your mother was the same way when she was young, too. I just couldn't stand it. She drove me wild, wearing those big old bloomers. It wasn't until she got married that she switched from cotton to rayon, like that diamond on her hand warranted a change in fabric."

I closed my eyes. Tried not to disrespect God. Found myself muttering a prayer but then stopped when I realized my error.

God had four hundred hands, and I could feel them all rummaging my skin at the same time. Three running through my hair, some massaging my back while others prodded my every part. For an instant, I felt encased in bliss and realized that this was why everyone loved God so much, why His creepiness was so far removed from the image portrayed in the Bible and all of the works generated thereafter. My breath stuttered, then wound so tightly that I had to gasp for any air I could find. I could reach the clouds. My every cell shouted with glee.

And then his mouth met mine.

I had never kissed a boy before.

Or a piranha.

God's frightening teeth took horror to a new level when He attacked my lips, tearing into them like a wolf with a fresh kill. His fingers held me, thousands of grappling hooks ripping every muscle. The brief pleasure I had enjoyed fell aside, and this time I could not find breath because my fear had hidden it so well.

When God stopped I gasped. He patted me on the back, acted concerned that I was practically drowning in my waterless room, lungs full of panic and unable to process my newfound oxygen.

"Well, that's enough for one night. Keep your promises, Lucy. Stay in the house. Don't kill yourself trying to escape her."

His eyes widened and I felt myself, naked, sprawled in front of Him, then as He turned my clothes became visible again.

I wiped the blood from my lips.

Changed back into my nightgown.

Crawled into bed.

Mom was on her own tonight.

Chapter 34

Evelyn

He tricked me, my devil.

Led me by the hand like a star-struck child. With him I had gathered hundreds of souls. Caused unfathomable pain. Even giggled uncontrollably as he brought down the bolt that took out my own mother.

Dare I say I'd fallen in love? With him, our whole lifestyle, the torment of being his wench?

When I began to notice his distraction, I was infuriated. Had I grown too old for his desires? Was I not willing to do anything he commanded, no matter how vile? Did I not protest enough? Had he tired of my devotion? Did he only want a woman he had to tame into submission, not one stretching the boundaries of her own soul to remain by his side?

First it was a shriveling of our camaraderie. I remember it exactly. We were in Cambodia, trolling the rainforest, a breathtaking adventure on its own. But when we stumbled upon a group of men hunting deep within the veil of the trees, we decided we would have days of fun and take their minds long before they took their final breaths.

Kind of a vacation for us, if you will. A safari.

Our adventure started with almost jokily hiding their supplies, making weird noises that set their hair on end, playing old childhood ghost-story games that paralyzed them with fear.

I had taken over while my lover tended to his more professional duties. He had left me like this many times, running off to some backward country to motivate insurgents or help a politician wallow in the sleazy alleyways of his own mind. I was used to that.

But when he came back, when I had all five men staggering around in pain and fear, while I had spent my time moving them like puppets through the dense foliage and waiting for my companion to come back and help me finish them off, when he came back he was bored.

We were in the heart of action.

"Look at that fool!" I laughed, pointing at one wretch as we watched from our seat in the canopy.

The man was minus a foot. He had lost it the day before, when our game of cat and mouse had ratcheted up a notch and he barreled into the river in an imprudent attempt to escape me. A Siamese crocodile, who had been eyeballing us for quite some time, decided to make a snack of him. The hunter had a healthy set of lungs on him and had survived the croc's attempt to roll and drown him. Of course, it didn't hurt that I was at the other end, yanking the creature's tail. I wasn't about to let him steal my new toy.

I wasn't done playing.

The hunter was on a slow trip to Hell. His mind was disintegrating, unable to handle both the fear and agony of his condition. He hobbled through the difficult terrain, his leg bent at the knee, the flesh below it ragged and yellowing. Still, he fared better than his companions.

One had become a pincushion. Only hours earlier he had suffered a vicious attack of hornets, thousands of them leaving their mark on his skin. He was barely alive, hunkered down by a tree, begging death to find him.

"Oh, you do it." My lover waved his hand at me.

"But I've been waiting for you to finish him off."

I probably shouldn't have spoken so boldly. My prince was quick to scold me, his taloned hand raking my cheek. "You do it!"

And I did.

I finished while he sat back, criticizing my work, punishing me when he deemed fit. Which was often.

His distraction was obvious. I couldn't help but wonder, what had happened on the global front? The big picture? But I dared not ask.

"I'm bored with this."

Our time together, done, just like that. We were in Cambodia and then back in the States, standing in the back yard of my niece and her family.

"Now, this is entertaining."

Her child played among the flowers. What was she, five? Maybe six?

"She's a relative." I didn't understand yet why we were here.

"Oh, I know. She's one of my good girls. Look at how sweet she is. Don't her eyes just shine with delight?"

He lit up like a proud parent. I hadn't known him to go after such young flesh, unless he was unnaturally hungry. But this time my lover stared at the girl like she was the next in line to join his harem.

Was I jealous or just indignant? Did it bother me that he stared at her innocent flesh and wanted to own it?

The answer was clear.

I was enraged. Joan looked up at us, invisible to her, her eyes piercing my heart, as if she could see straight through me, even though she didn't know we were there. I wanted to crush her skull. Dig out her eyeballs. Let her know that he was mine!

"This is the one," My master informed me, his face beaming.

My heart dropped.

"Really? The one to replace you?" I asked.

Joan's long hair rose with the wind, flying back from her face. She twirled in the yard, spinning around in circles, until dizziness overtook her and she fell upon the ground in hysterics.

"No. The one who will bear her. Look at her fine skin. The happiness in her eyes. I can't wait to destroy it!"

For a second I felt relief. He wasn't here to convert Joan to his wicked ways or to covet her body. We were just there to look at the child. To laugh at her future death.

"She will grow up to be beautiful." Although disappointed, I tried to sound supportive.

"Well, until I get my hands on her. Then she won't be much of anything after that!"

He suddenly became very interested in me again. I had my uses, and I understood that.

But I couldn't shake my sorrow.

He rattled on about Joan endlessly. Her perfection. Her glow. Her eagerness to please, one of his favorite qualities in girls and women.

I put on a good act but knew he could see straight through it.

For months we spied on the child. He spiced our days with occasional forays into soul-catching, but neither of us had the same passion for it. My companion was obsessed with his new plaything, and my heart shriveled each time we visited.

"Did you really believe I'd choose you?" He asked me once, after a week-long tryst with his friends had left me close to death.

"Yes." My honesty turned instantly into shame at my weakness.

"But you are nothing without me."

Did I know that already? Somewhere, in the recesses of my heart, I understood this to be the complete truth.

My flesh was wracked with pain. Every breath I took seemed to be my last. Yet he insisted I continue to give him pleasure. Was he the only thing that kept me alive?

"You have served me well, Evelyn. Even when you were a teenager and I wore your father's flesh, you gave yourself to me. You have done what I've wanted and born up to the consequences when you've let me down. But being a whore doesn't make you the woman I've been looking for. Taking orders doesn't make you a leader. Flinging souls into the abyss is fun, especially when you work as a team, as we have. But what we've got going is a war. You need wits. You need backbone. You need aggression. And you, quite frankly, fall short in all three categories."

I tried to let go.

To whisper myself away.

But I knew it could never be so easy.

He would decide when I would die.

And it certainly was not now.

Chapter 35

Lucy

I approached Mom in darkness. She was moaning in her sleep, and I thought it would be rude to flip on the lights and wake her. I also didn't want her eyes to open to the treachery of my hair. Stealth and I had become good friends.

Her room was trashed. If she had been killing chickens again, she had had to chase these all over the furniture and maybe up a wall or two. The chair from her vanity caught my left foot while I tried to tiptoe into her room, and my tray with her breakfast went flying. I lay, sprawled on the floor by her bed, waiting for her belt or something worse to meet my skin after making so much noise.

"No! Not again! I can't take it anymore!" Mom started sobbing. Her voice sounded like my fifth-grade teacher's, scorched and scratchy after decades of heavy smoking.

I was terrified. Did I let her know it was just me? Did I take ownership for breaking into her bedroom and dropping oatmeal on the floor? Or was comforting her the better solution?

"Please, just kill me this time," Mom begged.

"It's only me, Mom. I thought you were sick and I brought you breakfast, but I fell over this chair and dropped it."

"Brandy? Sweetheart?"

My heart plummeted. Now my betrayal had doubled. I was skulking about in the dark, hiding my appearance, and I wasn't my sister, the one she loved.

"No, it's me, Lucy," I practically whispered.

She met me with silence.

"I don't want to be served by the devil."

"I'm not the devil, Mom. I'm sorry I woke you up. I was just trying to take care of you."

"Get out of here. Go! Get away from me!" Mom raised her head from the pillow, but didn't have the strength to hold it there for long.

"Be careful if you walk over here. I can't see to wipe up the oatmeal...."

A pillow landed against my head.

"Leave, you wicked spawn! Just let me die in peace!"

"Okay, but if you decide you need anything, I'll get it for you. I'm sorry you don't feel well today."

I backed out of the room. Made sure Tippy was in the hall before shutting the door. Worked my way downstairs with the wooden tray, eager to make my own breakfast.

"I can't let you out, sweetie. But I'll put these newspapers over there and you can go on them."

Tippy and I both knew Mom would get furious with her for going in the house, even though it wasn't her fault. We both stared at the big windows in the living room, and for once I wanted to throw a chair through one and climb out. But I remembered God's words and kept my promise.

"I don't see how this can ever end well," I told Tippy as I filled her bowl.

We sated our hunger and went on a survival walk through the kitchen. Granola bars, dried fruit, Milkbones, and some of Mom's favorite beef jerky all went into baggies so I could stash them under my mattress. We found a few more plastic bottles in the trash and filled them with water.

"This time pack the right things," Tippy insisted.

"What do you mean by that?"

She nodded at the knife drawer.

I agreed, it was definitely time. And this was probably the best opportunity we'd have to find a good weapon.

I snuck over to the drawer, in case Mom was listening to the floorboards creak and knew exactly where I was. Furtively pulled it open. Almost screamed when I realized it was empty.

"Tip, they're gone!" I whispered.

We checked every place in the kitchen, but couldn't find anything sharper than a regular dinner knife. As the day progressed, Tippy and I snooped through the downstairs and never found a sign of the whole array of kitchen paraphernalia we used to have.

So we went to the attic.

An amazingly bold move on my behalf. Tippy stood at the end of the ladder after I pulled it from the ceiling, standing guard in case Mom came. But, for some strange reason, I wasn't even nervous about that.

Just the darkness and creepy crawlies that awaited me at the top of the mini-stairway.

The chickens were back and moved through the walls until they were gathered back by the attic door. They knew it was a forbidden zone in our house, and my behavior gave them quite a bit to squawk about.

I had never been in this part of the house before. My nerves were chattering as I made my way up the steps, slowly gathering my courage as I went. The flashlight in my hand wasn't as powerful as I wanted, and I found myself encased in darkness when I finally made it to the top.

Most of it was hot pink insulation. As I moved the spotlight back and forth, I kept expecting enormous child-eating rats or even some wintering raccoons to jump out at me, but overall the place was boring. Mom had stashed a small pile of boxes not far from the entry, but that was it. No corpses, no secretive KKK robes, no drug labs.

Maybe the attic had always been off-limits because the insulation might make us sick. Or, possibly, the place was so boring that it had just never entered conversation in the first place.

But since I had managed the steps and braved the whole event, I decided to rifle through the boxes anyway. How long had it been since I'd openly defied Mom and snooped through her things? Probably my entire life.

Time to live on the wild side.

I crawled to the boxes, staying as silent as possible. In my excitement I had completely abandoned my quest for anything sharp that would possibly save my life in the battle with Mom that was sure to come.

The cardboard was old. Waxy. My hands felt uncomfortable, just touching it. Like the act of snooping was so filthy it would rub off on my skin, leave me covered in big boils or coat my palms with hair.

But that didn't stop me. I plundered with ease, like I was destined to find these boxes and unveil their contents.

The first lid came off in no time. The box was empty, except for a couple of papers scattered at the bottom. I scooted it aside and pulled the next one closer. This cardboard was falling apart, but the box had weight.

I don't know what I expected: lost family photos, the signed confession from whoever killed Jon Benet, the original Constitution. But I was sadly disappointed. It contained neither dinosaur bones nor the lost cutlery from our kitchen drawer. From what I could tell, the box was filled with documents from my grandmother's life. Her old tax returns, insurance papers. Nothing exciting.

The last box was almost as empty as the first. Since it was taped shut, I shook it a bit and heard something bang around inside. I determined it was worth going through all of the trouble to open it.

Quietly I undid the seal. Thankfully the glue was old, the tape brittle. I fantasized that when I finally got it open, the box would contain something marvelous like an emerald necklace or a huge wad of hundred dollar bills.

But no such luck.

I pulled out a book, leather-bound and tied with what looked like an old black shoelace. When I flipped through it, I discovered it was some kind of diary written decades before I was even born.

I almost threw it back in the box. My grief at having found nothing of great significance in the attic caused me to just about give up.

But then I remembered my boredom. Days of watching chicken drawings play out on the upstairs walls could only keep me entertained for so long.

I put it on the attic stairs, where I grabbed it when I was ready to head back down to Tippy. She huffed off, exhausted by our adventure.

I hated to disappoint her again. As Tippy made her way to our room for a nap, I slid down the wall by the bathroom and thought about all the opportunities I had missed: the screwdriver in the junk drawer, the snow globes in the living room, the glass jars I could break into shards ready for stabbing. They were all downstairs and my energy was waning at best. I didn't want to stand up and waste calories on such an excursion. At this point I didn't think I'd even make it to my room again.

I vowed to get them the next morning. Mom didn't seem to be going anywhere. Tippy and I weren't completely starving or lingering on the verge of death anymore, but we tired easily.

Too easily.

The shoelace slid off the journal.

The chickens all gathered behind me as I began to read. Almost immediately their squawking took on a fevered pitch, but it quickly blended into background noise as Evelyn's story consumed me.

Chapter 36

Joan

The rooms were different, but at the same time, evil conjoined twins that had me in a strangle hold.

My body sprawled on the bed. But instead of sheets, I could feel the touch of our brand-new plush carpeting. My mind knew it was soft, but to my tortured flesh it felt like a cheese grater.

Curtains kept the sun at bay.

The darkness, my best friend, sat vigil while I decided whether to survive or decay.

Brandy, ever diligent, tried to bring me food and make me well again.

Only this time you were Brandy, and I couldn't handle being near your devil's stench.

Lucyfer.

Your brief foray into my room made me want to peel off my skin. I could smell him in your every cell. Were you working in tandem? Had you made me your personal captive this time?

Like before, I could barely speak. Sleep found me and kept me pleasantly occupied, but then I would wake up and the sweaty smell of nightfall would remind me instantly of what I had endured.

I couldn't remember if my husband still watched from the new eye blasted into his forehead. If my mother's final gasp of breath had crossed her lips fifteen years ago, or last night?

I called my daughter. The good one. The one who, years ago, had finally done as I had asked and gone across the street for help. Two days after the corpses started rotting.

The neighbor, according to the police, reported my child as announcing with pride that her mommy was going to have another baby and that she was really sick. If Brandy hadn't been wearing so much of my blood, the old man who answered the door would probably have sent her back home and never thought anything of it.

But the scene was so similar to my tomb today. Alex, dead. Mom, tortured and catching flies in her open mouth. My body a canvas of blood and semen, the sight horrific but dotted with the activity of a child—the crayons and scribbling paper Brandy had dragged out of the moving boxes in her room, the jar of peanut butter lying by my head, the water she had given me out of the cereal bowl she had filled in the toilet when she couldn't reach the tap.

My eyes shut. Closed to this world.

I had wet the bed. How pathetic was that? My legs couldn't recall the simple method used to transport me to the bathroom. They didn't understand movement. Urgency. Grace.

Instead, I stay silent and still. Let the blackness consume me. Not like a shark or giant snake, but like a veil of fragrant poison, slowly taking away my ability to breathe.

I had lived in this same cloud for months after you joined me.

My cousin Jasmine buried them. Kept Brandy while I lingered in the hospital. Put my husband in the ground and sent him on his way before I even knew my own name again.

During those months I swam through seas of sorrow so deep no one else would have survived. But you did. You latched onto my bones and gnawed, did laps around me while we floated through the black together, emerging only to show me your red tresses and that horrible deformity you inherited in your eye.

Jasmine brought Brandy to visit, but even then I couldn't shake the swarm of nagging memories that hounded me. My precious daughter never asked about her Daddy, didn't seem concerned with the stitches that kept my face together like Frankenstein's monster, or even ask when I was coming home. All she wanted to know was when you were arriving, so she'd finally have a sister.

My cousin suggested I tear you out. And how I wanted to! But the darkness beckoned, the black hole I called home, and I would run to it for weeks on end, emerging when it was really too late to take care of you. And what if you weren't his? What if you belonged to my husband, the love of my life, the man who had watched while his hired man practically pulled my womb from my body to make it his own?

She buried my family. Raised my daughter while I remained in bed, my mind a burned out husk, and felt you lay root in my soul.

But after my cousin mentioned the word *abortion*, she was taken out of the story. Obliterated. Her children additional victims of the semi that crossed into her lane and totaled her car.

Brandy, by the grace of God, was on a play date at the time.

Her smiling face the hands that reached into my abyss and pulled me up again.

Without me, my daughter would go into foster care. Jasmine had been our only family. The last one. I could no longer wallow in my own despair. I had to resume my role as a mother.

But no one could force me to care about you.

I stood up and said hello to the world I hated. Found a job. Made us a new home. Hobbled through life like a robot, completely devoid of passion and sentiment. Did what was needed to survive.

When they pulled you from my body, I immediately saw your hair and wanted to die.

When you left my room today, I saw the same thing. If I had been able to move, I would have grabbed the ax and been done with business. But my legs had completely forgotten what it meant to have a duty. To be obligated to protect the universe.

To be a mother with a child to kill.

I closed my eyes and welcomed the black back in.

Surely this time he would let me die.

Chapter 37

Lucy

I wouldn't let sleep catch me.

The day had been too quiet, with Mom locked in her room. The threats of violence and irrationality that were her trademark were hidden away as long as I didn't open her door. Tippy and I worried about her, and wanted to help, but at the same time our new-found freedom was addictive.

The second I opened Evelyn's diary I felt jumpy. Plucky would straighten her feathers behind me, and I'd practically scream with fear. Tippy called me a frog, all fidgety and ready to leap. But my dog had no idea what the book was about, and I refused to let her call me a coward again.

I couldn't put it down. Her language was stilted and sometimes hard to understand, especially when each page was dotted with foreign words or quotations, but I got the drift. Boy, did I get the drift.

This woman was scary. No wonder the attic was off-limits. I wouldn't want my children to find this book, either. Mom would beat me senseless if she knew I was reading it. But then again, that box hadn't been opened in decades. Maybe Mom had no idea this Evelyn woman even existed.

Evelyn began with thoughts of her sister. Laughing at her. The feminine weakness she wore like a badge, and how belittling Evelyn found it. She thought very highly of herself and expounded on her own intelligence, her independence and ability to take command. She discussed her tours of Europe, going on a safari, even an affair she had had with a woman in some remote area of Russia where they had lived for several months.

Then she had met a man and fallen completely in love with him.

A beast, really, from her description. Brutal and sadistic. No one I would ever want to meet.

At first I couldn't decide if the book was fact or fiction. My experience with popular culture was limited to conversations the other kids at school had around me. I had listened to them discuss scary movies, where people were butchered and raped and cut up and even eaten, but I had never seen one of these films. Sometimes I read the magazines in the library and learned about serial killers and people who committed horrible acts of violence. Kids who came to school with guns and killed their classmates. Parents that locked their kids in cages and sold them to men for sex. People who lit other people on fire just for wearing funny clothes. Or dragged them behind pickup trucks because of their skin color.

These things seemed surreal to me, but other people incorporated them into their everyday life without batting an eye—watching violent movies, reading the countless books that promoted a deviant lifestyle, living with a complete lack of morals that I found utterly devastating.

When Evelyn moved into the story of her first encounter with her new boyfriend, I was convinced she was an evil storyteller. They didn't meet on a date, or at a church function, or a neighbor's barbeque. Evelyn was in an alley attacking a woman, and he jumped in to help her.

Literally, jumped into her skin and muddled the lines of reality. Two souls contained by one body. Two souls mauling the poor woman that Evelyn had found so attractive.

Together they tore her apart. Ripped her to shreds. Used their fingers like knives and shredded the poor woman. Evelyn described it in minute detail; the transformation of her own body as her hands turned into his talons, as they slid through her victim's pale skin and into her gut, Evelyn had taken the time to maul the woman's breasts, cut off her nipples, fling them across the alley for the dogs to eat. When she ran from the scene, Evelyn had left little intact. The dead woman's intestines spilled into the alley, her spine tossed behind a building as the killer made her way home. I hated her, this Evelyn woman. Why would anyone even consider something like that? She enjoyed it. Couldn't wait to do it again.

And again.

The chickens bickered in the walls around me. Swatted at one another. Fell out of the woodwork and onto the floor, only to hurry back again into their charcoal formation.

For a second, I thought about my reality. How headless fowl that went from drawings to living, physical entities and back again didn't seem that odd to me anymore. Maybe Evelyn wasn't weaving a bold, nasty tale. Maybe I was. What other purpose could the chickens have in my life but to symbolize my own break with sanity?

That got me laughing. So hard that my dog ran into Brandy's room, tucking her tail and hiding from my hysterics.

Maybe Evelyn and I were a lot more alike than I wanted to admit. But, however horrible, her world was certainly much more exciting than the one where I sat watching chickens, waiting for Mom to either die or kill me.

The woman in the book loved blood. However demented her world, I easily fell prey to it. My eyes wouldn't leave the book. I was mesmerized.

I practically screamed when something started thumping down the hall.

Big, bass-drum vibrations, making the very floor beat like a giant heart.

I dropped the book, tried to hide it in case Mom was coming, but the only place suitable was in my waistband.

The hens squawked louder, more frenzied, twelve of them issuing a warning cry I couldn't understand.

Then one voice stood out above the rest, and the birds all flew over to the corner by Brandy's door, scurrying to be part of the action.

One of the decapitated heads started screaming. A horrid noise, shrill and full of agony. I worked my way to the banister, the pounding noise accompaniment to my every step, and found the bloody neck flopping in the pile of chicken parts. With my toes, I moved it aside from the rest of the garbage and felt my heart pinch as I saw the desperation on this chicken's face. Her eyes were wide and panicky. Her beak, cracked from the careless way her head was flung over here, emitted a curdling cry.

The other chickens were attacking.

After reading Evelyn's story, I thought for sure they were coming after me. As if they were her minions and she didn't want me to know the private details of her blood-drenched life.

But they gathered in the corner, all of the girls pecking away at one headless chicken. From the side it looked like Ms. Antoinette, already bloodied and battle weary. The others were killing her.

I tried to shoo them away, but they crawled into the walls and took her with them. Her protests filled the house. No matter how hard I tried, my hands couldn't enter the paint to pull her back out of the plaster.

They fluttered their wings and stabbed poor Ms. with every bob of their necks, staining some of her feathers with blood, pulling out others and decorating the walls with them.

Her severed head never stopped screaming. At one point her body broke free of the others, and I couldn't help but cheer her on, trying to get her to jump out of the drawing and back into my world, but Ms. was too weak to move that quickly. The hens ripped her to shreds.

Just like Evelyn and her first victim.

The other girls were vicious, like a clique at school, intent on making the weaker one suffer. Just because she was headless. Maybe they were jealous that she hadn't had to see the weird world they inhabited or because she maintained her weight without ever having to eat anymore.

As Ms. Antoinette took her last breaths, I stroked her head and tried to make her feel more comfortable. Loved. I promised over and over that I wouldn't eat her. Mom and I weren't going to have any chicken dinners for quite some time.

I was exhausted when she finally passed. Tippy was already on my bed, acting like nothing had happened, when I collapsed against my pillow.

* * *

The house sat silent, backed up against the woods, surrounded by the devastated fields.

Occasionally it would shriek when the wind chilled it to the foundations or creak when stretching its frame, but otherwise the place was a tomb.

Mom didn't make a sound. I wondered if she was alive.

The walls were empty, void of all fowl and their related activities.

I forgot to eat. Even Tippy stopped harassing me about keeping her bowl full. During one of our forays downstairs, I realized that it wasn't so much that we couldn't remember to stop by the kitchen and load up plates of tasty treats, but that the plates themselves were empty.

We were out of food.

How long had it been since we'd had a real meal? The fog hovering in my head didn't allow for such deep thoughts. I found some stale crackers on the top of the refrigerator, and Tippy and I feasted on them.

"How about a stick of butter?" Tippy asked.

I shook my head.

The refrigerator wasn't just empty, it was clean. Clean like it had only been during my first months of captivity, when I'd had my chore list and scrubbed every day.

How long ago had that been?

Was Mom still alive?

We sat on the floor, in front of the cabinets that held all of our cleaning supplies. Tippy, as usual, crawled onto my lap, stole part of my heat to help her thin body stay warm.

When I stroked her fur, I realized that she hadn't been outside for days. Where had she gone to the bathroom? I hadn't run across any accidents anywhere.

Still, I knew that when Mom finally got up, she would punish me for any violations of the house rules Tippy had committed.

We drank more water.

We had had a lot of water lately. Not that we complained; Tippy and I were not far from the days when water was the hottest commodity around. Right now it helped ease the hunger pains.

My thoughts returned to Tippy's bathroom habits. I found myself staring lustfully at the door. I crawled to it, put my hand against it, half expecting an alarm to sound at my audacious behavior. None did.

The wood had ice on the inside. I scraped it with my fingernails, and then realized that maybe that was why everything looked so unfocused. The glass was coated with it as well. Thick and flakey, just like the windshield on the mornings Mom used to drive us to school and Brandy and I had to clean it off for her.

No knives, no food.

After I managed to stand back up and walk to the junk drawer, I scavenged for a useable tool. Of course we had no ice scrapers in the kitchen. But I did find my old library card, the one I hadn't used in at least five months, and walked it back to the door.

Removing the ice did little for my vision. The world outside was still as white and ice-infested as the inside of our door. Snow piled high, up to my eye level.

Could this be a dream?

Tippy and I moved into the living room, where we slithered next to the curtain so as not to draw attention from any cars driving down the road.

Not that they could see us. The front porch was cocooned. Had Mom come out here while I was sleeping and made a rectangular igloo? If I stood in the middle of it, would I feel like a lone ice cube, shivering in the freezer?

We went upstairs. Tippy hurried ahead of me, but I had to resort to my hands and knees after the third step. The wobbliness I had experienced after the purification episode in the basement was back again.

If my family had been normal, this would be unbelievable. I could hear my sister behind me, shouting that school would be cancelled for at least six weeks while the snow melted. Brandy would have danced up and down the hall, Mom laughing at her excitement, Tippy joining in, her nails clicking on the hardwood floors as she bounced from leg to leg. How long had it been since we'd had a blizzard? A blizzard where the wind had forced walls of snow around the house, so high it covered the gutters, so thick I'd never be able to shovel us out, even when I'd been strong and a star on the swim team?

How had I slept through it?

The car was completely buried.

No knives, no food, no car.

But I could still see the shed.

When I caught sight of the metal roof, the sunlight kissed the top of it.

The fucking thing had winked at me.

Mom must still be alive.

Chapter 38

Evelyn

Joan, Joan, Joan. She was all he ever talked about.

Did he want to go to the beach and play shark anymore? No. Brutalize the already scarred women of the Congo? No. Cause a few racial uprisings in the south, a bit more tension among the folks fighting in Europe? Well, on occasion. Political uprisings were one of his greatest addictions.

He was content to keep me on my knees, remind me of my place in his life. I stayed glued to his side. Waiting to act on his every command. Sometimes I had difficulty remembering—was I paying rent in this room? Had I been traveling again? Or was I spinning in some loop where the two of us were invisible to the world and I was no longer burdened with social obligations?

His conversation narrowed to simply Joan. His new find. His little treasure.

She made his blood boil. He didn't look at her as the potential mother of his heir; he saw her for what she was. The harbinger of doom. The portent of his own demise. The little bitch whose daughter would eventually send him on his way.

Sometimes, the darkness settled on his face and I could see his weariness. How many years had he gone full throttle? My lover never rested. His work was unending. Yet he refused the idea of retirement.

I wondered but did not ask: where would he go, when his story was finally told? Would he serve in Hell for all eternity? Would his soul be released? He was, after all, only performing the duties of his job. How would his time end?

But as soon as these thoughts crept into my head, he heard them. Exploded with a rage I never knew possible. His tirade led us straight to a school play-yard outside London, where he introduced a young man who had just lost his job and his girlfriend. The man opened fire on the children high up on the swing sets, picking them off as they shouted with glee…and then with terror.

I was pleased with the bloodshed and hoped more would follow.

But none did.

He took the rest of his anger out on me.

Joan, Joan, Joan. We sat quietly while she played dolls in her bedroom. Joined her at a slumber party, with three other annoying children cackling over cookies and board games. Threw spit balls at her teacher and laughed while the boys in the back row got chastised.

I tired of discussing her hair ribbons, her bobby socks, or how cute she'd look with a pair of scissors lodged in her heart.

If he'd let me, I would have volunteered to take pictures after I'd punctured her chest, but that was out of the question.

What would happen to me in the end? The years I had passed with my lover were memorable, but their end was near. Would I be strung up in the bowels of Hell alongside him or be left on my own? Would Joan's daughter use me as an advisor or would I just flounder through eternity with nothing to do but wait for it all to implode in the end?

My lover lost interest. Focused solely on the child, his rage increasing by the day. He sent me others to entertain, kept me chained to the bed for what seemed months on end. On the rare occasion he even left me a female, knowing my preference for Spaniards. How fantastic it felt to be in charge. To wield the whip rather than taste its heated kiss. To suck the life straight out of tortured skin.

Those were the days I would miss the most. My fist in the bloodiest of places. My teeth finding flesh and ripping it clean of the bone. My unbridled power.

At those moments, I knew the truth. I was destined. Taking over the crown was my role. No Joan or child of Joan's would ever be as powerful or blood-thirsty as me.

I came up with a plan. Vague, as my thoughts had to be, as someone was always listening.

I would not let go that easily.

Chapter 39

Joan

The blackness let go for just an instant. Took its claws out of my back and let me breathe again.

Alex was gone, Mom long dead. Again.

My thoughts instantly flashed to Brandy, whether she was hiding somewhere or if he had gotten to her, too. God help her if he had.

Then reality trickled in. I remembered my room. Smelled the horror of my own bed. Knew he'd been watching me. Breaking me. Slowly killing me.

I moved my legs. They responded, but not well. When I slid off the bed, I fell to the floor. I did not get up with any speed.

We were close to the end. You and I.

I wanted to just let go. Join my loved ones. Forget about you and your plight.

But I had a job to do.

I was propped against the bed. Half standing, half willing myself to go back into my comatose state. Maybe I could just disappear. Forever.

The stench of my room overwhelmed me. How had I sunk so low?

Then I remembered his face.

Your face.

I had a job to do.

My legs held this time. On my feet, I clutched the dresser and found my watch.

We had seven more days.

Chapter 40

Lucy

When Tippy and I got out of bed, morning had not yet arrived.

She stumbled when her feet hit the floor. Took a nose dive, then flailed when all four paws slid away from her body. Tippy looked like a cartoon deer caught on a frozen pond.

My lack of grace was even more amusing.

I had to cling to the walls to keep my knees from giving way. My journey to the bedroom door took me past funhouse floors, where the hardwood tilted every direction and I could hear demonic laughter through the ceiling.

We looked at each other, ashamed to be bumbling around again, worried that our bodies were failing us. Neither of us wanted for water. But how long had it been since we'd eaten?

The beef jerky was gone, a much-needed meal after our last field trip to the kitchen had yielded stale saltines and nothing more. We had dozed off before gorging on the granola bars, but for the life of me I couldn't remember how long ago that was.

Our emergency stash sat idle in my dresser, but was so paltry it wouldn't last us three days if Mother locked us away again. Tippy and I both knew it was there, growing staler by the second. But neither of us was ready to dig in. To eat that food meant we were completely out of options. That Mother had finally won.

I dared not turn my head to look out the window. My balance was precarious at best, and I wasn't about to destroy it by moving sideways so I could get a glance. How would my heart take it if the snow hadn't melted yet?

In the hallway we took a break. Tippy stood, her breathing labored. My thighs quivered like gelatin, the sensation sending me into hysterics.

"Hey, look, Tip. It's like walking in high heels! Can you imagine dancing like this at the prom?"

"Let's cut the antics and just get downstairs." Tippy, as usual, was all business.

I put my arms out straight, imitating a tight-rope walker, trying to maintain my balance.

I tried to remember when we had fallen asleep. Had we just been so comfortable, with Mom locked away this time, that the two of us had cuddled ourselves into oblivion? Instead of hours, had Tippy and I lost days while we wiled away our lives in bed?

The kitchen was miles away. Tippy let loose the second she hit the linoleum, and I couldn't have cared less. Mom wasn't around to scream at us. For all I knew, she was dead.

At this point, I really didn't care.

Yet I went to the cupboard with every intention of feeding her. If my legs were Jell-O, hers were worse. Granted, she had more body fat and hadn't toured Hell like I had this year, but she was looking pretty rough as of late.

"There's the door, Lucy." Tippy pointed with her nose.

"What's your point?"

"My point is, I think you like it here. Like this."

"You heard what God said!"

"God specifically discussed windows. Not doors."

"Tippy, God implied all escape efforts. He wants me to stay here until…the end."

"She's going to kill you. And you know what? When you're gone? Who's going to feed me then?"

"Is this your hunger talking? Because in the whole scheme of things, Tippy, I look at you as a lot more than just a mouth I need to feed. How about saying to me, who will love me? Who will talk to me? Who will cuddle with me under the blankies when it's cold outside?"

My dog remained silent. She oozed over to her food bowl and bumped it with her snout.

"I get the hint!" I had been clutching the edge of the counter for support and knew how much we both needed to eat. Through the wavy fog in my brain, I felt like we had lost at least two days during our sleep fest. Food, at this point, was the most important thing.

Yet I knew we had nothing. No knives, no food. No car. With the sink to steady me, I was able to turn and look out the window. Through the darkness, I could spy the light on the edge of the shed. That meant the snow had either blown away from the steel building or had melted some while we slept.

But beyond that, nothing.

No moonlight. No stars gazing down at me. No lamp illuminating the side of the house and our driveway. No Christmas lights on the Hanley's house.

My heart sank. We had missed the big day.

My dog knelt before her bowl. Her fur was falling out, her eye drained of joy. I had failed her. Again. Christmas had always been her favorite holiday, the morning she woke up to a sock filled with chew treats and new toys, the day she ate human food without Mom complaining.

Tippy needed to eat. And I needed to give her a present.

I resumed my search with renewed determination. If this kitchen held even a crumb of food, I was going to find it.

But when I opened the cabinet door, I fell backward.

Every shelf, full. Top to bottom. Neatly straightened and facing out, just like in the grocery store.

Can after can of chicken noodle soup. A brand I didn't even recognize, a generic, I supposed, proclaiming "Home Made!" I thought of Mother's bedroom walls and shut the door.

The cupboard above the sink, where Brandy and I used to find our morning cereals, brimming with the same cans, all shiny on the edges, all beckoning me to open them.

Chicken in big letters.

"Just give me something!" Tippy barked.

She didn't care. To her, the chickens were some fairy tale that I had created to help us pass our days. She laughed when I told her Sissy was on the bed with us, found it hysterical when I worried about the wall drawings.

I took down one can and opened it. Slopped it into her bowl, without even heating it. Usually I took care to make Tippy's food a bit more palatable. But today I didn't have the heart to bring it to a boil.

As soon as she started slurping up the broth, the upstairs came alive. All the hens were in the hallway; I could hear their feet scratching on the hardwood floor, like they were doing a line dance or having a mixer where everyone was chatting or scurrying about.

When Tippy started to chew, the screams began. Dozens of them, all different pitches, a cacophony of horrors raging through the kitchen. I opened the remaining cabinets but was confronted with display after display of the creepy cans, the word CHICKEN big and bold in the middle of the label.

Then I realized that the noise was coming from my left.

The refrigerator.

My fingers gripped the handle, but I didn't want to open the door.

Tippy continued licking her bowl, oblivious to my problem. Even with her excellent hearing, she didn't notice sudden turmoil. Or the non-stop cries that came from our appliances.

The freezer contained nothing but cans. Matted with ice.

When I cracked the refrigerator door, the screaming crescendoed.

And there they were, the heads. Why Mom had chosen to put them here, unless she just wanted to terrify me, I could not guess. They were boisterous, some tainted a pale green, others dripping fresh blood from their wounds. I recognized Ms. Antoinette's sweet face immediately, barely visible under the other heads mounded on top of her own, pushed all the way in the back corner on the top shelf. Her beak opened and exploded with her anger. If she'd had wings, I'm certain she'd have been pointing one at me, accusingly.

I'd promised not to eat her. And here I'd gone and fed her to my best friend.

I closed the door. Didn't know what to do. The damned chickens wouldn't shut up, and I was starving. I wanted more than anything to find something to eat.

My whole body bolted upright when Mom's voice creaked from behind me.

"Merry Christmas, Lucy."

"Huh?" I asked, when what I really wanted to do was die at the sight of her.

Mom looked wretched. Like she had been in a car wreck and miraculously survived. Her face was mottled eggplant, her left eye drooping and bloodshot.

"So it's a few days late, but we can celebrate now, I guess." When she smiled, Mom flashed me one less tooth than usual.

"That'd be great."

"Let's see what we can make for dinner."

She pushed me out of the way and opened the refrigerator. There, on the top shelf, sat a plump chicken, ready for the frying pan.

Her scabby arms reached for it. "Well, I guess that answers my question. I don't even remember buying this one."

I was aghast. That the heads were gone. That Mom was up and talking to me. That Christmas had evaded me and I hadn't made Tippy a thing.

When I glanced at my dog, Mom was feeding her another can of soup. Mom's socks were wet from walking through the enormous pool of pee Tippy had left on the kitchen floor, but she didn't even seem to notice. Mom moved to put the can in the trash, and I caught glimpse of her neck, bruised and decorated with slashes, crisped with infection.

Everything was surreal. The piss, the chickens, Mom and the flesh that seemed to be rotting right on her, my mental state.

She pulled out the frying pan. Found some potatoes in, of all places, the flour canister. Had I looked there? Why would I even try?

The world swooned about me. Snow started to fall. Right there, in the kitchen, the room crowded with flakes. They were huge and filled the room, Mom's hair turning white as if she had donned a fancy Christmas wig, Tippy almost swimming through the pile. I couldn't believe our luck, that God would cherish us enough to shower us with this bizarre holiday treat, but Mom and Tippy didn't even notice.

When I stuck out my tongue to catch one of the big flakes, I gagged.

The sudden storm wasn't snow at all.

Feathers. Everywhere. Thousands and thousands of them, covering the kitchen, my family, even the bird Mom was preparing.

Mom caught me off guard when she turned to me, anger flaring in her good eye. "What the hell happened to your hair?" Her body tightened as she realized I no longer looked like Brandy.

"God—"

Mom shut me up with the skillet.

When it hit my head, I realized that she was still alive.

Definitely still alive.

But I, probably, was not.

* * *

Tippy. Pippy. Nippy. Zippy.

Where was my dog?

I reached for her, but found only my hip bone. Her little body was not beside mine.

Tippy. Slippy. Clippy. Skippy.

Where was I?

I couldn't see. Could open my eyes only for a split second. My head held a rock band on a stage surrounded by ten thousand jack hammers, all vying for attention.

The smell of wood. Had she put me in one of her old trunks? Was I in a cabinet? The closet?

A casket?

I freaked at the thought of the shed. Banged against my comforter with my feet, trying to kick my way out.

Then I realized that I wasn't freezing cold. That the shed would not give off the scent of wood. And that my bedding would only be in one place. My room.

My breathing calmed. I recalled the small bookcase I had, pushed against the windowless wall. My dolphin poster, hanging above my headboard. The rag rug I had found at Goodwill, the many colors complementing my pink and blue wallpaper.

I couldn't move. Couldn't lift my head, or I knew it would crack open and spill my brains out like yolk into the pan.

The pan. Mom had clobbered me with the frying pan. No wonder the parade of elephants stomping around in my head wouldn't go away.

But where was my dog?

Tippy. Toppy. Tappy. Tuppy.

Chapter 41

Tippy

I became an earthworm, tunneling through the snow. My stamina wasn't what it used to be, but I was propelled by the thoughts of my girl. Locked away, again.

Dying.

We were all doing a pretty good job of that. Once my tummy was full I could smell it everywhere. The very walls oozed the sweet sticky stench of death.

But you were still alive, this I knew. After your mother had gone to bed, I'd sat outside your door and listened to you breathe. Whatever she'd done to you had left you sleeping for nearly a day.

Whatever she'd done to you had left me panicked for nearly a day.

Burrow, burrow, burrow. Maybe I wasn't so much an earthworm as a rabbit. Or a badger.

Yes, I was a badger. Not cute and meek. Not an eyeless, limbless, bit of fish food.

I ate fish food for breakfast.

As a badger, I was no longer cold. The snow tomb was my safety. My paws were ten times more powerful than a house dog's. In fact, I didn't have to burrow anymore. I was so brawny I could swim through the snow-packed yard.

And swim I did.

When I ran into the shed, I turned to the left and came up for much-needed air. Your mother tended to forget about me when she left me outside, and while it usually annoyed me, today I needed that extra time. First I had some personal business to attend to, as I was horrified by the presents I'd left under the dining room table and didn't want to put myself in that position again.

Then I needed to find my friends.

I yowled. Put on my best warrior stance, even though my lips barely crested the white ocean surrounding the house, and tried to appear brave and strong so they knew I'd never falter.

Perhaps, in my weakened state, I was not loud enough.

A badger has no difficulty maneuvering through the densest soil. Would my friends consider me worthless if I could not pull myself completely from the snow?

This time I burrowed around the backside of the shed. Found the stump of an old elm tree that had gotten some weird bug in it and died. Stood on it and was able to push most of my body into the cold morning air.

When I howled again, I got a better response.

They were hunkered down in the trees. More than twenty of them. More than fifty. More than I could possibly count.

My army. I gave instructions, draining the last of my energy as I shouted to my soldiers. They would have to brave the remnants of the blizzard. I had. And they had quite a size advantage on me.

Not to mention thicker pelts.

The time was here. The time was now. At any moment I might need their help. And I wouldn't be able to open the door and escort them in.

I didn't believe in God. At least, not this beast that visited my girl, Lucy. I didn't care about His rules concerning the windows. And this would be the only way they could get in.

Not an easy task, given the freak weather conditions.

But at least no one would see them coming.

The big guy huffed back at me. They understood the urgency; they welcomed the challenge.

In the end, I thanked them for their service. Let them know how much Lucy loved them, and shared her gratitude as well. Put my badger face back on so they'd know I meant business.

Going home was easier. My tunnel had held, and I slid on my belly half the way to the door.

She was waiting for me when I made it to the back porch.

"Get in here, you damned dog. What do you think I am, your personal butler?"

Her foot pushed against my butt, causing my wet paws to slide across the linoleum.

I gave her my badger's eye. Grumbled, low and with a hearty warning.

My plan was in action.

Chapter 42

Lucy

The dark never gave way.

For a while, I was convinced she had locked me in a wooden casket. Was I already underground? How had she managed to dig through all the snow and the soil, frozen beneath it?

Maybe she'd been waiting all this time to kill me. Maybe Mom had dug my grave months ago.

But none of it made sense. When I finally managed to raise my head off the pillow, I made my headache a hundred times worse by vomiting over the side of the bed. Not that I had anything to bring up but bile. But that's when the dots started to connect.

I was on my own bed. In my own room. When I stretched out my arms in all directions, I couldn't find the walls of the coffin she had locked me in. Surely if she'd buried me alive, she'd have tucked me into the smallest space possible.

How could I be buried if I was in the house?

I rolled off the side of my bed. Worried, for a second, that I'd broken my arm, but it held my weight when I crawled on all fours to the closed door.

Strength evaded me. Just the simple task of turning the handle became an extraordinary chore. I couldn't balance my body and reach for the knob at the same time. Eventually I gave up and wedged my face between the knob and the door. Turned the handle. Found myself locked inside. Again.

My heart tripped. This time the door had no give in its frame, like it had before. It felt welded shut. No air seeped around its edges. Only a thin line of light eked over the threshold.

My fingers made their way across the wallpaper. Past the section Tippy and I had pulled down. Over the closet door. To the corner.

The smell of wood was stronger here.

I started on the wall with the window. Almost knocked the ceramic angel off its perch, the one Brandy had given me years ago for my birthday, a promise that someone would always look over me in my sleep.

When I hit the window frame, I knew. She had boarded it over. Taken the planks piled up in the basement and nailed them over my only escape. Mom had performed excellently. The seal allowed not even the faintest bit of light to seep through, the wood so thick and tight I'd never be able to pull it off with only my hands.

I couldn't imagine Mom's carpentry skills being this proficient. She had always used Brandy for the manly work around the house. But then I remembered who might have helped her.

God, intent upon my not escaping. His only son, a carpenter. Would He have called upon him to ensure I did not get out?

My despair came out in full force.

I made it back to the bed. Didn't have it in me to cry anymore. Just curled under the blankets and went to grab my girl, so I'd have someone to share my sorrow.

But Tippy wasn't there.

Where was my dog?

* * *

The granola bars were a lifesaver. I ate two, parceled out some water, took a mental inventory of everything I had hidden in my room.

Six packs of raisins. A couple boxes of dried soup, which might not be bad with a dab of water and a vigorous shake or two. Four more bars. Twenty containers of water, all shapes and sizes but enough to keep me going for a while. Some old hard candies I'd found while on my great search for weapons. The plastic bucket of pretzels Mom had thrown out when they expired but that had made their way into my closet before she hauled the trash to the cans beside the shed.

The pretzels were rock hard and would probably break my teeth, but at this point that didn't matter. What did I need teeth for if I had nothing to eat? No one to talk to?

Tippy and I had stashed several batteries. In fact, Brandy had for some reason kept an entire box of them in her room and we had confiscated it for our own. The flashlight would come in handy in the pitch black that was now my life.

Otherwise, all I had was Evelyn's book. No dog. No chickens. Just a world full of blackness and no one to share it with.

* * *

Sounds amplified in my gloomy cage. Mom rattling around downstairs. Tippy making an agonizing trip to the top of the steps, then turning around to go back. I could hear Mom cleaning. She used the vacuum, ran water in and out of the sink, opened the back door time and time again. Was she shoveling? Had the snow melted enough that she could maneuver through the arctic wilderness to the car? Would she be able to get to the grocery store for food?

Not that I'd get any.

But Tippy needed to eat. Something besides the cans of tainted chicken soup.

I set up the closet the same as before. Hoped God wouldn't jump in again. How embarrassing if He materialized and landed in my slop bucket!

With nothing to do but lament about my situation, I grabbed Evelyn's book and opened it, without shame this time. Tippy was not around to give me her one-eyed look of disapproval. Mom would have to bust down the door to see me with it, and even if she did decide to free me again, I'd have ample warning to tuck it back under my mattress.

Funny how much I needed a friend, and the only one I had left was this deranged woman and her scary, secret lover.

I pulled my blanket off the bed and plopped on the floor next to the heating vent. Sitting against the far wall, I could hide the trickle of light I needed to illuminate the diary.

Not that anyone would be looking.

So much movement made me dizzy. With my head balanced against my knees, I swallowed the discomfort. Once my eyes could focus, I opened the book back to where I had left off.

Horror in the Himalayas. The two of them, Evelyn and her man, taking out the kindly Sherpas helping some hikers from Australia make it to the top of Everest. The poor Aussies were lost without their guides, a blinding snowstorm relentlessly dogging their every move.

They were separated from each other. Terrified. Driven nearly mad by the cold and confusion, the drive to survive the treachery of the mountains.

Evelyn took pride in her destruction of the men. She slid up behind one and pushed him off a small ledge, watching him tumble but catch himself on a boulder. His left leg was broken, the bone sticking out of his thigh. While the man fought to climb down to their camp, his compound fracture slicing through muscle and skin with every movement, Evelyn made his plight worse.

She shoved him into an ice cave.

This time his hip was demolished. Shattered. Excruciatingly painful.

He screamed for quite some time, while Evelyn reveled in his pain. When she joined him on the ledge where he had landed, precariously perched above an endless abyss below, the hiker had thought she was an angel, sent to help him.

She started with his ear. Biting it off. Sticking her tongue inside the hole, then slapping it with her hand until his eardrum exploded.

Evelyn turned the man on his back, jumped on his injured leg, sat with all her weight on his shattered pelvis. She chuckled over agony.

In the end, the hiker slowly strangled to death on his own entrails. Evelyn had been kind enough to hang him, intestines wrapped around his neck, from one of the pitons he used to climb the mountain.

She watched while her boyfriend raped the next man to death. Acted as his personal cheerleading squad, the dutiful lover, assisting him as needed, inflicting more pain here and there when she wanted in on the action.

The third man suffered the most.

Evelyn cut his lips off with his own pocketknife, then went to town on his tongue, which they split in two and devoured while the hiker watched in horror. She made love to her boyfriend after removing one of her victim's eyes, wallowing over his body and covering herself with his blood.

They kept him alive for several days, feeding on his living corpse. Evelyn went so far as to compare their love fest to that of newlyweds, the festivities of their holiday abroad interrupted by fits of deviant sex and gastronomic delicacies.

I turned off the flashlight before shutting the diary.

Crawled over to the bed, my blanket in tow, wishing desperately for Tippy to keep me company after reading of such atrocities.

The kids at school wouldn't be afraid. They would have laughed at the part where they gnawed off all his toes, screeching with delight. I could hear their cries of "That's awesome!" and "What a trip, man!" as they listened to Evelyn's story.

But I wasn't like that.

I shuddered under my blanket. Pined for my sweet puppy, thinking about the man with his missing eye, and Tippy with hers. Wondered what kind of story Mom would write when I was gone. Would she be proud that after eight years of keeping me in storage, my bones were picked of all meat by the rodents that shared my room? Or would she simply burn down the house, and all evidence of my presence, before running to Rome, where she could live in hiding and pen her memoirs of being a murderous mother?

* * *

Eight raisins and a granola bar do not make a very hearty meal.

I toyed with the idea of having an enormous feast: pounding the rock-hard pretzels until my teeth shattered, despite the fact that the salt on them would only worsen my condition. Or do nothing for me when, sixteen days from now, I was reduced to bones and a couple drops of blood after I had starved to death.

Earlier in the day I had felt a bug on my arm and devoured it without even knowing what it was. A tick? Probably not, in this cold weather. A beetle? A roach? We had never had those in the house. Maybe another silverfish, Tippy's favorite meal when we had lived without food before?

Time eluded me. The weaker I became, the more I slept. Or felt I slept. Or, at least, wanted to sleep. Perhaps my dreams woke me in twelve-minute increments; I would never know. When I drifted off, it was in complete darkness, except for the light slinking under my door. When I woke up, everything remained the same. Did that mean twenty-four hours had passed, or ten minutes? I did not know.

I got my book and returned to the heated spot on the floor, blanket pulled all the way over my head this time, trapping the heat and making my body use fewer calories to keep it warm.

When I went to scratch Tippy, I remembered she wasn't there.

I couldn't bear to think about her future. Or lack thereof. For all I knew, Mom had tired of chicken noodle soup and was making brunch with my dog as the main treat.

Evelyn would certainly do that. That and much, much worse.

"Yeah, but she was a good old broad. We had a lot of fun together." God's voice came through the pitch black of my room and practically made me jump out of my skin.

"You did?" I asked, unsure if He was a hallucination or not.

"Until I tired of her, sure. Evelyn kept me company for many years."

I put my marker back in the book, closed it tight.

When it hit me, my head flung back so hard I knew I'd probably dented the wall. "You mean…this is about you?"

"Who else would it be, Lucy? Don't I match her description pretty well?"

In my mind's eye, I could see God twirling around in front of me, modeling His rugged look. His red hair.

"I guess so."

"Well, you don't sound too impressed."

"I thought…you'd be different."

"Really, Lucy? You thought I'd be what…not like the other guys? The ones who want to do this to you?"

I struggled for about seven seconds before I realized it wasn't worth the effort. Eight raisins do not equal endless energy or strength. I could never fend Him off.

God was all hands and tongue again, His rough touch invading my every inch.

But then He stopped.

"I just thought God would be about…love. Not all of this death and destruction."

My words were met with static.

And then He started to laugh.

Demonic. Room-filling, dead-rodent breath yowling.

I pissed myself.

Chapter 43

Joan

The dog forgave me.

She had to, if she wanted to eat.

I watched her put her nose against your door, take a sniff, walk away. Since she didn't linger, I hoped you had already died. That was a nasty hit you took to your head, knocked you out cold for several hours. Well, that and the Benadryl I poured down your throat. What a useful elixir that turned out to be.

The snow put a damper on things. But I managed. Found the wood stacked up in the basement, where we had left it years ago. Boarded the window shut. Double-boarded it, in fact. I figured you might stand a chance of ripping one section off with your demon-nails, but as weak as you were, two would be impossible.

And the door...well, let's just say that neither of us would be getting through that very easily.

The ax lay beside me in bed. I didn't fret that the red-headed man would be back. In fact, I hoped he'd use it on me and end our time together once and for all. But I was ready. For you, for him, for whatever it took.

I pictured Aunt Evelyn the day she died, in the kitchen. Pointing her finger at me, just a child. Thinking that if she pronounced my future, the women of the family would just take me outside and hang me with my own belt.

What I would have given for that to happen.

Six days. I could last that long. Even if he came back and shredded me, I could linger through that pain. Just to make sure. Just to know you could do no harm.

And what would I do when it was over? Find Brandy? How would I ever explain the truth to her? That I sent her away to spare her this wrath? That I had loved her with all my heart, her life a blossoming memory of what should have been shared with her father?

No. When you were gone, I would be as well. One day Brandy would return to this house and find nothing but cinders.

Ashes to ashes.

Dust to dust.

Chapter 44

Lucy

The Great Wall of China. The Grand Canyon. Niagara Falls.

Places I would never see.

Fly to the moon. Win a million dollars playing the lottery. Hold my newborn in my arms, right after delivery.

Things I would never do.

I thought of Brandy, alone in the world, and hoped that she would have all the opportunities I would not. That she would fall in love, travel the globe, have a fancy career if that suited her. Maybe she would pop out a bunch of babies and name one after me, once she heard that I was gone.

Dead.

Starved to death in my own bedroom.

The pretzels were a life saver. Scraping the salt off the sides practically killed me, as I had no energy left. But then I thought about the survivors of the Holocaust, forced to perform excruciating labor in the freezing cold with maybe a piece of bread to keep them going every day.

Removing salt became much easier after that.

Hours ticked away while I tried to stay alert. Boredom and hunger cavorted around my room, holding hands; I had no desire to play with them.

I contented myself with the book. Although I must admit, even it had a hard time capturing my attention. The killings became mundane. The sex, another story. One I couldn't begin to imagine. God, who brutalized Evelyn. Angels He brought along to share in the fun. Six men, two men, five dozen over the course of a week. God demanded and Evelyn performed.

Not what I had ever expected.

My energy level waned to nothing. To the point that turning pages became exhausting. Keeping the flashlight poised so I could read a physical feat on par with an Olympic event.

Skiing. Ice skating. Riding a horse.

Things I would never do.

Scotland. Hawaii. Amsterdam.

Places I would never see.

* * *

I couldn't move when He came back.

"I had to check up on you, Lucy. You holding together okay?"

God curled up behind me. His contact made me yearn for Tippy, to have my cuddle-buddy back in bed with me.

Instead, I was stuck with this creature.

"Don't hold back anything, Lucy. I know what you think of me."

I was glad we didn't have to converse. My lips had lost all desire to move. My voice seemed decades away, lost in waves of time that I couldn't even comprehend.

His hands, now familiar, coursed my body.

"She wanted to kill your mother, you know. Evelyn."

My curiosity tilted its head. But I did not move.

"She was jealous of her. Of a little girl. Can you believe that? We had a good thing going, the two of us. She just wanted more than I could give her. Typical woman."

Not worth my effort to respond.

"But the old broad really crossed the line when she told your grandmother to murder Joan. Pissed me off! I killed her right then and there. In front of your mother, so she'd know how much I needed to keep her around. I wrapped my hand around Evelyn's heart so tightly the organ nearly burst. She was toast in seconds."

His words overwhelmed me. I tried sifting through them, sorting them into patterns, digesting them raw. Nothing worked. I was too tired to understand.

"You really are in bad shape. Are you hungry?"

He laid a plate of food on my nightstand. A baked potato, prime rib, green beans. Not my absolute favorite, but not chicken, either.

This time I didn't hesitate. I figured I knew God well enough to eat His offering. After all, He had been groping me for weeks now, and I deserved something for my trouble.

Behind me, He laughed.

"Is that how you justify it? Well then, here...."

God tossed me flat on my back, just as I was reaching for a bean. I had nothing left but complacence. Whatever He wanted, He could have. Just to get it over with. Just to push it further toward the end.

Was this, perhaps, a ritual I had to complete in order to have access beyond His gates?

He radiated heat. Where I had imagined love and passion, God was about dirtiness and His own greed. I gasped when His teeth bit me. Thought of the nice stories people told in church about Him while He ripped my clothes and parted my body.

"Would you please quit calling me God? It really ruins the moment, you know. I am not THE father, Lucy. I am YOUR father. Get it straight!"

And then it hit.

My anger. My energy. My defense.

I rose from beneath him, flung the red-headed man across the room. My thoughts were primal. My instincts on high alert. My motivation back in the saddle.

"Get the fuck off me, you pig!"

"Woo-hoo! Now, that's the way I like 'em. Hot and feisty. Not limp and pathetic."

The man whistled and came back at me.

I felt myself expand. Became a tree, a whale, a typhoon. My attacker was unable to touch my skin.

"Ok. Battle over. You win this time." He put his hands up in defeat, but I did not back down. I was on high alert; this might be a ruse.

"Ask your mommy sometime how much she likes it. Boy, did we have fun making you, my treat. Bet she's never even told you about it."

The questions that popped in my head made him chuckle.

"Oh, Lucy. You are so blind to everything. I'll be back, soon. You can just lay there and starve yourself, I don't care."

Chapter 45

Evelyn

Stupid, mindless little vixen.

Joan, Joan, Joan. Sticking a pair of scissors straight into my ear canal seemed preferable compared to his obsession with my great-niece. What did she have that I didn't? What did he see in her?

We stopped everything. He had minions to do his work, spreading hatred throughout the world, causing pain and misfortune. We didn't need to do that anymore. He was bored with his same routine, even with the wars that flourished in the east and the discord he had planted on our hottest continents. The only action he liked was watching me, punishing me for not being her, for lacking the magnetism that made him ready to sow his seed.

I was tired of our routine as well. Where I longed to laugh and savor our time together over fresh meat straight from the prison yards or pluck some young thing from the filth of less-developed countries and help her find the freedom her soul desired, we instead watched the youngest woman in my family sing at her Christmas pageant or go door to door selling baked goods for her school fundraiser.

I saw no end.

When I couldn't take it anymore, I acted. Never let the thoughts settle in my head, knowing he would read them. Just let them skittle across the periphery of my brain, a water bug on the move, barely discernible except for the slight ripple of its wake.

My sister requested my presence at the annual family get together. Who knows why she carried out the ritual of inviting me, since we rarely spoke and I had not attended one of those catastrophes since Father passed away.

Imagine her surprise when I showed at her doorstep. Suitcase in hand. A changed woman from the one I had been years before, when I had returned home shortly before Mother's death.

Did I need to look dowdy to keep up the ruse? My hair remained braided, a heavy rope that coursed the length of my back, but it was now woven with gray. I stood before her and ran a mental list of places I had been, atrocities I had created, beasts I had known and let ravage my body.

What was left of my soul.

She shrieked, and I feigned joy at the sight of her. My sister, the weakling. Had Dad ever caused a ruckus among the cattle while defiling her in the barn during the morning milking? Had he darkened her backside with whips he fashioned from the tender branches of trees?

All these years later, and this was the first place my mind went, to the questions I could never ask in polite society. But in my heart I knew he wouldn't have touched her. My sister was about simplicity, girliness, divine purity.

Things I had never known.

I acted befuddled by political trends, divulged the secrets of the great cultures where I had spent some of my better years, reminded them of my high integrity and intellectual pursuits. My sister, so silly, let me prattle on, as she was wont to do. Our entire relationship a hoax. Knowing, somehow, that we would never set eyes on each other again.

Which was fine with me. I couldn't believe we had spawned from the same union. Her fingernails, long and painted, her hair coiffed and so full of spray that I could barely inhale around her...my sister was definitely my mother's child.

I wore boots. Plodded when I walked. Paraded around in the britches that had startled the world when I gave up the skirts Dad liked for their easy access to my more favorable parts.

Did she know, my sister? Could she hear us in the barn, the field, even in the back of his truck? Did he know what it was like to have her stare up at him from her spot on the floor, on her knees like he had taught me?

She handed me my tea, remembered how I liked it. Introduced me to neighbors, even drove me to the plot where Mother had become one with the soil, the scene at the cemetery one only my sister could create, with a small bench and angel statuary all around.

Dad would have gotten such a kick out of that. I wondered if eternity next to his much-despised wife was more than he could handle, or if he enjoyed his position, whispering tales of our debauchery to her, year after year repeating stories of our times together. Once even in church. In the basement, in the room where we stored the choir robes.

My moment came when the girl-child joined us in the kitchen. While the entire family was crammed inside my sister's house, the rain keeping everyone from croquet or kickball. My tea had grown cold. My brain parched from day after day of this fraud.

I crawled onto my high horse. Put on my best routine. Reminded them all of the reasons I had spent my life traveling the globe, tracking down all the women who had been here before.

Then I pointed fingers. Spelled out the future. Joan would bear his child.

Joan would bring the beast into this world. She was destined, the one he wanted for her future fruit. The past two thousand years had led us to this day, here in this kitchen, where the family must decide what to do with the one who would live out the curse and bear the horror that would rule the darkest parts of creation until the end of time.

Joan needed to die.

Her death would end our responsibility. Her blood would pay our due. She could not be allowed to grow fertile, to open her womb to his seed.

But before I could lead the charge, he heard me. My time was a passing fog, the click of a pen, the cluck of a hen.

Across the room, he stood and waved at me. Walked past Joan, patted her head.

Strode right up to me and yanked me out of my chair. Put his teeth against my neck. Reached through my rib cage and grasped my heart.

Squeezed.

I could have screamed with terror, but I knew it was coming. My plan had but one flaw.

The creature I thought I was deceiving was the devil.

The man who crushed my heart was my father.

I collapsed the moment he touched me. Not out of fear. Not out of any clause of weakness, like my sister would have subscribed.

What brought me to my knees was love.

I was finally in his arms again.

Chapter 46

Lucy

The floor sweltered. When my toe touched wood, the sizzling sound alone made me pull back. The blistering was instantaneous and viciously painful, as if the wound was full of razor blades.

Sweat pooled on my skin, soaked into my sheets. For a second my mind flashed on the fact that they had barely dried after my accident the last time God had visited.

Or Godless, as I now liked to call him.

Even the bed frame seemed afire. I tried to sit up by grabbing a post, but my hand jerked back, and I had to shake it to dissipate the heat.

Not knowing what to do, I curled my knees into my chest and lay the day away. My eyes had adapted to the dark, but my time was lonesome all the same.

The dresser exploded. Like a bag of microwave popcorn, it banged and expanded, banged and expanded, until it was a complete and utter mess.

I didn't become hysterical until flames crept from the base, rolling up the sides. My brain was too sluggish to connect the dots. But when the top drawer slid out, fire coursing over my entire stash of food, I jumped off my bed and made a sad attempt to salvage it.

Deep-fried foot.

I screamed, more out of desperation as I watched my few last morsels turn to ash before my eyes, although the pain on the sole of my foot indicated that this wasn't going to be an insubstantial wound. A series of popping sounds came from under the bed, startling me. At first I thought they were gunshots, but as I watched the steam pour from the floor, I realized that he had destroyed my water bottles as well.

My life-force boiled on the hardwood floor.

Above me, he laughed.

Disgusting, yellow-toothed, child-molester hysterics that crept up my spine and set my teeth on edge.

But this time they didn't fade. As though he had produced his own album of insane giggling and put it on a loop for me to endure.

No knives. No food. No sanity.

* * *

No one had ever come.

The darkness deepened as I realized this.

Not Mrs. Winchell, from church, who had often hinted about my home life as she saw the bruises on my arms and face. I could remember her softness, the bosom that entered a room ten steps before her, the teddy-bear sweetness of her eyes. Her concern. The reminders that I could always stop by, talk to her about anything.

In the months I'd been locked away, she'd not dropped by. Had she asked Mom for my address in France?

None of my teachers. Not that they were busting down the door before I 'moved,' but why hadn't the principal at least come to verify my whereabouts? Why had a phone call declaring I'd suddenly packed up and moved been acceptable?

What about the neighbors? Did they gossip about my family but stay on the outskirts so as not to interfere with our problems?

The kids at school? By now I was old news. My name crossed few lips when I was a full-time student. Why would anyone notice me? Be interested in my life?

My death?

Because that was all I had left. No food. No water. No strength.

I wondered what would happen when they discovered my body. Mom would never pay for a funeral, a casket, even a headstone. I'd be lucky if she cared enough to leave the clothes on my body when she dumped my corpse in the lake by the landfill.

One of the coolest funerals I had ever seen, back when we still had television, was in New Orleans. Hundreds of people, walking down the city streets, playing jazz, the procession intensely personal and celebratory. Women wailing. Raising their arms, as in prayer, or just a heated discussion with those in Heaven. You could tell they loved the man who had died. He was revered. Honored.

Missed.

I was no one. Had always been a loner, a loser, a tag-along for Brandy. No one had come to check up on me. No one would notice when my last breath passed.

Tears I couldn't afford to waste came down hard. My heart strained. The prospect of my own death was something I'd only noticed peripherally, the thoughts of how it would occur almost romanticized with my popularity at school. If I contracted a deadly disease, like leukemia, would people swarm to me out of sympathy, be my friends as my spirit waned? Would Brandy and I make headlines across the nation if we went to Mr. Wyckoli's and he had snapped? Met us at the door with a hatchet and cut us into tiny pieces?

Would people care about me after the fact? When they realized how sweet I was? How quiet? Would Velvet Bradshaw weep because she knew too late that we could have been the best of friends, and now we'd never have that opportunity?

Death had always been elusive.

But now I had to stare at it face-on.

And all I saw was Brandy. My sweet sister. My best friend. I longed to run into her arms, feel her strength, her love. Was I such a horrible person that I had to be denied the simplest of things, her camaraderie, her chuckle, the kiss she always planted on my forehead when we went to our separate rooms at night?

I wouldn't miss Mother. Not much, anyway. When it came right down to it, Brandy was my mother. Had been as long as I could remember. She was my only source of love, until I found Tippy.

One of my most cherished memories was my tenth birthday. How fabulous to reach double digits! I could barely contain my excitement. Other girls my age celebrated with slumber parties or had their parents book the big room at the pizza parlor, even took groups roller skating or to the zoo.

Not me.

My mother forgot.

When I awoke that morning, Brandy slopped together some oatmeal. Tippy and I went outside for her morning stroll. Mom slept in.

I kept waiting. For something small. A card. A spontaneous trip to the book store. A good wish or two.

Mom said nothing.

Brandy took the hint. Asked for money. Told Mom she wanted to take me on a field trip for my birthday. I could see Mom's eyebrows rise and felt my shoulders wilt. My big day, and she hadn't done a thing. No gifts. No cake. No big banners across the dining room door frame.

I barely felt alive. I hadn't asked for Hello Kitty invitations. I knew how much Mom hated to be nagged about upcoming occasions, so I had never mentioned how much I wanted my own diary or one of those slip-n-slides to put in the side yard so Brandy and I could play during heat waves.

Could Mom not see how much I desperately wanted to call the girls in my class and have them sleep over on the living-room floor, eat our fill of popcorn and chips, drink all the soda we could?

But I never would have told her this. Mom would have shut me up with a fast smack across the cheek or one of her terror-inducing glares.

We got on our bikes. Rode to town. Just being alone with my big sister, her long dark hair floating in a stream straight behind her as she pedaled like an Olympic racer, relaxed my heart. She had not forgotten.

She loved me.

We went to the church. Not what I had anticipated for my birthday. Not that I didn't like the building or the people in it. I had wanted something more exciting, more glamorous than our usual Sunday activities on the day I hit the big 1-0.

But Brandy was smart as a whip.

She led me to the basement, which creeped me out because we had to search for the light switches. My emotions were in turmoil.

Turning ten and the excitement of such a grand moment, coupled with my trepidation at wandering around in the dark church basement, waiting for critters of all sorts to bite my ankles or grab me and take me to some backwoods cabin, only to suffer some fate more horrible than having a mother who couldn't care less about my special birthday. It all made me jittery.

When I finally turned on the lights, the people jumped out, scaring me so badly I almost fainted.

"Surprise! Happy Birthday!"

Brandy stood across from me, beaming. She could read my heart. She knew how much I had wanted a party. To be queen for a day. To celebrate my life.

The women decked me out with a tiara and sash proclaiming my status as Birthday Girl. Most of the kids at my party were from my Sunday School class. Brandy had arranged for their mothers to bake goodies and plan games for my big day. Like she knew Mom would never do for me.

She and I held hands through most of the afternoon. We played the old standards, pinned tails on donkeys, ran around the church lawn in a heated game of tag. I was shocked when they all gave me presents. Card games, books, a stuffed hippo. My loot pile so big Brandy and I had to stuff both our backpacks full to carry it home.

We had had a glorious day. An unimaginable day. Brandy had thrown me a birthday party. None of the other mothers had even asked where mine was, and it didn't matter. My sister had rocked my world.

On the way home, we stopped for pizza. Brandy paid with the money Mom had given her, and we even had enough for breadsticks.

"Don't say a word," my sister warned when we returned home.

How I missed her. Brandy hadn't been gone very long, and I had withered away into nothing without her.

Did she think of me? Why hadn't she called someone?

That was what it narrowed down to. When it was most important, my sister had failed me. Left me behind. To die.

My death promised to be uncomfortable. Long and drawn out, rancid fart flavored taffy. Completely coated in the slime of solitude.

My head ached. Already my thirst was overwhelming. My hunger so acute it could cut glass.

No one had come.

And no one would.
Where was my dog?

Chapter 47

Joan

Could it really only be four more days?

You'd stopped moving around much. Unless your room was infested with rats, I'd heard your footfall on occasion. The last time, I'd been quite surprised. You hadn't taken a step in at least a day. My heart saddened at the thought of you still up there, breathing. Why couldn't you just let go?

I made my own preparations. Took the box of photos, the ones from the happy years of my short marriage, and decorated my bed with them. Alex and I after our engagement party, which included two couples from his work and my mother, everyone's eyes sparkling. Was it the alcohol, or the joy we inspired?

Pictures of our first house. The small one, where we had papered the walls with love. I blushed at the memories of our sex life before Brandy came along. The night Alex came home from work and I had left a trail of rose petals, from the front door to the bathroom. My husband preferred white wine, and I had balanced his glass on the table in the hallway, right next to a single stocking, the leg trailing over the edge of the ebony wood, the toe pointing toward the bathroom where I was waiting.

The water hot. The bubbles frothy. When Alex joined me, half the contents of the tub spilled onto the floor. We laughed hysterically.

He moved me from the tub to the kitchen, where we polished the counter. In the living room we shared his favorite recliner. Under our sheets, we created Brandy.

How could anyone take him away from me?

Pictures of Brandy. Newborn, in her high chair, wearing her first Halloween costume. Her proud papa, holding her in the crook of one arm, balancing her on his shoulders, tossing her into the air and listening to her scream with glee.

We had been happy, the three of us.

My mother. I recalled who she was before my father's funeral, how she quietly fell apart afterward, refusing anyone's help or attention. How I had needed her after my own husband's death, but she was gone then, too. Lost in her own world. Banished from mine.

I stopped taking pictures after you came along.

Why would I want to record your existence? The school took care of that each year. On a few occasions I had splurged and taken the two of you to the mall for photos with Santa, the Easter Bunny, even the baby lions that came on tour one summer. But this was only because I cherished images of Brandy. Not you. You were just along for the ride.

The pile of pictures shifted when I moved my feet. One remained in place, noticeable now where before it had been buried under the others. It caught my eye because of its color. Black and white. How old could it be?

Someone had taken it at our family reunion.

The tragic one where Aunt Evelyn had died. Right there, at the kitchen table, after pronouncing my horrible fate.

The picture showed almost the entire room. The counter with the bar stools. The table, all six chairs filled with the women of my family. My naïve self, clinging to Mother's leg. The refrigerator, the coffee pot.

And leaning against the stove, a strange man dressed in work pants and a denim jacket. His face slightly blurred by the camera. His gaze focused on me and my mother.

No mistaking his face, even though it was obscured. The red-headed man.

I dropped the picture. Picked it up again and stared harder. Across the table, Evelyn had a foul look on her face.

She was looking directly at him. Watching him watch me.

She had known, all right.

And he had been the one to tell her.

Chapter 48

Lucy

My body melted onto the floor.

He had turned the heat off, but his laughter still haunted my room. So loud no other noises permeated the persistent cackle. I couldn't tell if Mom was moving around, whether Tippy ever made it up the stairs to check on me.

The chickens could have taken over the entire upstairs, and I would never know.

Somehow I survived. Days wrapped around themselves, so I had no idea how much time had passed, but my mind told me at least a week had dragged by, its hind legs shattered and weighing it down.

Images floated past in the darkness. The convertibles carrying the homecoming queen and her court. A water slide, dripping with children. Crocuses. The family of owls in our back yard. Brandy asleep in her bed, curled up with her stuffed rabbit, the blankets tucked perfectly around her chin.

Mom. Screaming at me. Her palms flying out to greet my face. Her lips curled up in glee as she kicked my backside while I tried to crawl away. Back when things were good enough I could have walked out the front door and never returned.

If only I could do so now. I would open the door in a split second, key or no key. Throw a chair through the downstairs window. Remember that a shard of glass makes as potent a weapon as the knife I could not find.

I had to escape. But I couldn't even stand.

The light under my door beckoned, a beam of hope in an otherwise pathetic existence. I found the strength to crawl across my floor, push with my knees and bury my face in the old rug by my bed, slide across the room like it was lathered in Crisco.

Then I came to the most fantastic realization.

Waiting for death to come. Pushing myself into the light.

Maybe this light was the final one. All I had to do was understand what the true God was telling me, the symbolism He had placed in my room. My ultimate quest. To find the light.

And here it had been staring at me all this time.

Godless turned up his soundtrack, which solidified my epiphany. Why else would he try to distract me? To ridicule me with his maniacal laughter? I had to have finally made the right decision.

When my head rested against the bottom of the door, I tried to relax. I was on center stage. Celebrating my moment. The grandest occasion of my life; not the joy of being escorted down the aisle to meet my future husband, not the cap-and-gown fest of getting a PhD, not even a medal ceremony when I broke all records in the butterfly at the Olympics.

There would be no national anthem playing for me.

I was about to give myself to God.

The real one.

The one who was waiting for me, with open arms and the splendor that was not this life.

Flat against the floor, I pushed my fingers under the door. Spread them open, reaching in all directions to try to grab the beam that would take me into forever. I held my breath and waited to be sucked under the frame and into the radiance, riding it like a high speed train going non-stop to the golden gates.

Something slimy ran over my fingernails.

I pulled my hands back. Listened to the guffaw as it ridiculed my attempt to meet death on my own terms.

Then the sensation nudged my brain.

Had I been locked up for so long that I had forgotten?

I pushed my hands further this time, under the door until my knuckles became wedged against the wood.

And found her precious face.

Tippy. Waiting for me outside my door.

God had answered my prayers after all. I wasn't abandoned. My best friend had found me, in all my disgust and shame, and was slathering my fingers with kisses.

My lips were too parched to part. Could she hear my thoughts? I thanked her for coming. For being here to see me off. Promised her Mom would take care of her, even if she kicked her around on occasion.

We were soul mates, Tippy and I. Why had I ever worried about the girls at school not liking me, when I could never have found anyone more worthy of my friendship than my dog?

Had I had any moisture left in my body, I would have collapsed into tears. I sent Tippy my best apologies. She had, of course, been right. The window was my best opportunity and I blew it time and time again. Had my naivety made me believe that he was the one, true God? My immaturity? Mom had sold me on the idea. He creeped me out, but who was I to question him?

My fingers rested on Tippy's paws. She pressed her head against them, licking my skin in what I hoped was forgiveness. Would she even be here if she still held a grudge?

At that thought, I felt her leave.

My heart caved in.

Was God teasing me? Punishing me for my earlier decisions? Was He upset that I'd fallen for Godless's routine?

I couldn't scream her name. I had nothing left. My tongue had long ago become an old piece of jerky. My throat, the earth after a sudden sandstorm.

When I reached back out to check for her, my angel had returned.

Tippy put a cloth on my hands.

The thought didn't register for several seconds. Then I realized my skin was wet. That water was running onto the floor, a stream coming straight where my face was pressed against the wood.

I flattened it out, pulled it in with me.

What a brilliant beast.

She had pulled the dishtowel off the stove, where it hung on the door. Soaked it in her water dish. Carried it to me.

I sucked the sweet liquid out of the cloth. Wrung it out, letting it waterfall down my throat. Put my left hand back where I could find my dog. Wrapped my fingers around her paw, holding it tight, hoping she understood exactly how much I loved her.

We clung to each other this way. When I shoved the dry rag back under the door, Tippy took it away and brought it back again. Kept me sane and eased my discomfort at the same time.

I had my second epiphany of the day.

When I reached under the door I had been searching for God.

And this time, I had found her.

Chapter 49

Joan

Twenty-nine hours.

I was manic with joy. My body had forgotten the bruises, the areas where I needed stitches. Everything was fitting perfectly.

My wedding dress hung in the closet, removed from over a decade of storage. I couldn't believe it when I tried it on and the zipper closed. Two children and a lifetime of distress later, and the damned thing had more give than the first day I'd worn it.

Who had I been back then?

Who was I now?

Starting my life with Alex had been a whirlwind of time ago. Walking down the aisle to his outstretched hand, dancing after our ceremony, the first night we spent as husband and wife. He held my hand constantly. Waltzed with me in the kitchen. Listened to my every word, intent upon the details of my life. Our short time together a never-ending honeymoon.

Alex stole my heart and never returned it.

All I wanted in this world was to feel his body wrapped around mine. Smell his scent, a dab of Eternity and the slight musk of his sweat. To feel safe again. Loved. Cherished.

But what if he was repulsed by what was yet to come? Would Alex turn his back on me? The thought of spending eternity without him infuriated me. I picked the ax up, threw it back into the floor. Listened to the wood beneath it crack. Did it again.

All that I had endured.

That fucking red-headed man. He had destroyed my life. Taken away all of my love. All that made me happy. What had I done to deserve this? Because I was born into the blood line? Who cared about the freaking family curse? Why had I been selected to bear the greatest burden of all?

I would take care of matters. First Lucy, then myself. If she was even alive.

All I had to do was look at her flaming hair and know where she came from. That would make this job much easier. Imagine him in her body, the man that ruined everything, and my fury would emerge. He had killed my husband. Slaughtered my mother. Left me all but dead. Come back after all of this time to flaunt his power over me.

And I would get to end it all.

Payback is a bitch.

I hoped Alex would forgive me. I didn't have to worry about Mother; she had always known it would come to this. My battle was almost won. I had waited, strategically, until the last moment. When he wouldn't have another opportunity to put his seed in another one of us. Because who was left?

My daughters.

A picture of Brandy, laughing over a game of Pictionary at the kitchen table, flashed through my thoughts. On her piece of paper, a sharply rendered drawing of a man with horns sticking out of his head.

Bastard.

What if he had had her? What if he had treated my sweet child the same way he had me?

Here I thought I'd been protecting her. And I'd put her out into the clutches of the very beast that had decimated my life.

This time I threw the ax at the wall. Watched it stick for a second, then fall to the floor.

Oh, Alex.

Could he ever forgive me?

Chapter 50

Tippy

The smell was everywhere.

Pouring out from your room. Sitting thick on your mother's skin. The floor reeked so badly of it that I couldn't clean it off my paws, no matter how hard I tried.

But you were with me. Barely. I could feel your hurt even though I couldn't see you. Joined you the best I could, wanting to put my head on your shoulder and lend you my courage. Touching paws was the best I could do.

I couldn't imagine my mother treating me as yours did. She had a kennel, but no one locked her in it. Her humans would say, "Dolly, go to bed." And Mom would. She liked her special spot. With the big fluffy pillow in it. And all of her toys.

But her bed had no bars on it. Fresh air. A door that opened all the time.

Yours had nothing. I had almost given up all hope when you reached for me. Your fingers scared me at first, and then I understood that you had heard me calling for you but you couldn't see me. My tail wagged. Knowing the smell hadn't taken you over. Knowing you still loved me, even if I was on the outside.

I couldn't stand the thought of life without you. Days of silence, only to be kicked out the door when your mother remembered that I had to go outside to pee.

She had forgotten to feed me. But I had found a secret supply of old treats, hidden in the cabinet under the kitchen sink, where I liked to hole up sometimes. They were like eating the rocks straight from the driveway and smelled like the sickness in your eye, but I didn't have it in me to complain anymore.

I didn't know what to do.

I rested my head against your hands.

And then she came back to me. Dolly, my mother, the wisest of all.

"Tippy, your girl is dying."

Yes. But how could I stop it? I had an army. They were ready. But they were fighters, not door-busters. How did I get them up the stairs and through the door?

"You don't."

I begged for her help.

"You know what to do, dear. What does she need?"

When your mother boarded up the window, I had witnessed it. Thought about the times we had feasted on snow. About how afraid I was when you went out on the roof, terrified you would fall off and die, leaving me alone. Now you couldn't get outside at all.

"Water."

"Then get her some."

The gap under the door was small. Even if I could find a glass of water, I wouldn't be able to wedge it through.

"Tippy. Think. What water do you have?"

My dish. But my teeth couldn't hold onto it well. I could not drag it through the kitchen, let alone up the stairs.

"What else could you use to carry the water?"

What would fit under the door?

Your sister had once slid a piece of paper under there, back before she left. When you were being punished, and she wasn't allowed to speak to you. Instead she wrote a note. The paper had fit. She pushed it under the door and your mom didn't even notice.

But paper wouldn't hold water.

"What else, Tippy? Think harder!"

And then it hit me. Washing dishes. When you and your sister finished, you always hung the rag over the sink and it would drip for a long time, the sound driving me crazy, the constant pinging of water against metal.

But I couldn't reach the sink.

I kissed your fingers. I was trying, Lucy, really I was.

When you scratched my cheek, you gave me another thought.

The cloth you kept at the stove. Easy access. Something that even I could reach.

I jumped up and ran down the stairs. Pulled the cloth down, soaked up all the water in my dish, hurried as best I could so as not to lose anything on my trip back to you.

When I laid it down, you didn't move. I thought I was too late. That in the minutes I'd wasted catching as much liquid as I could, you'd left me.

Then you pulled it in. Gave me one hand to hold. Asked me for more when you pushed the rag back to me. My dish was empty, but I knew where there was an endless source nearby.

The bathroom.

It took all I had left to stretch and get it in the big bowl, but it worked. I was proud of myself. Ran back three more times, keeping my girl alive.

Later, when you were sleeping, I snuck back to my secret hiding place. Curled up for a nap, hidden so your mom wouldn't hurt me.

When I bit into another one of my treats, my mom came back for a visit.

"You did a very good job today, Tippy. But what else does Lucy need?'

My tooth crunched the answer.

My biscuits were square and very thin. Small enough to shove under the door.

I mustered my strength. Put two in my mouth. Hurried back up to your cage.

My girl would never die.

Not while I was on the job.

Chapter 51

Lucy

In the end, I apologized to God as well.

How had I confused the two?

I'd thought I was being good. Following orders. Believing when everything Godless had said was dreadful. Wasn't that part of the Old Testament? God says hey, go kill your son, and you do it because He gave the direction? Even after reading about his travels with Evelyn, I hadn't questioned his origins. Just had faith, because Mom told me that he was God.

And he was the opposite.

Tippy had given me a whisper of strength. Just having her nearby was uplifting. I appreciated her efforts to keep me from starving, but it was almost too late.

In the end, I didn't want her to see me this weak. If she could have crawled into my arms and I could have just fallen asleep, holding her, that would have been a different good-bye. As it was, I backed up as far as I could go, reaching the far wall, where I could lay on the floor and keep a watch underneath the door. If I could see Tippy, I would at least feel like I wasn't leaving alone.

The time had come. Everything in my body told me I'd hung on too long as it was.

The worst was my mind. At times I thought I'd been having strange dreams, even nightmares, only to realize that I wasn't asleep. Or maybe I was in some loopy world where I was asleep, dreaming that I was dreaming, and not asleep. My ideas were a labyrinth. I didn't have the wherewithal to fight my way out of it.

Her paws were gone.

I couldn't even hear the laughter anymore. Had he turned it off?

Birds filled the room. Not my chickens. Black birds, mammoth shadows fluffing their wings, waiting for me to go. To escort me somewhere? Had I heard that before, that animals welcome you into the next world? Or were they just hanging around because they, too, were extraordinarily hungry, and I would soon make a tasty meal?

Tippy. Why couldn't I just hold her once more?

I spilled my last ounce of strength, sent an urgent thought to Brandy. She needed to come home. She needed to rescue my dog. Take her away from Mother. Find her a new home, if necessary. Mr. Wyckoli would love her. She needed loved.

And then it came. Sudden and unexpected. A breath-stealer.

A crisp flash of light, in the middle of the door.

Followed by a wave. My eyes shut at the sight of it, overwhelming, the light blinding me after so long spent in my room. Somehow I had expected death to be more subtle. Sleepy even. A black mist, coiling around my body while my eyes were shut and my senses on vacation.

Not this. This boisterousness. This high activity. The brightness screamed at me, not in a welcoming way, but with a pointed finger and the diaphragm of an opera singer. My bones wanted to flee. To find shelter. To desperately cling to the darkness, cower in its corners.

Instead I reached out for God. Thankful He had forgiven me.

Reached out, despite my fear, to end the pain. Begged Him, as I went, to take care of Tippy.

But I didn't move. The floor held me captive.

I realized that she was shrieking.

Mom, tearing down the door. She was moving furiously, but it all came at me in slow motion. Like she was twirling in a big ball gown. Eyes blazing. Hair a wild bird's nest.

Holding an ax.

Her weapon assaulted the door again. Splintered the wood. Broke it open and ushered in the hall light. It beamed directly upon me.

The craziness had finally consumed her.

But I didn't much care. I couldn't move. I had made my peace with God. Tippy had forgiven my weaknesses. I had nothing left.

Mom put her ax down and pulled sections of the door apart with her bare hands, until she looked like a wedding photo, the harried bride framed by the outline of the door.

I tried to smile at her. Thankful that our game was finally over. I didn't begrudge the fact that I'd lost.

Then they returned. Their song joined me in my room seconds before I saw them. My friends, the chickens. The hall held nothing but Mother, and then suddenly they appeared.

Dozens of them, all with heads. Bigger. In a steroid rage. Clucking furiously, their beaks enormous, they were as wound up as a cellblock in the middle of a prison riot.

I smiled, because they had not forgotten me. But despite the chaos and the dance Mom was doing with her weapon, I still couldn't move.

They attacked her. Pecked at her legs, just as they had done to Ms. Antoinette. But this was much more vicious. The birds dug into her flesh. Stabbed her with their sharp beaks, clawed at her feet with their talons.

Mom reached for the ax, swung at them. But they did not give up. Their mouths were the knives I could never find, slicing into Mom's calves. Esther buried her face in the skin behind Mom's kneecap, pulled away a bit of muscle, pink and flimsy like a worm. The rest soon followed her lead.

Mom gave a warrior's cry. Brandished her blade, crushed the heads of some of my defenders. But they ripped her legs to shreds. Mom fumbled. Fell down in her big, white dress, the blood from her wounds soaking into the fabric. Red blossoms appeared at her thighs, then her torso, as the birds continued attacking.

Mom tried to crawl away. I hadn't realized that, in all the drama, I had inched forward for a better view. With her heading away from my room, I had a clear path to the stairs.

Could I make it?

She wailed in agony. They were pecking at her face. I turned away, not wanting to see what the chickens did to her eyeballs.

Looked back at the stairs.

At my sister, working her way up.

She had come back! She had remembered me!

But something was off. Brandy didn't hurry to Mom's rescue. She marched up the steps, slow and steady, moving with a swagger, as if she had all the time in the world to fix this horrible scene. Couldn't she hear Mom screeching? See the ruckus in the hall? She was the only one among us not incapacitated, but I thought even I could hobble faster than her.

When she passed, Brandy paused and winked at me.

Her eyes were weird looking. Black. The irises almost doubled in size.

My gut woke up. Almost came leaping out of my throat, terrified of the creature standing so close to me. When I had fantasized about Brandy rescuing me, I always thought I would jump into her arms and never let go. Now I just had the urge to set myself on fire so I could escape her.

This beast was not my sister. She had grown taller, filled out and fluffed up. I had seesawed with sanity for so long that I worried for a moment that I had finally fallen off the board, but this woman was more enmity than love. The tendrils of her malice squirmed around her shoulders and patted my cheeks as she strolled past.

But nothing stunned me more than her hair. It flowed like blood from her head, rancor pulsing through every crimp and curl. Brandy wore it proud and red, just like mine. She flipped it at me when she turned her head back to Mom and her battle with the chickens.

This time our mother saw her favorite daughter. She reached up when Brandy neared her, but then her face showed shock and a profound terror.

My sister picked the ax up off the floor. Wedged her feet between the hens, scooting several aside. She wore boots and walked with the lumbering weight of a man. It didn't faze her that the birds had pecked huge holes in Mom's body. That blood was trickling down the hall, coating the hardwood floor.

"Guess what, Mom?" Brandy asked, calm as could be while the chickens devoured our mother. "Wrong daughter."

The ax came down. As if Brandy had been practicing for this her entire life. I gasped in horror as Mom's head rolled to the side and her empty eye sockets stared at me.

Somehow I was on two legs. Moving down the stairs. Propelled by terror.

But I was wobbly. Weak. Followed by a madwoman, my sister, the one I had loved so much.

"Is that any way to greet your sister?" Brandy chuckled behind me. What had happened to her while she was gone? Had it been so long and terrible that she had turned into a mother-killer? "Lucy? For real, I just saved your life."

"The chickens—"

Shock struck full force. I made it to the living room, was desperately clinging to the back of the couch, fighting for balance. The door was not too far away. Had the snow melted? Could I get outside? How did Brandy make it here if it hadn't?

"Came in handy. How else could I keep an eye on you?"

"What?" My lips were so dry that I could barely open my mouth.

"They make excellent cameras. Did you know that dog of yours likes to sniff your dirty underwear? How funny is that? Or Mom? She can't pass up a Bloody Mary now and then. Good thing a little liquor puts her right to sleep. Who knows what she would do to you when she's plastered if it didn't? Whoops. I guess I should be using the past tense. When it comes to her, anyway."

I inched my way toward the front door. But Brandy moved step for step with me.

"Why did you come back?" I had been content to die at the hands of Mother. She had always hated me. But Brandy?

"Oh, come on, little sister. You're my back-up plan. Someone had to be around to take over for me in case I…failed…to take office. But in a few minutes, I'll be crowned. No need for your services after that."

The black birds flew down the stairs, swarmed the room. Were they a hallucination? For that matter, was Brandy?

She explained it to me in my brain. Our silent communication, which I had thought was because we were so close, such good sisters, was Brandy reading my ideas and placing her own back in my head.

Pictures of the women who shared my blood surged through my mind. The strange affliction in their eyes, like my sister's, like mine, an image she flashed that I had never even seen in myself. Yet Brandy had it in both eyes.

Because she was Her. The one who would take over. The she-devil my family had killed each other over, trying to prevent her from rising to office.

Centuries preparing the perfect gene pool. Getting it just right. A master plan.

"I'm sorry, sweetheart. I promised to take care of you, and I did. But now it's time for me to move on. I don't really need you anymore."

Because Brandy was ready to take over from the man with red hair. The one I had mistaken for God. The one who, like my sister did now, made my skin feel like it was full of flaming snakes.

Then Brandy showed me Mom. Her horrible life. How my sister, barely more than a toddler, had sat in the corner of the room while the devil took Mom and created me. Brandy lunching with the red-headed man while her grandmother watched, Mom passed out and the other woman screaming, her death imminent. She scrolled through our years together, Mom's craziness propelled by the games Brandy played with her. Tormenting her. Keeping her cage rattled.

Keeping me in pain.

"Someone had to divert her attention away from me. You were the perfect scapegoat. She was too stupid to even consider the fact that I was Her. Talk about gullible."

Brandy laughed, as maniacal as her father. As *our* father.

She raised the ax.

In that instant, three things happened. Tippy howled, the loudest and angriest cry I'd ever heard her make. For a split second, I thought that Brandy had killed my dog. I straightened, ready to fight back. Nobody fucked with Tippy. Not while my lungs still held air.

The weapon flew at me. Flinging blood off its blade.

And the windows burst.

With the shattering of glass, I heard thunder. Hooves. Dignity.

The buck jumped through the window, shards flying the length of the room, and right into my heart.

He entered me. His antlers slid through my back and out my chest, my arms raised from the force, my head swinging up so that I was eye to eye with my sister.

In an explosion of strength, we combined. Struck Brandy with our antlers, forcing her to release the ax. I dropped my head and we rammed her. Prongs straight through the gut. With so much strength that Brandy was impaled against the wall.

My sister clutched at the air. Slapped her hands against our forehead. Steam slipped between her lips, the stench of her breath like the rotten corpse of a cow festering in the smoldering sun for days on end.

The seconds flittered between us, flies darting between goodies at the picnic table, Brandy's lungs somehow managing to pull in air despite the damage done to them.

I took my lesson from the drawings on the hallway wall. Spoke the names Tippy and I had given the headless children.

Callie. William. Fred.

The buck stepped back, but his strength remained in me.

I grabbed Mom's weapon.

Wiped her blood away.

Went to my sister, transfixed on the wall. The deer surrounded us. I could hear their chanting, urging me to finish the job.

I remembered her loving me. Brandy, always my mother. My best friend.

"I love you."

Tippy barked. She would never lead me astray. I thought of the times I'd not tried to escape, to get both of us to safety. How she'd smuggled me food. I would never do wrong by her again.

I swung the weapon. Watched the deer back off after we were all sprayed with blood.

Brandy's eyes spread wide. Her mouth opened; she wailed and put Ms. Antoinette to shame. Was she calling for her father? *Our* father? Would he come to challenge me once he knew his replacement was dead?

The ax felt comfortable in my hand. No wonder I had never found a knife. I wouldn't have known how to use it properly. But this handle fit perfectly in my grip, came up over my shoulder with the ease of a feather pillow, and landed time and time again on my sister's face.

She was nothing when I finished. Not human. Not monster. Just a spray of blood, up the walls and across the ceiling, a clump of tissue that would never scream again.

I was horrified at my actions. When I realized what I had done, I dropped the ax and backed away from her body. Felt the vigor of the buck's body leave my own. Watched as my sister's blood dripped from my hair and over the carpet.

When I collapsed, the buck caught me. Let me lean against him. Lowered himself to the floor where I could be safe.

Tippy curled into my arms. We stared at my sister's body, the blood-soaked wad of flesh that had once been her beautiful face, knowing what this meant. What she had explained, just moments before.

I was her backup.

The next in line.

I watched as the birds moved one by one toward her corpse. They were much larger than I first noticed. They ripped into her flesh. Devoured the sister I loved, leaving nothing in their wake.

Had she sent them here to take care of me?

Tippy touched noses with the deer. One by one, she spoke to all of them. The buck bent down and snorted next to my ear. I ran my hand over his muzzle. Thanked him. He had jumped inside my body, joined us. His courage and power. Life savers.

The others had been my friends, as well. Why had I ever worried that I was alone in the world, when my life was full of these magnificent animals?

I wanted to run off with them, but did not know where my new role should take me. From what Brandy had shown me, at midnight I would take over the dark side of the world. I would be Her, the one no one dared call by name. Would Tippy fear me then?

What would I ever do? I couldn't live like Evelyn. Didn't want to be heartless like my big sister. If they hadn't been trying so hard to kill me, I would never have hurt anyone in my family.

But I wouldn't have long to question things. I grabbed Tippy, pulled her close. Even though I had been infused with the deer's strength, I could feel it waning. I wanted to be ready.

From the broken window, I could hear the wind. Calling my name.

Beckoning.

We rose, the two of us. Tippy and I were a team. Where I went, she would follow. No force on earth or otherwise could ever keep us apart again. I would make sure of it.

I opened the door. Walked onto the snowless porch, down the cement stairs. Didn't even say goodbye to the house as we made our way through the side yard and out toward the field.

Wind whipped around me, wound itself in my hair, danced along my cheeks. I could hear it whispering to me, letting me know that it had missed me as well. That the Earth Herself had mourned while I had been locked away.

Behind me, the structure burst into flame. Fire licked up its sides, a giant campfire lighting up the winter landscape. The blaze reflected in Tippy's eye, making it look like the deformity in my own.

We walked into the darkness. Through the graveyard of obliterated corn stalks. Past the stream, the safe spot where our friends, the deer hunkered down, and to Mr. Wyckoli's house, his light still on, the cackle of his television set invading the silence of the night.

I paused. Wanted to say something to the poor guy, tell him why we had stopped coming over, why we had abandoned him.

Instead I watched his program through his dirty kitchen window. Saw the glittery ball as it dropped on its annual countdown. Listened as the crowd roared with excitement, welcoming the New Year. The new millennium.

The new me.

The End

www.ingramcontent.com/pod-product-compliance
Lightning Source LLC
Chambersburg PA
CBHW050356260626
47156CB00003B/757